THE SAPPHIRE ECLIPSE

AMY HART

ISBN 978-0-473-56553-4 (paperback)

ISBN 978-0-473-56555-8 (EPUB)

Winter Song Press

Cover design by Deranged Doctor Design

For Clare,
for loving every version of this book

I'D ALREADY DIED ONCE. It had been unexpected and violent and was seriously low on my list of things-I'd-like-to-experience-again. But school mandated therapy tried to make me relive it every Wednesday at 8:30 p.m.

"How are you feeling tonight, Emily?" Mr. Green, the school psychologist, shifted in his seat, the burgundy leather of the two-seater couch creasing under his large frame. He crossed his legs, and his left foot swung up and down in an uneven rhythm.

I looked away. "Fine."

"You know I can smell it when you lie," he said mildly.

"Okay, mostly fine, then." My gaze was fixed firmly on the window beside me. The enclosed courtyard outside was lit up against the dark night, and even though it was small, it looked like freedom. Because anywhere I didn't have to talk about myself, or what I'd been through, or what I *was*, was a million times better than this.

"And your classes?" Mr. Green continued.

I shrugged. "They're okay, I guess. I've got a lot to catch up on, but …" I bit my lip, the unspoken words hanging between us like a lie. I had more than a lot to catch up on—I had an entire lifetime worth of history and skills to learn. "I'll do the work. I'll figure it out."

Mr. Green paused and typed something on his laptop, the keys tapping softly in the silence. "Is there anything specific you'd like to talk about tonight?" he asked when his fingers finally stilled.

I looked at him then. I could've talked about school, about missing my family, about not being human anymore. I could've told him how scared I was that the people in charge at The Paranormal Program—an institute I'd spent six months at after being changed, an institute designed to transform newly turned supernaturals into productive, responsible members of society—had gotten it wrong. That they'd sent me here by mistake. But I opened my mouth and nothing came out, so I silently shook my head.

Mr. Green pulled back the sleeve of his gray tweed jacket and looked at his watch, the stainless steel bright against his dark brown skin. "You've got fifty minutes left. We don't have to talk if you don't want to, but you know it won't do you any good. Not in the long run." His brown eyes were serious. "I'm here to help you, Emily. But I need you to meet me halfway."

"Maybe I could—" I stopped as the cat flap in the door at the back of the room swung open. Within seconds,

Fred, a miniature dragon with blue scales and leathery wings, was bounding toward me.

"Sit," Mr. Green said firmly, his command stopping the small creature in its tracks. He handed a dried apricot to the expectant dragon, who devoured the treat in a single bite, then he patted him on the head. "Good boy."

"Can he sit up here?" I asked.

Part of me felt like I should've been scared of Fred. I mean, he was a dragon, complete with sharp teeth and a spiny tail, but he was so small and cute he seemed more like a puppy than a fire-breathing reptile. He panted with excitement, his tongue slipping out of his mouth, and I felt a grin slide across my face.

"You know, he doesn't greet everyone like this," Mr. Green said. "Go on. Invite him up."

I tapped my leg twice and Fred leaped onto my lap. He turned around in circles, his claws scratchy even through my jeans, then he lay down and curled his wings around his body. He yawned, sending a wave of apricot-scented breath in my direction, before closing his eyes and settling down to sleep.

Mr. Green uncrossed his legs and shifted the laptop onto the couch beside him. "What was it you were saying before we were interrupted?"

"I think—maybe I—" I ran a hand across the thick scales on Fred's back, and his body vibrated. I'd never imagined that dragons could purr. I'd never imagined that dragons were real. "You know what, it's fine. Maybe I can just come back next week?"

Mr. Green raised his eyebrows.

"I've already told you about the attack. And I've told you about what happened at The Paranormal Program. What more do you need to know?"

"I need to know how you're coping." Mr. Green leaned forward, his hands clasped together, his elbows on his knees. "You've undergone some major changes in the last nine months, and it's my job to help you navigate the effects of these."

"Navigate the effects? Really?" My blood hummed beneath my skin, and I knew I should pull myself back, but I couldn't stop. "You make it sound so academic. I get turned into a vampire, then I'm locked in a cell at The Paranormal Program for six months until I can control my newfound desire for blood, and then I get sent to boarding school with a bunch of other supernatural kids. I have to start junior year all over again. My family thinks I'm dead, and there's no cure for what I am. It's not some sort of theory. It's my life!"

Mr. Green considered me carefully. "And how do you think you're dealing with it?"

Ugh.

This was why it was easier not to engage.

"I'm dealing with it fine."

If fine includes spending most of my time trying to ignore what I am.

Mr. Green's eyes narrowed. "You're not scared of losing control?"

I straightened abruptly and Fred opened one eye, then

leaped down onto the floor. "Sorry, little guy." I tapped my leg again, but he didn't hop back up. Instead, he shot me a dirty look, stalked across the room, and settled himself at Mr. Green's feet.

I wiped my hands on my suddenly cold lap and stared at the floor. I needed to change the subject. Losing control had been one of my biggest fears when I'd been at The Paranormal Program. I'd had nightmares about killing my family, about draining their blood and still wanting more, more, *more*. It had taken me longer than most to learn how to manage the hunger. Some people never managed it at all.

"It's not an uncommon fear," Mr. Green said. "Especially for someone in your position."

I pressed my lips together.

"You were human for seventeen years," he continued. "It's going to take some time to adjust. But the warden at The Program gave you a glowing recommendation and —" He stopped suddenly, a curious expression on his face.

I sat forward. "Is that smoke?"

The fire alarm went off in the hallway outside, and I jumped.

"Outside." Mr. Green scooped up Fred and grabbed his laptop. "Now."

We dashed out into the corridor and made our way to the main exit alongside a handful of other students and staff. Mr. Green's office was part of the school medical center, a small building near the campus entrance, and as we passed various rooms along the way, I looked for the fire but couldn't see it.

My fangs tingled in my gums.

There wasn't a lot that could kill a vampire, but fire would definitely do it.

"Quickly," a voice boomed from behind us. "You need to move to the assembly area."

I looked back to see who had spoken and almost stumbled, my fear suddenly muted. "Who's that?" I said to Mr. Green.

"Dr. Norlgren." Mr. Green increased his pace. "Come on. This isn't a drill."

But I didn't want to.

I didn't want to do anything other than stop and stare.

There was something about Dr. Norlgren … He looked uncomfortable in his fluorescent-orange fire warden's jacket, the heavy material hanging limp around his thin elven frame, but that didn't matter. His skin, light green and smooth, shone as if millions of tiny diamonds had been caught beneath it. It was the most captivating thing I'd ever seen.

I took a step toward him. I wanted to touch him. To feel that shining light beneath my fingertips. My fangs slid out, but I barely noticed. I took another step, my hands rising in front of me.

"Emily."

It was more than a want.

It was a need.

"Emily Sanderson." A voice broke through my reverie, and I tore my gaze away from Dr. Norglren.

"Mr. Green?" My voice was strange and dreamlike, and I turned around, but the doctor had already gone. "Where's Dr. Norlgren?"

"Checking the rooms. He's the fire warden for this level." Mr. Green's dark brown forehead wrinkled in a frown. "Are you feeling all right?"

I lowered my hands. "I—I don't know."

"Come on." He took my arm and led me to the exit as smoke drifted around us like blackened fog. "We'll be safe in a minute."

We emerged into the night through a heavy set of arched doors, and I glanced over my shoulder as I hurried down the stairs to the path, hoping to catch another glimpse of Dr. Norlgren. I didn't know why he shimmered —none of the other elves at school did—but I didn't care. All I knew was that I had to see him again.

"Are you feeling better?" Mr. Green asked when we were a safe distance away from the medical center.

I looked back at the building and saw flames dancing bright and tall through one of the arched windows on the upper level. A shiver ran across my skin. This could've been bad. Like, *really* bad.

"I guess." I drew in a deep breath and smoke-tinged air filled my lungs. "I've never been in a fire before." My fangs brushed against my lower lip, and a shiver of hunger ran under my skin.

The warden was wrong. My control isn't good enough.

I drew in another deep breath and tried not to cough as I forced my fangs to retract. We were outside. We were safe. Everything was going to be okay.

I followed Mr. Green and the rest of the medical center evacuees toward the fire assembly point—the playing fields on the other side of campus. Most of them talked quietly to each other, the dark aniseed scent of their shock coloring the air around them, but I hung back just a little, silently observing the school that was now my home.

According to the school's website—accessible only via Supenet, aka the internet for supernatural beings—Mistwood Academy was concealed from human eyes by powerful magic. It was tucked away somewhere in a remote area of Washington State, and even though it would never be home, I had to admit it was beautiful. With its tidy gardens and tree-lined winding paths, it almost looked like a picturesque village, but the buildings were too imposing, their Neo-Gothic heaviness shifting the atmosphere from quaint to full-on spectacular. It was so different from anything I'd seen growing up in suburban Michigan that I was still getting used to all the pointed arches, vaulted ceilings, and elaborately decorated flying buttresses. Not to mention the huge, stone, *living* chimera that kept watch over every building.

My life was a dream and a nightmare.

Still, the five-hundred acre campus had everything we needed and more. We had state-of-the-art academic, arts, and sports facilities, as well as a convenience store and a coffee shop. There was even a huge forest, used mostly by the wereanimal staff and students. The entire campus was a secret world, a world which came to life at night. The school day didn't even begin until the sun went down.

The group I'd been walking with broke apart when we got to the playing fields, and Mr. Green pulled me aside. "We'll reschedule your appointment for later in the week," he said, shifting Fred in his arms. "Or I might be able to fit you in tomorrow."

I patted Fred on the head and shrugged. "Later this week is fine."

I watched the two of them melt away into the crowd, then set off to find the assembly point for my dorm, Worthington Hall. There were only eight dorms at the school, so it shouldn't have been difficult, but no matter how many times I circled the field, I couldn't find the right sign. Weaving my way through the center of the crowd, my heart stuttering in my chest, I searched instead for Miss Lassila, the housemistress, or Ms. Emmerson, the matron. Somehow I ended up back where I'd started, standing beneath one of the huge spotlights at the margins of the crowd.

"That's weird," I muttered, moving forward to try again.

My fangs prickled.

The hunger grew louder.

I pushed both it and the fangs away and made my way back through the crowd, but within minutes, I was standing once more beneath the same spotlight.

What the hell?

I turned and headed up the small, tree-covered incline that sat not too far from the edge of the field. Maybe I'd be able to spot the Worthington Hall sign from up there.

"Emily…"

It was a whisper, sinister yet beguiling, and I whipped my head around, searching for whoever was there. "Hello?" I said. It came out overly loud, sharp and feral and dangerous.

"Emily…"

"Who's there?" I demanded. "Show yourself."

"Emily…" The whisper was higher. Sweeter. A twisted invitation. "Come and play."

I shivered, yet found myself turning. I took one step, then another, moving farther up the slope. Everything about it felt wrong. But I couldn't stop myself. I was no longer in control of my own body.

"Who are you?" I said.

I took another step.

"Come and play, and I'll tell you."

Fear burned through muscles I couldn't command. My legs moved again. And again. Another step. Another withdrawal from safety.

"Tell me who you are," I ground out through gritted teeth.

I tried to turn, but nothing happened. A scream, rough and hot, scalded my throat.

I'm losing control.

"Emily!" It was another voice, deep and solid and familiar. "Emily Sanderson!"

I wobbled and my knees hit the ground. I reached forward—*on purpose*—and my hands scraped against dirt and grass.

I was free.

"Emily!" Mr. Green yelled. "Are you up there?"

"I'm here!" I pushed up to stand, then ran back down to the edge of the field, my feet almost skidding out from under me as I stopped in front of Mr. Green.

The psychologist's hands wrapped around my upper arms, steadying me. "You weren't there for the register check. Did you get lost?"

I looked back up at the tree-covered incline. Moonlight played lightly against the leaves, casting shadows on the earth, but that was all there was. Dirt and grass and trees. I hadn't seen or smelled anyone else up there. Had I imagined it?

There's been a mistake.

"Are you all right?" Mr. Green's forehead wrinkled. "Did something happen?"

They let me out too soon.

"It was nothing."

I couldn't tell him what had happened. If Mr. Green had any reason to think I was hearing things that weren't there, he'd send me back to The Paranormal Program. And I couldn't go back. Not again. Not after what had happened to Michael Miller.

Mr. Green picked up Fred, who'd been running

around in circles by his feet, and led me across the field, his expression serious. I'd told him once about Michael Miller, the only other person in residence with me for most of my time at The Paranormal Program. He'd been a regular man. A husband. A dog-owner. An accountant. Until he'd been turned into a werewolf.

Michael Miller had failed The Program.

There'd been circumstances that had led to his failure. Ones that weren't any fault of his own. But he'd never recovered, and now he was locked up in the penitentiary cells at the back of the building, hidden away from society forever.

I could never go back.

But what if the warden was wrong?

Mr. Green stopped in front of a brightly painted sign. "Here you go. Worthington Hall."

I nodded stiffly. "Thanks."

After a quick word with Miss Lassila, Mr. Green left, moving on to wherever he was supposed to be.

I didn't hear the voice again.

2

"You're late." Miss Lassila frowned as she ticked my name off the class list. She was a haltija, a house sprite, and she only came up to my waist, but she was formidable and strong, and I didn't want to end up on her bad side.

"I'm sorry," I said quickly. "I couldn't find the meeting spot."

Her lips pursed. "Well, it's here. Where it always is."

She marched away and I turned, just as Haven Montgomery ran up and threw her arms around me. "Em!" she squealed, her peroxide-blonde pixie cut tickling my chin. "Where were you? Did you get my messages? We've been looking for you for hours!"

Haven was my roommate and a witch and possibly the coolest person I knew. She was coming top in all of our classes, played flute in the orchestra, and could perform spells that even the teachers admitted were hard. She had at least ten piercings and five tattoos—all delicate floral pieces—and she dressed to her taste, not to trends. She could've been intimidating, but she was just too cute. Everyone said so.

I extricated myself from her grip and pushed my hair back behind my ears, the long brown strands falling back behind my shoulders. "I forgot my phone."

"How could you forget your phone?" Cayley Rodriguez, a succubus who lived across the hallway, strolled toward us. Her hazel eyes were sharp, and her all-black ensemble even sharper. "How can you do *anything* without your phone?"

I lifted my shoulders in a shrug.

"Not everyone needs to be connected twenty-four-seven." Haven pulled her phone out of her pocket and checked the screen. "Just most of us."

No matter what was going on, Haven and Cayley made me feel like I could almost belong at Mistwood Academy. That I wasn't just the new kid. The ex-human. The one who'd been attacked. Most of them had been born into this life—even the vampires.

They'd had their whole lives to learn control.

I glanced across the field at the tree-covered incline. I needed my cello. It always calmed me down. It centered me in a way that nothing else could. As soon as this was over, I could slip off to one of the practice rooms and—

"Why did they have to do a drill tonight?" Haven said suddenly, breaking into my thoughts. "It's way too cold for this." She slipped her phone into the pocket of her vintage pink trench coat, then rubbed her hands together,

her cherry-red nails bright against her pale white skin. "Do you think they'll notice if we leave?"

"We can't," I said. "It's not a drill."

"What?" Haven's blue eyes widened. "Are you serious?"

"How do you know?" Cayley leaned toward me, her expression bright. "Did you hear someone talking about it?"

I shook my head. "I was there. There was a fire in the medical center. Upstairs."

"Shit," Cayley said. "Did you—"

"Shhhh." Haven raised a finger to her lips, and the stem of the pink rose tattoo that graced her wrist peeked out from under her sleeve. "Incoming."

I almost groaned. I could smell the three of them before they even came into view, a sickly combination of werewolf and liberally applied perfume.

"Look, it's Haven, Cayley, and Ella." Courtney Beckett flipped her long honey-blonde curls over her shoulder, her lips curled up in a sneer. Her hands-on-hips pose was echoed by Vanessa and Danielle, the two werewolves at her side. Together, the three of them were striking, all model-tall and beautiful, though their charm was only skin deep.

"It's Emily," I said.

Courtney frowned. "Emmaline? I thought your name was Ella."

Breathe.

Don't let them get to you.

"You know what my name is."

Haven waved a hand dismissively. "Goodbye, Courtney."

"You don't want to talk to us?" Vanessa pouted, her pink lips glossy beneath the floodlights that lit up the field. "We were only teasing."

"Logan would talk to us if he was here," Courtney said.

Cayley snorted. "Only out of obligation."

I hadn't met Logan. I knew he was a werewolf, and he was one of Haven's best friends, but he hadn't been in school for the past three months—he'd missed the entire start of junior year. I didn't know why, only that it had something to do with pack business.

"Shut up, succubus." Danielle stepped forward. Her copper-colored bob swung around her face, highlighting her strong jaw and angular cheekbones. "You don't know anything. You're not one of us."

"Enough," I said. It was barely past breakfast and my patience was wearing thin. "Don't you have somewhere else to be?"

Danielle turned to me, her hazel eyes narrowed. She was a walking disaster, a war that needed to be fought. "No one was talking to you, mosquito."

Breathe.

My predator was a scream in my chest.

Control it.

Danielle took a step toward me, and power—electric, sharp, dominant—swirled into the space between us. She expected me to look away. My human side wanted to. But my fangs slid out, and I gave her a smile. "Is this what you wanted?" I said.

Danielle's fists clenched.

I could hear her blood, churning in her veins.

Take it.

Take it.

Take it.

"She's not worth it," Vanessa said, putting a hand on Danielle's arm. "None of them are."

Danielle didn't move.

Courtney pursed her lips and cast an assessing glance over the three of us. "Come on. Let's go." She spun on her heel, and Vanessa followed suit. Danielle stared at me for a moment longer before joining them.

"Thanks for stopping by," I said sweetly.

Courtney glanced back at me and glared before turning her attention to Haven. "My father informed me that Logan gets back tomorrow. Don't expect to see him. The alpha's been talking to him about the company he keeps."

Haven raised an eyebrow. "Logan's family don't have any issues with me. If you knew even half as much about him as you think you do, you'd be aware of that."

Courtney huffed and stalked away, her shoulders stiff with anger. Vanessa and Danielle strode after her, both of them flipping us the bird as they left.

"You okay?" Haven said when they were gone.

I nodded and willed my fangs to retract. "I'll be fine. What's their deal, anyway?"

Haven grimaced. "Too many years of being told they're better than everyone else."

"And too many years of getting everything they want," Cayley added.

"Except for Logan." Haven smiled. "Courtney will never have him."

The conversation moved on, from werewolf drama to theories about the fire, and I tuned out. I looked up at the stars, barely visible through the floodlit haze, and wondered for the millionth time how my life had come to this. I'd been nearing the end of junior year when I'd been turned, attacked behind the journalism room at school after music practice, my life drained away and replaced by something else. Something I'd never wanted.

I never got to finish school with my friends.

I never got to say goodbye to my family.

But I was given something that most people in my position never are—a new start. I was still alive, even if that life was totally different than what I had expected. And that could only be a good thing. I just had to remember that.

"Emily." Cayley bumped my arm with her elbow. "Are you even listening?"

"What?"

"Do they know what caused the fire?" Haven asked.

"And did they get everyone out in time?" Cayley added.

"I—I don't know." I thought of Dr. Norlgren checking all the rooms, a shining beacon through the smoke. Even in my memories, I was drawn to him, a moth to a flame.

Cayley tilted her head, her long brown hair falling over her shoulder. "What aren't you telling us?" she demanded.

"Nothing!"

What if they think I should be locked back up?

But I had to tell someone. Cayley and Haven had been supes all their lives—maybe there was something about the situation I'd missed. Haltingly, I told them everything. About Dr. Norlgren, about the voice, about the way my body hadn't been mine to control. They were both quiet, uncharacteristically so, and by the time I was finished my stomach was in knots.

"What is it?" I said. "What's wrong?"

Haven ran a hand through her hair, her forehead wrinkling. "I have no idea about Dr. Norlgren. He's just a regular elf. But the whole voice thing? That's different. I know what that is."

She didn't say anything else.

"Are you going to tell me?" I said. "Or do I have to guess?"

Cayley sighed and shook her head. "She'll get there eventually. You know, after the obligatory dramatic pause."

Haven rolled her eyes. "Have you told anyone else?" she asked me quietly.

"About the voice or about your fondness for dramatic pauses?" I tried to ignore the tightness in my chest.

"Just answer the question," she said.

"No, I haven't told anyone else. Just you guys. Why?"

Haven and Cayley shared a worried glance.

My fangs slipped through my gums. I'd never seen either of them this uneasy before. I was trying not to panic, but all I could think was that they were going to tell me I was broken. That something within me was *wrong*.

They'd send me back.

It's just one of those things. Sometimes the change just fails to take.

That's what the warden had said about Michael Miller.

That's what she'd say when she locked me up. I'd be put in a cell next to the werewolf who'd eat anyone who came near him, or the half-man half-tiger, or next to Kitty —the living nightmare—who'd offered me a cure that never existed. She was the one who'd destroyed Michael's life, who'd offered him too much power. He'd almost killed one of the guards. And I'd wanted to kill Michael.

Pull it together.

"Is it bad?" I said, my voice low. "Will they send me away?"

Cayley held up a hand. "Wait. You didn't do anything wrong."

"Someone did a spell on you," Haven said. "It was magic. *Dark* magic."

I blinked. "What?"

I still didn't know as much about the supernatural world as I would've liked to, but I did know that dark magic was bad. In a you-could-get-expelled-or-locked-up-if-you-even-think-about-doing-this kind of way.

"But who would've done that?" I said. "And why?"

Haven shrugged. "I could do—"

A magically-enhanced female voice cut through her reply. "Quiet please, students." It paused until everyone fell silent. "You may all return to your classes. You will be released dorm by dorm, beginning with Emberfield. Please wait for your dormitory to be called, then make your way to your second period class."

I look at Haven and Cayley, my head swimming. "What do I do? Should I tell someone? I can't just go to class and pretend this didn't happen."

"I'll do a spell," Haven said, her voice calm and steady. "And when I confirm that someone used magic against you, we'll tell a teacher. Or maybe Miss Lassila. But we'll have to do it soon, before the residue wears off."

"Now?" I said, pushing the sleeves of my sweatshirt up to my elbows. My skin was too tight, my clothes too constricting. I didn't know why anyone would want to perform dark magic on me. I wasn't anybody special.

"I can't right now. I've got a physics quiz." Haven tapped one heavy-booted foot on the ground as she thought. "What about third period? You're free, right? I'll skip Advanced Incantations and we'll do it then. There'll still be enough of the magic left."

"Worthington Hall," the voice announced. "You may go."

"What about me?" Cayley said. "Do you need me there? I've got Photography, but—"

"No," Haven said firmly. "You can't skip. You've already missed too many classes this semester. They're going to hold you back if you're not careful."

"Fine." Cayley's hazel eyes flashed, but the half-smile that curved her lips showed she wasn't really angry. "Tell me what happens, okay?"

I nodded, wishing there was no reason for it to happen at all.

I leaned back against the plush cushions that were scattered across my bed and sighed. I'd only been waiting five minutes, but it was five minutes too long. My stomach clenched, and I picked up Minikins, the stuffed toy cat I'd had since I was a baby. I needed Haven to do the spell. I needed to be *sure*.

Because what if she was wrong?

What if it wasn't dark magic at all?

My phone beeped, and I snatched it up. It wasn't Haven, but the message made me smile. It was a photo of Cayley, grimacing as she sat in the photography lab. Courtney sat on the stool behind her, glaring at someone off screen. Beneath them both was the added text: SEND HELP!!!

The door swung open before I could reply, and Haven burst through, a whirlwind of light and energy. She dropped her bag on the floor and barreled over to her desk, the ends of her coat swinging out behind her. "Sorry," she said as she pulled a book from a stack that was a whisper away from toppling. "Mr. Timmins kept the entire class back after the quiz. Apparently we're squandering our potential and aren't working hard enough and will never get accepted into a decent college. You know, the usual."

I set my phone back down on the bed beside me and frowned.

"Don't worry," she said, seeing my look. "He wasn't talking about me." She moved over to the large wooden trunk that guarded the foot of her bed and lifted the heavy lid. It opened smoothly, swinging up on silent hinges, and revealed almost everything Haven kept to execute her spells. She removed a polished quartz crystal, a vial of liquid, a few bags filled with herbs I couldn't identify, and a small glass jar. After rummaging around for a few more moments, she stood, a bright smile on her face. "You ready?"

I straightened. "You got permission for this, right?"

"Well ..."

"Haven!"

She waved off my concern with a flick of her hand. "I do this sort of thing all the time." She set everything down on her desk and shrugged off her coat. "You know that."

There was a rule at Mistwood Academy that said no student was to perform magic without permission. I mean, plenty of people did, usually without getting caught —there were ways around almost everything if you knew what you were doing—but I didn't want to get Haven in trouble.

"You could get suspended," I said. "Or expelled."

She poured some of the herbs from the bags into the

jar, then sprinkled a few drops of liquid from the vial on top of them. "They won't actually do that. It's a stupid, outdated rule that was put in place decades ago because someone didn't get what they wanted and started making trouble. They lost control and almost killed someone. But I'm not going to do that. And neither are you."

My breath caught in my throat.

"It's almost ready." Haven stirred the ingredients together with a thin silver rod and the earthy scent of magic flickered around us. "Go, sit over there."

I went into the middle of the room and lowered myself to the floor, watching as Haven set five wide candles down around me. She turned out the lights and lit the candles with a whispered command.

"Is this really necessary?" The smell of wax and flame drifted through the room, and shadows flickered along the walls. There'd already been one fire that night—I wasn't sure I could handle another.

Haven's nose wrinkled. "Sorry. I'll get a stronger result in the dark."

I didn't even know what was supposed to happen, but I kept quiet so Haven could begin. With movements that somehow managed to be both fluid and efficient, she poured the herbs from the glass jar into one hand, picked up the quartz crystal in the other, and began to chant. The words were Latin, so I didn't understand them, but as she spoke, she lifted her arm and let the herbs drift over me. They floated down, landing in my hair and on my clothes, smelling both delicate and sweet, grounding me.

"Vox in tenebris ..."

A light shot out of the crystal and the air around me began to glow, yellow and soft and warm. My limbs tingled, and without knowing why, I stood. Static electricity sparked around my whole body, and I bit back a gasp, not wanting to break Haven's concentration.

"Lux in tenebris ..."

The static charge intensified and the light changed, gradually shifting from yellow to purple. A series of crackles and pops rang out. Smoke filled the room, and I coughed as its strange, sulfur-tinged aroma hit my lungs.

And then, as suddenly as it had begun, it was over.

3

"WHAT DOES THAT MEAN?" I whispered.

The light was gone. The static electricity was gone. The smoke was gone.

Haven's fingers tightened around the crystal in her hand, which was now a streaky gray. "It means it was dark magic."

I wasn't sure whether to be relieved or horrified. Deep down, I hadn't really believed Haven when she'd told me the voice was part of a spell. I'd been convinced there was something wrong with *me*. But I hadn't lost control. And I wasn't going to be locked away. *This time, anyway.* We had proof that what I'd experienced had been caused by someone else.

Someone else who'd controlled me.

A flush of heat crept over my skin. Why hadn't I considered what that meant? I'd been manipulated before, back at The Paranormal Program, when Kitty had come into my dreams and played on my fears, but no one had ever assumed control of my body before.

They could make me do anything.

My heart thundered in my chest. The room was too small, too pitched, and I raised my hands to steady myself. Sweat slipped across my skin, which was already too cold, too inhuman, too *wrong*.

I couldn't breathe.

"We'll tell Miss Lassila," Haven said. "She'll be able to find whoever did this."

My fangs snapped out.

I pressed my fingers against my eyes, trying to find my center, trying to find control. But my stomach was churning, and the hunger was a fire in my veins. Haven's blood, type A positive and copper-sweet, flowed just beneath her skin.

I need it.

I stumbled back toward my bed. "You have to go. Now."

"It's okay." Haven's voice was steady. "You can handle this, Em. Stop fighting it."

Drink.

"I can't." My hands clenched into fists at my sides. "Just go. Please."

"No."

I hit the edge of the bed and thumped down on the mattress, the predator inside me screaming to be free.

"Breathe in and out. Nice and slow." Haven edged slowly toward her nightstand. On the surface she looked calm, but her gaze never left mine and the sooty scent of fear was a stain on her skin. "Let the hunger flow through you and out of you. Breathe it away."

My fingernails cut into my palms.

"Breathe," she said again, firmer this time, as she opened her nightstand drawer.

"I want to," I whispered. "But it's too strong."

Suddenly, Haven threw something toward me, and my hands shot up to catch it.

"Eat it," she said. "Now."

I tore open the packaging, and the sweet smell of chocolate hit the back of my throat. I shoved half the bar in my mouth and chewed, hoping it was enough to quell the hunger.

"Feeling better?" Haven said when I was finished.

I set the crumpled wrapper down on the bed, shame twisting through me. "Thanks," I whispered as I picked up Minikins and buried my face in his fur.

Haven's blue eyes softened. "Don't mention it."

I held Minikins close and breathed in the remnants of my past, of my home, of my humanity, to reminded myself who I was. Yes, I was a vampire, and I needed to drink blood to survive, but I was still Emily Montgomery, the same girl I'd always been. Responsible. Creative. Loyal.

And I'd almost attacked my best friend.

I stayed very still, clutching Minikins to my chest, until the last strains of the bloodlust faded away. When I looked up and saw Haven sitting calmly on her bed, my face flushed hot.

"You're not the first person this has happened to," she said, "and you won't be the last. It's nothing to worry about."

"But—"

"But nothing," she said firmly. "Anyway, I don't want to rush you, but we need to tell someone about the spell. I'll see if I can find Miss Lassila or Ms. Emmerson and we'll go from there. Do you want to come?"

I shook my head.

"You wouldn't have hurt me." Haven's boots thudded against the floorboards as she made her way across the room. She blew out the candles as she went, then flicked on the overhead light before stepping out into the corridor. "I trust you, Em."

She closed the door behind her, and I flopped back onto my bed and closed my eyes. I knew Haven was capable of defending herself—she had more power than half the teachers at Mistwood combined—but I never should have lost control.

I sat up and grabbed a banana from the fruit bowl I kept on top of my nightstand, peeled back the skin, and took a bite. The bloodlust was still a song in my veins, an itch beneath my skin, but if I ate enough food it would keep it at bay—I hoped—until I could visit the dining hall.

I wish I had my cello.

I took another bite, put my earbuds in, and chose a song off my phone at random. Any distraction was a good distraction.

"Hello?"

I screamed and threw the phone across the room. It almost hit the boy who was climbing in through the window above my desk.

"Who the hell are you and what are you doing in my room?" I demanded.

The boy caught my phone with one hand, then smiled, his brown eyes brightening. "I'm Logan. Logan Adams." He swung his legs over the desk and landed nimbly behind the chair. "You're Emily, right?"

I picked up my fallen earbuds and glared. "Yes, but that still doesn't explain what you're doing here. Or how you got past the chimera patrolling the roof. This is the third floor. How did you even get up here?"

Logan's smile broadened. "I came to see Haven."

I glared even harder as I took my phone from his outstretched hand. "You'll get us both in trouble."

He didn't look concerned.

I tried to ignore the way his messy brown hair fell over his forehead, and the dimple in his left cheek, and folded my arms across my chest. "Weren't you supposed to be coming back tomorrow?"

He raised an eyebrow. "Keeping tabs on me already?"

"I—"

"Shit." Logan froze. "Ms. Emmerson's coming." He turned back toward the window, but it was too late. The door was already opening.

"Mr. Adams." Ms. Emmerson's mouth turned down in disapproval at the sight of Logan. "What are you doing in Worthington Hall?"

"Sorry for the intrusion, Ms. Emmerson." Logan smiled at the house matron. "I needed to borrow some study notes from Haven. I've missed the first three months of school. I've got a lot of catching up to do."

"I'm well aware of your situation," she said sharply. "And I also know that your teachers have been providing you with plenty of work to do at home."

Logan started moving toward the door. "Well … it looks like you're all very busy here, so I'll be on my way now."

Ms. Emmerson held up a hand. She was tall and thin, a witch with pale white skin, long gray hair, and an aquiline nose, and though she was usually pretty nice, she was also scary enough to stop Logan with a look. "Detention, Mr. Adams. For one week—no, two—starting today." She wrote something on a small yellow card and handed it to him. "If I see you up here again, the consequences with be dire. Do you understand?"

Logan nodded, his gaze drifting to meet mine. The corner of his mouth lifted in a lopsided grin, and I couldn't help but smile back.

"Nice to meet you, Emily," he said as Ms. Emmerson led him out the door.

"Wish I could say the same," I retorted, lifting my hand in a wave.

I heard him laugh as he moved off down the corridor.

Haven closed the door and started cleaning the mess left over from the spell, sweeping up the remaining scattered herbs with a small brush and pan. It was strangely mundane, given what they'd been used for. "So, that was Logan," she said, tipping the herbs into the trashcan by the door.

"Yeah, I gathered."

Haven paused, though the herbs kept trickling over the edge of the pan. I wasn't sure if it was gravity or magic. "I didn't know he was getting back today," she said.

"Does he come up here often?"

"Do you want him to?"

"I—uh—" I picked up the remains of my banana and the candy bar wrapper, just so I'd have something to do. I definitely wasn't thinking about Logan's floppy brown hair. Or how good his butt had looked in his jeans.

"I saw the way you looked at him," Haven said.

"The way I looked at him?" I balled up the candy bar wrapper and threw it, with the rest of the banana, across the room. To my surprise, they both missed the trash can completely.

"Wow, you really are distracted," Haven said. "Are you feeling okay after … you know, everything?"

She had a good point. Vampirism had taken a lot from me—namely, my *life*—but it had also given me a whole host of new abilities. I was practically invulnerable, I healed fast, and I could see perfectly in the dark. I could hear almost anything, from a pulse to the barest whisper, and I could smell everything. Shampoo, laundry detergent, emotions. None of it was secret. I'd mostly gotten used to the constant assault on my senses, but some days it was still a lot. I also had improved speed and reflexes, and I shouldn't have missed that shot.

I grabbed the wrapper and the banana skin and deposited them directly into the garbage. "I'll be fine," I said quickly.

Ms. Emmerson flung open the door, her movements like fire, and I swiftly moved out of the way. "Now, girls," she said sharply as she strode into the room, "I am thoroughly unimpressed with the two of you. I shouldn't have to reiterate the rules: you are not permitted to have boys in your room, and you must never perform unauthorized magic."

I glanced over at Haven, whose gaze cut to the candles still laid out on the floor.

"Sorry, Ms. Emmerson," she said.

"Sorry," I echoed.

She regarded the two of us carefully, her chin tilted down and her hands on her hips. I hadn't often seen her angry—maybe once or twice, and never directed at me—and I didn't like the way her blue eyes stared right into my soul. "You need to feed now," she said suddenly, and I flinched.

"What about the spell?" Haven crouched down and picked up the candles. "The residue will wear off soon."

"It can wait a little longer." Ms. Emmerson stepped back into the hallway, her long brown dress swirling around her legs. "Come on. Let's go."

Five minutes later, Ms. Emmerson, Haven, and I walked through the large, arched doors into the dining hall. While every building at Mistwood Academy was architecturally impressive, the dining hall was the most extravagant of all. The ceiling was high and vaulted, and the floor was paved with encaustic tiles featuring geometric patterns in plum, emerald, and gold. The walls were decorated with mosaics featuring images from myth and legend, and stained glass windows glittered up above.

"Come along," Ms. Emmerson said, flicking her long silvery braid away from her shoulder. "Quickly."

Haven and I followed her to the feeding room, a small chamber that branched off the main dining hall, hidden behind a heavy wooden door.

"I won't be long," I said before slipping inside.

The feeding room wasn't nearly as impressive as the main dining hall, but it was still more beautiful than anything I'd ever seen when I was human. Delicately-colored oil paintings graced the walls, and large arched windows offered a view to the garden beyond. I took a seat at one of the small wooden feeding tables, tucked behind a tasteful maroon curtain, and waited for the teacher in charge to assign me a Nutriment.

I was the only student in the room, and I drummed my fingers lightly against the table as I waited, wishing I was already done. Even after nine months of drinking blood—at first multiple times per day and now two or three times a week—I still hated it. I probably I always would.

"Hello, Emily. I'll be your Nutriment for today." The

curtains opened and an auburn-haired human woman walked through. She sat down opposite me and smiled, then placed her arm on the table. "My name's Jennifer."

I swallowed hard and forced out a polite greeting. Jennifer smiled encouragingly and moved her arm closer. I'd fed from her before. I knew she'd chosen to be there and would be paid handsomely by the school for her services, but it still felt so wrong. I leaned forward, taking in her scent—she was type AB positive, my favorite—and I wondered if she had to lie to her family about where she was. For the most part, humans didn't know about our world, and the ones who did, the ones we fed on, were bound to secrecy by magic. It wouldn't be safe for them, or us, if our existence was public knowledge.

"It's okay," she said. "I'm ready."

Breathe.

I picked up her wrist and closed my eyes. It was easier that way—I could pretend she wasn't human. She didn't even flinch when my teeth broke the surface of her skin, slipping down into the vein. I'd been taught how to make the experience pleasant for the Nutriment. Enjoyable even. But I didn't want it to be pleasant for me. I couldn't lose myself that way. I was scared I'd never find my way back.

As soon as I was done, I released her arm and set it down gently on the table. "Thank you very much," I said, ignoring the part of me that still wanted more. "Have a good night."

The Nutriment gave me a hazy smile and reached for a

cookie from the tray the supervising teacher placed down on the desk in front of her. "I will," she said.

I left the room as quickly as possible, keen to get away from the smell of her humanity, the smell of her blood, but what was waiting for me next wasn't really any better.

"I have to what?" I said to Ms. Emmerson as she escorted us from the dining hall.

"You have to go to Mr. Olaru's office." Ms. Emmerson walked briskly, her ankle boots clacking on the cobblestone path. "He wants to see you both to discuss the incident."

"But the residue—" Haven said.

"Will still be there when you're done," Ms. Emmerson said, her words clipped.

"Will you be coming in with us?" I asked.

Ms. Emmerson shook her head. "There's an issue with one of the freshman back at Worthington that I have to deal with. Unfortunately, it can't wait." She looked at her watch and increased her speed. "I'll catch up with the two of you later."

We got to Mr. Olaru's office more quickly than I expected. Unfortunately. I'd only talked to the headmaster a few times, but it was a few times too many. He was a vampire, and he was old, though no one seemed to know exactly where or when he came from. There were rumors, of course, a couple of which suggested he'd been around since before the Iron Age, while another claimed he'd been turned in Europe in the thirteenth century.

Either of them could've been true.

"Do you think anyone will notice if we leave?" I whispered to Haven as we sat in the small reception area outside the headmaster's office.

"Yes," she said. "They would."

"But—"

She stopped me with a level stare. "I'm gonna give you the benefit of the doubt here, because I know you're still new to … well, basically everything, but someone used dark magic on you. *Dark magic.* We can't do nothing about it."

I looked down at the floor and sighed. "I don't want to talk to him."

"Mr. Olaru?" Haven grimaced. "No one wants to talk to him. Ever. But sometimes we have to."

A telephone beeped, and Mr. Olaru's gray-haired assistant looked up. She pointed across the room with a gnarled, arthritic finger. "You may enter."

Haven grabbed my hand. "We'll be fine," she said firmly.

I wished I'd worn something more somber.

Mr. Olaru's office was exactly how I remembered it—dark and unwelcoming. Heavy drapes covered the windows, the steel-gray fabric hanging in folds that stretched from ceiling to floor; the only illumination came from two antique lamps, one standing beside a bookshelf at the back of the room, the other sitting on Mr. Olaru's desk, its shade dark and textured.

"What do you want?" the headmaster demanded. His

voice was a weapon, sharp and slick with blood, and a shiver prickled over my skin.

"There was an … an incident," I said, forcing myself to meet his gaze.

"With magic," Haven added. "Dark magic."

Mr. Olaru pointed to the two wooden chairs that sat facing his desk. "Sit. And explain yourselves."

Haven and I did as instructed, and by the time we were done I was certain we'd made a terrible mistake. Mr. Olaru seemed barely human at the best of times—his skin was paper thin, almost translucent, and he held himself with an unnatural stillness that always made me think he was more predator than man. But now he seemed like nothing I'd ever seen before. His lips were pulled back in a grimace, and his pale-blue eyes seemed to glow from within.

"Why didn't you tell me about this earlier?" he snapped.

Because I thought I was losing control.

And because you're terrifying.

"I—uh—we—" I stuttered.

"We had class," Haven said smoothly. "And we weren't certain it was anything at all."

Mr. Olaru nodded, his face shaded and hollow in the lamplight. His fingers were steepled beneath his chin, their bones too close to the surface. "Perhaps your initial assessment was correct. The grounds are warded and are well-protected by the chimera." He turned his attention to the computer on his desk and pressed a few buttons. It seemed strange that he knew how to use a computer at all. "We have had no alerts, magical or otherwise. I believe what this is, is a waste of my time."

"But, the spell—" I began.

Haven cut me off with a glance. "If I may, sir," she said, "is it possible for one of the teachers to perform a residue spell? Just to be certain?"

Mr. Olaru's nostrils flared, though the rest of him remained motionless. "Are you telling me how to do my job, Miss Montgomery?"

"No, of course not, sir. It's just—"

"Silence!" Mr. Olaru barked. "I do not have to explain myself to you. Return to your classes. And if anything like this ever happens again, you will inform me immediately."

I stood so fast my chair almost tipped.

"In this case, however, you need not speak of it again," he continued. "Not to me, not to your teachers, and not to your peers. The faculty will execute a series of wide-reaching spells to search for residue, but we will deal with the situation quietly. There is no need to cause unnecessary alarm."

"Yes, sir," Haven said quickly.

I echoed her words, then we both turned and scurried from the room. Neither of us spoke until we were halfway across campus.

"As soon as they do the residue spells, they'll see that I'm right," Haven said as we reached Worthington Hall. "I guarantee it."

4

As soon as I walked into orchestra practice, just after my last class had finished, I knew Haven's mood had improved. She was standing at the far end of the music room with Logan, her hands moving quickly as she talked.

"Hey," she said when she saw me. "I was just telling Logan what happened in Biology. I accidentally let the toad out of its enclosure and it hopped behind Mr. Carter's desk, and when he went to get it he—" She broke down in giggles, unable to continue.

Logan grinned at me. "This is her third attempt. I don't think we'll ever find out what happened."

Haven wiped her eyes, her shoulders still shaking with silent laughter. "It was so ridiculous."

Mr. Longley—a tall, thin elf who was head of the Music Department and also our orchestra conductor—clapped his hands and the room fell silent. "Rehearsal starts in five minutes. Finish your snacks, finish your gossip, and get set up."

"I'll be back in a minute," I said to Haven, who'd finally recovered. "I have to get my cello from the storeroom."

She nodded, then glanced quickly at Logan before meeting my gaze. "Did you hear anything else about … you know?" she said quietly.

I shook my head. "I'll talk to Ms. Emmerson about it later."

I set off for the storeroom, winding my way around various instruments and their owners, and was almost out the door when Logan ran up behind me.

"I'll come with you," he said, stepping to the side as a senior walked past with her double bass. "I need to see if my viola's still there."

"You didn't take it with you over summer break?" I asked, surprised.

Logan shook his head as we ducked out of the music room. "I was a bit preoccupied at the time." He ran a hand through his dark brown hair, leaving it even messier than it was before. "I hope I didn't get you guys in trouble earlier. You know, up in your room. I've never been caught before."

I almost said it was fine, but I hadn't decided if it was or not, so I chose not to say anything. Logan seemed okay —and he was cute as hell—but it didn't change the fact that he'd come into my room uninvited. It was my safe space, the one place I could relax and let things go—even with a roommate. What if he'd arrived five minutes earlier? He would've seen me struggling with my bloodlust, ready to attack Haven. It would've been a disaster.

"I'm sorry, okay?" He opened the door to the storeroom, then looked back at me, his dark eyes serious. "Honestly. Haven didn't have a roommate last year—I think we both got used to doing whatever we wanted, whenever we wanted. But obviously it's not just *her* room anymore. If you don't want me coming up, just say the word."

"It's not that I don't want you there. It's more that—"

"Coming through!" Mia, a statuesque dryad with wild brown hair, slipped past us, her long peasant skirt swinging around her legs as she walked. "Good to see you back, Logan," she said. She grabbed her violin, its case adorned with brightly-colored stickers, and strode back out of the small, boxy room. "Your viola's in the back. I've been keeping an eye on it for you. It's not going to look after itself, you know."

Logan snorted. "Thanks, Mia."

"They can tell when they're unloved!" she sung brightly over her shoulder.

"I never know if she's being serious or not," Logan muttered.

"She smelled serious enough to me." I went into the storeroom and took my cello from its usual spot.

Logan disappeared down the back. "I think it's a dryad thing. It's like she can commune with them or something. You know, 'cause they're made of wood." He grunted and something crashed to the floor. "Shit. Anyway, about before—"

"It's fine." Despite how uncomfortable I'd been with having a stranger come through my window, Logan's apology *was* genuine. I could tell by the faint scent of mint leaves and sincerity. "Just give me some warning next time, okay?"

He stepped forward. There was a shabby black viola case under his arm, and dust clung to the tips of his hair. "You sure?"

I put out my hand. "Give me your phone."

Logan looked confused, but he unlocked his cell and passed it to me. I entered my details and smiled. "Now you can text before you come up." I passed it back, and Logan's fingers brushed against mine. Electricity shot through me and I ducked my head, hoping he hadn't noticed.

We made it back to the music room just before rehearsal started, and for the next hour I forgot about black magic, glowing doctors, and losing control. I even forgot about the cute boy across the room with the dark brown eyes and the abandoned viola. For a brief blissful moment, all that mattered was the music. I didn't know how or why, but my cello kept me grounded. I'd been playing since I was nine, first at the suggestion of my father, and then later because I'd grown to love it, and it had become even more important to me since my turning. It had become the only way for me to *feel*, to experience the full range of my emotions without the possibility of awakening the bloodlust.

When I played, I never lost control.

When I played, I could forget what I was.

Mr. Longley tapped his baton on his music stand. "Great practice today, people. Flutes, you know what you need to work on; violas, *one* of you knows what he needs to work on; and trumpets, you did great today. I can hear how much work you've put in since last week." He removed his glasses and tucked them in his jacket pocket. "Put the stands and chairs away, then get out of here. Enjoy the rest of your night."

Haven came up behind me as I put my cello in its case. Her flute case was already slung across her shoulder by its thick purple strap. "Do you want me to come see Ms. Emmerson with you?" she whispered.

I held my cello closer. "Can we just pretend it never happened?"

Haven raised her eyebrows but didn't say anything more. Instead, she looked down at her phone. "Cayley's having some sort of drama with her History homework and wants me to meet her at the library." Her words were short, full of barely-concealed smoke and impatience. "If you're not going to see Ms. Emmerson ..."

"Go and help Cayley. I'll get some food and maybe come find you after." I slipped my sheet music into its folder and stood. Logan's gaze caught mine from across the room, and my cheeks grew warm as I remembered the touch of his fingers on mine. I quickly glanced away.

"You and Logan should go together," Haven said, a little bit louder.

Logan frowned. "Where are we going?"

"The dining hall." Haven looked down at her phone again and quickly tapped out a message. "Cayley and I will meet you there later, and then you and I are going to go and find out more about what happened to you today. Whether you like it or not."

I glared at her swiftly retreating form. "Dammit, Haven," I muttered under my breath.

"I've said the same thing more times than I can count," Logan said as he walked toward me. "Shall we go?"

We stashed our instruments away in the storeroom and made our way over to the dining hall. The night was crisp and clear, and though the school was beautiful with its grandiose buildings and gently lit cobblestone paths, I longed for a glimpse of the sun.

I missed its warmth, its color, its life.

I missed *my* life.

Technically, I wasn't really dead, or even undead. I breathed and ate regular food and slept in a normal bed. I could see my reflection in the mirror. I could probably even have kids one day. But what I was living sometimes felt like a half-life; I was confined to the darkness, hidden away like something dangerous.

No, not like something dangerous.

I *was* something dangerous.

"Do you like it here?" Logan asked, his voice breaking into my thoughts.

I shrugged, not willing to tell him what I'd really been thinking. "It could be worse."

"I heard that was Mr. Olaru's first choice for the school motto," he said, nudging my arm with his elbow.

I bit back a smile and ignored the heat that radiated from his body. He smelled good, like forest air and wolf. "What about you?" I said. "What do you think of Mistwood Academy?"

Something indecipherable flickered in his dark eyes, but it was gone so fast I thought I imagined it. I drew in a deep breath, but he still just smelled like forest and wolf. There was nothing bitter about him, nothing that wasn't true, though he hadn't answered me yet. It was easy to lie by omission.

"It could be worse," he said with a grin.

I didn't smell any emotion at all.

We walked on in silence until we got to a narrow archway. I slowed to let Logan through first, but my foot struck a loose stone and I slipped. I braced myself for impact—not even my enhanced reflexes were gonna get me out of this one—but the impact never came.

"You okay?" Logan asked.

"Uh—yeah?" It came out muffled, and I realized I was crushed up against Logan's chest. His very warm, very solid, very inviting chest. I pushed myself back. "Thanks for the rescue," I said awkwardly, tucking my hair behind my ears.

"Anytime. Do you want me to—" He stopped, his expression hardening.

Perfume.

Sickly sweet and far too strong.

"Hello, Logan." Courtney stood behind us, her gray eyes flashing. Danielle was at her side, staring down at us in her usual aggressive way, while Vanessa lingered behind, making out with a dark-haired boy I'd never seen before. "I've been looking for you."

Logan turned and smiled, though it didn't meet his eyes. "Well, you found me."

"My father's been discussing things with the alpha," Courtney said. "He assured us that everything's going to plan." She stepped forward and placed a hand on Logan's chest. "And he assured us you'll hold up your end of the bargain."

"The bargain?" he said.

Danielle rolled her eyes. "You know what she's talking about."

"Yeah, but—"

"You don't want to anger my father." Courtney moved even closer, a challenge in her eyes, her body, her scent. "Or yours."

"Hey," called the dark-haired boy who'd been making out with Vanessa. "Are you gonna stand in that archway all night?"

"Probably," Logan said, though he took my hand and led me through the short passage, leaving it clear for Courtney and her friends.

None of them moved.

Something was wrong, though I didn't know what. There was too much tension, too much to see and smell and hear, and I couldn't figure out what was going on. It was clouding my senses—the sea spray of sadness, the bright flame of anger, the smoke-covered fear. Werewolf and perfume. Forest and hate. Whispers too low to decipher.

I glanced up at Logan. His shoulders were low, his pulse slow and steady.

"We should go," I said quietly.

Courtney's nostrils flared.

"I don't know why you bother with him, Courtney." Danielle set her hands on her hips. "Look. They're holding hands."

Logan didn't pull away like I thought he would. Instead, his fingers tightened around my own.

"I think it's cute." Vanessa giggled as the dark-haired boy licked a trail up her neck, his arm around her possessively. "But I always thought Logan was secretly in love with Haven. He spends all his free time with her."

"Maybe he likes them both," Danielle said.

Vanessa giggled again, but Courtney's entire body was tense. "Logan, you have to stop acting like this." Her voice was dark and bitter, like burned coffee grounds and spite. "I know what's been happening in the pack. You have to grow up and face your responsibilities. You know what that entails, and you know my expectations."

I had no idea what she was talking about, but I couldn't help the snort of laughter that erupted from my throat. "Your expectations? What are you, his mother?"

"Stay out of our business, mosquito," Courtney snapped.

Logan bristled, and a sudden flare of tension flowed through his fingers and into mine. "That's enough." He tugged on my hand and started walking away. I quickly followed.

"I won't be patient forever," Courtney called after us.

I glanced over my shoulder and saw Vanessa pull back from the dark-haired guy, who now had fuchsia lipstick smeared all around his mouth. "You should be careful," she said to Logan. "You're not Courtney's only option."

"He's barely an option at all," Danielle said. "We've all seen the scars. And heard the rumors."

Logan stopped and turned to face them. "Maybe they're not rumors." Then he smiled, showing too many teeth. His eyes glowed with a hint of amber. It wasn't what I'd expected him to do, but it worked.

Courtney and the others backed off, though Danielle's lip curled as she passed me. "I hope you like them crazy," she said.

I didn't say anything until they were a long way away.

"So," I finally said to Logan. "What was all that about?"

He released my hand and tugged down the sleeves of his hoodie. "It's nothing."

"But … the things they said. What did they mean?" I snuck a quick glance at him, then looked away.

"You mean, about me being crazy?" Logan shrugged. "You have nothing to worry about. I'm perfectly sane. I have the papers to prove it."

I wasn't sure what to say. I'd gotten used to being able to read people, to listen to their heartbeats, to savor the scent of a lie. It was one of the few things I liked about being a vampire. But Logan confused me. He could switch from serious to polite to flippant in the blink of an eye, his pulse remained steady no matter what was going on, and most of the time I could barely smell his emotions at all. I'd only met one other supe who'd been able to control their physiological reactions as well as he could—the warden at The Paranormal Program.

I breathed in again, reaching out with my senses, but still there was nothing but wolf and forest air. *What are you trying to hide? Scars? Rumors?* I didn't understand.

"Come on," Logan said. "The others will be there already."

I gave him one last glance, searching his face for something that would explain what had happened, or maybe something that would just explain *him*, but he gave me an easy smile and started walking. I went along with him, shivering in the cold night air, more out of habit than necessity.

"Did you really need Haven's study notes?" I said.

He shook his head. "No, but ... Wait. Do you feel that?"

My senses had gone on alert before he'd even finished the question. We stopped walking, both of us listening and watching. We were in the quad just outside the science building, and it was deserted, too quiet and still in a way that was definitely wrong.

My skin tingled. "Let's go."

We hadn't even taken two steps when a fine gray powder drifted down in front of us.

"What the hell?" Logan muttered, moving forward to get a closer look.

An intense white light flashed into the space around us. It was bright like lightning, but it lingered, sucking away the darkness until I couldn't see anything at all. I reached out in front of me, looking for something to anchor me, but all I felt was air, cold and empty, slipping through my fingertips.

Shit.

"Emily, come and play." It was a whisper, drawn out and familiar.

No.

No, no, no.

This couldn't be happening. Not again.

"Logan," I said, blinking as I tried to clear the spots from my vision. The strange light had faded, but I still couldn't see properly. "Logan, are you there?"

I paused, trying to follow the sound of his heartbeat, the heat of his breath, the smell of his blood. He was somewhere close …

I turned, blinking harder.

He was … *there.*

My vision cleared and I saw him, lying silent and still on the grass beneath a large ash tree. "Logan!" I yelled, trying to run toward him.

I couldn't move.

My body wouldn't co-operate.

My fangs shot out and I screamed, but no matter how much I tried I couldn't move.

"This way, Emily." The voice drifted around me like mist on the wind, and my whole body turned. I couldn't do anything to stop it. "Come to me. You have something we want."

I struggled against the spell, desperate to break free, but my feet moved forward, first one step, then another. Terror lodged in my throat. "Logan!" I screamed. My body kept moving. "Please, wake up."

He growled before he moved. From the corner of my eye, I saw him stand slowly, swaying slightly as he moved his head from side to side like he was searching for something. Then his growl deepened into something angry, something primal, and he began to strip, slipping his hoodie over his head.

"Logan," I said again, not quite sure what he was doing. "This has happened before. During the fire drill we had earlier today. It's a spell."

His gaze burned into mine, his eyes glowing amber. "How do I stop it?"

"I don't know." I tried to remember how I'd escaped earlier. Mr. Green had been searching for me and ... "Say my name. My whole name."

Logan growled again, louder this time. "I don't know your whole name."

"Emily Sanderson."

It didn't work. I kept moving forward, even after he said it at least five times over, unable to escape the hold of the spell. "Let me go!" I yelled.

"No," the voice whispered. "Not until you give us what we want."

With ferocious speed, Logan stripped off the rest of his clothes. For a second he was naked, all lean lines and tanned skin, his muscles taut below the surface. Then he began to change. His limbs contorted, his body cracking and shifting into painful-looking shapes that weren't anywhere near human. He didn't make a sound until the wolf stood there, large and brown and angry, and then the growl began again. He looked entirely animal, but I could see his eyes—Logan was there behind the amber gaze, the human still present within the predator.

And then he ran. He took off like a bullet, rushing past me in a streak of wind and fur. My body turned, not by choice, and I was able to watch him shoot through the night. He sailed over the top of the brick wall that edged one side of the quad and—

—an exhalation, a low-pitched grunt, from someone— something?—on the other side.

I tried to step forward, then fell, overbalancing as the spell suddenly stopped. The dirt was hard under my knees, and I pushed up quickly to stand. I ran to the wall and somehow scrambled over the top. Rough brick scraped against my hands, my ankles, but I got where I wanted to go.

Then I crouched down low and watched. Logan was still in wolf form, and he was fighting a man clad entirely in black. Even his face was obscured by a knit balaclava. He was tall and broad, obviously strong, and moved with the grace and confidence of a seasoned fighter. I breathed in deeply, searching for a scent, but there was nothing. I could smell the trees, the grass, the distinctive smell that clings to every school, but beyond that there was a void. Like a whole part of him didn't exist.

Is he a dream? Has Kitty done this?

He looked at me, his eyes gleaming with animal fire.

He started toward me.

I stood, legs slightly apart, anchoring myself firmly. I'd fight him. I wasn't entirely sure how. But I'd fight him.

I raised my fists.

Then Logan barreled into him, a growl tearing from his throat. I expected him to fall, but he weathered the impact with barely a flinch.

"What are you?" I yelled.

Logan tried again. He lunged forward, snapping at the man, but the stranger didn't seem bothered. He lifted a leg, the movement light, almost lazy, then kicked Logan hard in the side.

I shot forward. "Leave him alone, you asshole!" Logan didn't deserve this; he hadn't done anything wrong. And as far as I knew, neither had I.

The stranger paused, his leg already lifted to kick Logan again. "Make me." It was low and taunting, the rasping jeer of a man who clearly knew what he was. And who really didn't care.

I rushed forward, fangs bared, moving through space until our bodies collided. A starburst of lights flickered through my vision, and I took a step back, my hands flying up to hold my head.

"You'll have to try harder than that." The man laughed, rich and ugly. It was the kind of sound that crawled over your skin and burrowed into your bones. It was the kind of sound I never wanted to hear again.

"Who are you?" I said.

The man cocked his head to the side, studying me carefully with his eyes. "A delivery man."

I looked at Logan, who nodded almost imperceptibly. I didn't understand what he meant, but before I could do anything else, he bounded forward, moving faster than anything I'd ever seen. His jaw opened wide and the man in black yowled as Logan's teeth sunk into his leg.

"Get off, you bastard," the man rasped, shaking his leg.

Logan's jaw tightened.

The smell of blood filled the air.

Drink.

This was my chance. I darted forward and knocked the man to the ground. I threw myself on top of him and hooked my fingers beneath the edge of his balaclava.

"Not yet." He lifted his legs, pushing me up, then flipped us over. "It's not time."

Take it.

I struggled, trapped beneath his weight, and Logan bit down again. But this time the man was ready. He grabbed a small fabric pouch from his pocket and blew out more of the powder we'd seen before. It smelled like wheat and ivy and a handful of other things I couldn't identify.

"*Volant*," he whispered.

There was another flash of light, just as blinding as the first. Logan howled and I reached for him, but he was already gone. The sound of the impact was sickening; bones crunched and skin tore. I wriggled out from beneath the man and stumbled through the dark. "Logan," I called. "Where are you?"

The air shifted behind me.

"*Volant*," the man whispered in my ear.

MY EYELIDS FLUTTERED OPEN. "HELLO?" The word was barely a croak; my mouth was so dry my tongue hardly moved.

"Holy shit," someone said. "You're finally awake." It sounded like Logan. His voice was deep and low and filled with something confusing. Something I couldn't understand.

"Have I been asleep?" I mumbled. My eyes kept closing. I forced them open and turned my head to the side. "Logan? Is that you?"

"Yeah," he said. "It's me."

Lightning blasted through my skull. My stomach pitched and I closed my eyes again. "Where are we?"

Delicate footsteps crossed the floor. "Hello, Emily." It was a woman's voice, soft and lyrical, but I didn't know who she was. "Can you open your eyes?"

I blinked. "I'm so tired."

"I know you are," the woman said. "But I need you to open your eyes."

I did as she said, and the world came slowly into view, soft-focus and wrong, and wavering around the edges like it might disappear without warning.

"Very good." The woman moved around me, checking things and shifting things, talking quietly the entire time. I wasn't sure if I was supposed to understand her. Her voice kept drifting past me, soothing and soft and mild, like a lullaby.

Everything went dark.

"No, Emily," she said, louder now. "Open your eyes."

I blinked again. "Why? What's going on?" My lower lip split and I tasted blood.

"Here." The woman slipped a paper straw in my mouth. "Drink."

I tried, but I couldn't get my mouth and throat to co-operate, and water spilled over my chin.

The woman looked at me with concern and pulled the straw away. "Oh dear," she said. "You're bleeding again."

I lifted my hand and gingerly touched my lips, but the cut felt tiny. Not enough to be worried about. Confused, I looked up at the woman. She was petite and beautiful, with olive skin and long black hair tied up in a tidy bun. She was dressed all in blue—a short-sleeved shirt with a pocket watch hanging off it, and plain loose trousers, like … a nurse?

"You need a fresh bandage," she said, setting the drink down on a small table beside me. "I'll be right back."

I wanted her to stay. There was something calming about her, something that reminded me of home. But she walked off quickly and didn't look back. My gaze drifted to the wall, where a clock sat like a weapon, each tick a bullet through my skull.

Why does everything hurt?

"Logan?" I said.

"Yeah?"

I turned my head and saw him, sitting just a few feet away from me, propped up in a hospital-style bed. He was battered and bruised, his skin dotted with patches of dried blood.

"What happened?" I asked, each syllable splitting my lip a little more. "Are we in the infirmary?"

Logan frowned. "You don't remember? The quad? The guy in black?"

The guy in black.

The guy in black.

He'd taken control of me. Again. He'd attacked us and he'd—

"What's that?" Logan said as the machine to my left started beeping.

I closed my eyes.

"Make it stop," I whispered.

But I wasn't just talking about the machine. I pressed the heels of my hands to my eyes as the memories flooded through me. Light. Blood. Pain.

I can't breathe.

Gasping, I pushed myself up, my fingers clawing the

sheets, nails catching in the smooth white cotton. "Where is he?" I said. "*Who* is he?"

The nurse hurried back into the room. "It's all right." She checked the machine, then glanced over at the little plastic clip that sat on my finger. She set down the supplies she was holding and picked up my arm, her warm fingers quickly finding my pulse. "Everything's okay. You're safe now."

I wanted to believe her. She smelled like orange blossom, fragrant and true, but my head was spinning and the room was too small, too sterile, too *wrong*. I needed to leave. I shook off her hand, then tore the plastic clip from my finger. I was about to grab at one of the needles embedded in my skin, the one at my elbow, when she grasped my hands.

"You need to stop," she said gently. "You're safe. He's not here."

"That doesn't answer my question." I panted as the room spun around me. "Where is he? Who is he? Who are you?"

"I'm Ms. Park, the head nurse. I'm—"

I didn't hear what she said next. I leaned over the side of the bed and vomited all over the floor. Hot tears burned behind my eyes. "I'm sorry," I whispered, the fight going out of me. A sob slipped out from between my lips.

"It's okay," Ms. Park said. "You have a concussion—it's a completely normal physiological response. Just lie back." She helped me settle back down against the pillows, then lay a warm hand on my forehead. "I'll clean this up and get you some fluids. We need to get your heart rate down."

"But—the man—" I said.

Ms. Park smoothed my hair back from my face, and my tears flowed harder. "Your attacker was apprehended shortly after you were knocked out. You have nothing to worry about. You really are safe." She placed a small paper sick bag on the bed next to me, patted me on the arm, and left the room.

I wiped my eyes and stared up at the ceiling. The attacker may have been caught, but I didn't feel any better. My head was pounding, and my body ached like I was bruised all over.

I want my mom.

I covered my face with my hands as more tears spilled over my cheeks.

Ms. Park came back, carrying a bucket and mop, and began to clean up the mess. The sharp smell of disinfectant burned my nose and my throat, and I closed my eyes. My thoughts whirled as she washed her hands and hooked up some sort of IV drip to my arm, and I pushed down the panic that tightened my chest as she taped a gauze pad to the side of my head.

The hunger surged to life.

Ms. Park was a werewolf; forest and blood sang in her veins.

I tried to sit.

"Not so fast," she said firmly. "I'll be back in ten

minutes with dinner, a blood bag, and a Nutriment. Can you hold it together until then?"

No.

I took a deep breath and nodded.

"Good." Ms. Park checked on Logan, then gathered up the cleaning products and the empty gauze packet, and made her way to the door. "Use your buzzer if you need anything."

"My buzzer?" I said, but she was already gone.

"It's beside your pillow," Logan said. "On the right."

I didn't want to look at him. He'd just seen me throw up all over the infirmary floor. It was one of the most embarrassing things that had ever happened to me. Even worse than when I'd tripped in front of the entire class in sixth grade.

But he'd tried to protect me the night before. I had to know if he was okay.

I glanced to the side.

"Hey," he said softly.

I rolled over a little so I could see him better. "How're you feeling? I—oh, ow." I gasped as the dressing on the side of my head got caught on the pillow.

Logan winced. "Do you want me to buzz for Ms. Park? She might be able to give you something more for the pain."

I lifted my head and managed to disentangle some of my hair from the adhesive tape. "But pharmaceuticals don't work on us."

"Only the regular ones," Logan replied. "You're still

thinking like a human. We have witches. And wizards. They can alter the medicines enough to have an effect."

I patted the gauze back into place and my fingers came away stained with blood.

"Didn't they teach you all that when you were at The Paranormal Program?" Logan asked.

I wiped the blood off on my jeans, which were already dirty from the attack, and rolled over carefully. "I've had to learn a lot of weird-ass supernatural crap in the last nine months. You can't expect me to remember all of it. Anyway, I haven't had to use any medication until today. And I have a concussion. You're lucky I'm coherent at all."

Logan raised his hands. "Fair enough. Anyway, for what it's worth, I think you're really brave."

"Brave?" I snorted. "I wasn't brave. You took off after the bad guy first."

Logan's fingers tapped absently against his sheets. "That's not bravery. That's stupidity. But you, you've been thrown into this whole new life and you're facing it head on. You're going to school, you're making friends." He trailed off and his fingers stilled. "It's admirable."

"Oh." I wasn't sure what to say. No one had ever said anything like that to me before. "Thanks."

We both fell quiet. Logan started tapping the bed again, his fingers drumming some sort of syncopated rhythm, while I thought back over everything that had happened before the attack. "Who was the guy with Vanessa?" I asked.

Logan sighed, his gaze drifting to the ceiling. "Derek Watson."

"He seems like an asshole."

"He *is* an asshole. He hates pretty much everyone, but me more than most."

"Because?"

Logan's fingers stilled, and I wished I could take the question back. It was only one word, but it was enough to make his shields drop, just for a second. He was a whirl-wind of rotting leaves and sea spray, smoke and carnations. Anger, misery, fear, and shame. It was almost too much to bear. But then he gathered it all up, put it back inside and sealed himself off, though his gaze was still dark and heavy, like the bruise that ran up his jawline.

What the hell was that about?

"I didn't mean—" I started, but Logan shook his head.

"Derek's dad challenged mine," he said quietly. "For the position of alpha. It's why Thomas and I had to go home."

"Thomas? Your brother?" I'd heard Haven and Cayley mention his name, but I still hadn't met him.

Logan nodded, but the movement was stiff, like his entire body would fall apart if he relinquished control.

"And your dad? Is he—? I mean, did he win?" While I still had a lot to learn about the supernatural world, I knew that most werewolf alphas acquired their position either through lineage or through a fight to the death. And if Derek wasn't in line for the role …

"He won. This time. But—" Logan looked down. He toyed with a piece of stray thread on the sleeve of his hoodie, his fingers twisting in knots. "He almost didn't. He came close to dying. And Riley, his second in command, was killed."

"Shit," I said quietly.

Logan shrugged, but it didn't look right. His shoulders were too high, too stiff. "Thomas and I had to stay home to help Mom and make sure everything was settled."

"And your dad? He's okay now?"

Logan nodded.

"And Derek's?" I wasn't sure I wanted to hear the answer.

"He's still alive. My father prefers to settle things strategically. He won't let himself look weak—image is *everything* to him—but he won't kill unless he has no other choice. He prefers to win through intimidation and force." Logan sighed, and it was equal parts weary and annoyed. "In the end, Mr. Watson and his family, including Derek, were banished from the pack. Their parting gift to us was a brick through our front window."

I drew in a long breath and shifted my head carefully against the pillow. "That's so messed up."

"The brick or the whole situation?" His fingers still twisted around the string. "Because all of it's fucked up."

Ms. Park came back then, with two wooden trays of food balanced carefully in her hands. "There was more available than I expected," she said brightly. "I hope you're both hungry."

"Always," Logan replied. He smiled, but I could still

smell the faint scent of worry on his skin, leaking around the edges of his control.

Ms. Park didn't seem to notice. She placed the trays down on the over-bed tables, wheeled them into position, propped me up on some pillows, then nodded at the human woman who'd followed her quietly into the room. "This is Melanie, your Nutriment."

"I'm Emily." I extended my hand automatically; the polite greeting had been drilled into me at The Paranormal Program. "I'd like to start with the bag first, Ms. Park."

The petite nurse nodded. "Of course."

My fangs slid downward. I'd been holding the hunger in check since she'd left the room earlier, distracted by my conversation with Logan, but I didn't think I could manage much longer. She handed me the bag, and her gaze never left me as I opened it.

Careful.

Take it slow.

I tried to remember everything I'd been taught about bloodlust and control. About breathing and meditation and respect. *You can't lose control. Not now. Not ever.* I wished I had my cello.

I inhaled slowly through my nose.

"Take your time." Ms. Park's voice was gentle. "We're not in any hurry."

The bag was warm in my hands.

I started to drink, and Ms. Park moved a few steps closer. She was small, but she was powerful; the scent of wolf and forest and *life* surged through her veins. It could've been tempting, my predator against hers, a fight for supremacy, but I was injured, broken, my body weakened and in pain. I knew I couldn't win.

I finished the bag of blood—an option provided to vampires only when they were newly transformed or injured, partly for logistical reasons and partly for magical ones—and moved on to the Nutriment. The bag had taken the edge off the hunger and had dulled the pain of my injuries a little, but nothing compared to blood from the source.

I hated it.

And I loved it.

"Ms. Park," I said when the Nutriment had been dismissed, "why haven't I fully healed yet?" My body still ached, though the pounding in my head had reduced to a dull thud.

Ms. Park's brown eyes were gentle. "You were thrown into a brick wall at speed. You have a fractured skull, a concussion, three cracked ribs, and a large number of contusions. You're going to heal, but you're still very young, so it's going to take a bit of time. Maybe a day or two."

A day or two?

If I'd still been human …

"Now, I have to go and deal with a few other things, but I won't be far away," Ms. Park said, checking the monitor beside my bed before leaving the room.

I watched as she closed the door, then pulled the tray

of food toward me and wondered what to start with. There was soup and bread, chicken casserole, and a chocolate brownie. I finally decided to start with the soup, grateful I could still eat human food. It made me feel less … monstrous.

"Feeling better?" Logan asked when I was done.

"I guess." I set my spoon down on the tray. "So, what's your diagnosis?"

Logan's gaze snapped up. "What do you mean?"

I gestured at the room around us.

"Oh, right. From the attack." Logan pushed his tray away. "Similar to you, I guess. Concussion and a lot of bruises."

"Ugh."

Logan shrugged. "Happens all the time."

"I don't know how—" I stopped when I heard the distinctive voice in the hall. "Oh, no," I whispered. "It's Mr. Olaru."

The door swung open.

"Good evening," the ancient vampire said. He wore monochrome black—suit, shirt, and tie—and leather loafers, also black, that punctuated each step he took across the tiled floor. His face was pale, almost transparent, and although he was ancient, he moved with the ease of a predator.

"Good evening, sir," Logan said, inclining his head courteously.

"Good evening," I echoed.

Mr. Olaru glared at me.

I swallowed hard. "I mean, good evening, sir."

His expression didn't change. "I would like to extend my sincerest apologies to the both of you," he began, the words stiff but apparently sincere. "We have apprehended the culprit and he will be dealt with in due course."

Logan leaned forward. "Who was it, sir?"

The headmaster clasped his hands in front of his body and considered us carefully, his pale gray eyes first examining Logan, then me. He didn't say anything for what felt like a lifetime.

My head thumped dully.

When the answer came, it was without explanation. "The spell caster was Derek Watson."

"But … why?" I asked.

"And how?" Logan added. "Werewolves can't use magic. It always turns out wrong."

"Perhaps that is a good thing," Mr. Olaru said. "If it had turned out right, the two of you would not be here at all."

I didn't understand. Why would Derek have tried to kill us? He'd said I had something he—no, *we*—wanted. It didn't make sense.

"You're wrong," I said without thinking, my voice loud in the small room. "It wasn't just Derek. There was someone else. He said—"

Logan coughed, and I looked up, startled. Mr. Olaru was standing very still, watching me in the same way that felines do before they attack their prey. He was leaning slightly forward, his chin tucked down, shoulders raised.

I didn't move.

Don't look away.

His eyes narrowed, then the predator receded, though only a little. What looked out from behind his eyes was barely human. "I am not *wrong*, Miss Sanderson," he told me coldly. "We have the spells to confirm he acted alone, both in the quadrant and earlier out on the playing field." He adjusted the sleeves of his jacket, then clasped his hands together again. "That is all."

He stalked through the doors, leaving nothing but the bitter smell of ancient vampire behind him.

"This is ridiculous," I said to Logan. "Why would Derek have tried to kill us? I don't even know him. And why didn't he finish the job?" I pushed the food tray away, the smell of it making me queasy.

"I don't know."

"Fine. How did we end up here, then?"

"In the infirmary?" Logan picked at a stray thread on the bedsheet. "Mr. Green found us. He tackled Derek and restrained him, then called for help on his phone. We were sent straight here. I woke up on the way, but you didn't. For a second, I was worried you weren't gonna make it."

"It wouldn't be the first time I've died," I said quietly.

And then I burst into tears.

6

"OH, SHIT," Logan said.

I covered my face with my hands and dragged in a shaky breath. "It's fine."

It's not fine.

It'll never be fine.

"Do you need something?" Logan's words were hesitant, like he didn't know what to do.

I scrubbed at my eyes as the tears fell faster. Did I need something? It seemed like a simple question, and I felt like it should've had a simple answer. I could've asked for a drink of water. A tissue. A snack. When I was human, that might've been enough. But now? Now I needed my mom. And I needed people to stop trying to kill me.

The clouded scent of worry filled the room. "I can get Ms. Park if you want?" Logan said.

"I don't need Ms. Park. I just … I need a hug."

I hadn't meant to say it. But I didn't take it back.

Logan swung his legs over the side of his bed, padded softly across the tiled floor, and then he was sitting next to me. He smelled of wolf and warmth, wild and calm, and I melted against him as he put his arms around me.

"Can I stay here for a while?" I whispered.

What am I doing?

I don't know this boy.

But Logan held me close, his heartbeat steady, his arms secure. "Stay as long as you like."

I closed my eyes until the tears faded away, then I pulled back slowly, exhausted. "I'm not always like this."

"You have a good excuse."

"I guess, but ..." The predator inside me stirred, trapped and weak and angry. My fangs slid out, and I clenched my fists as I forced them back in. "I shouldn't have let this happen."

"The attack?" Logan said. "Or this, right here?"

I stared down at my jeans, at the blood and the dirt and the grit that coated them, at the tear in the knee that didn't use to be there. I smoothed down the loose denim threads, though I knew I'd never be able to fix them. "How did Mr. Green find us?" I said, deliberately ignoring Logan's questions. "There was no one else around last night. It was like Derek's spell made everyone disappear."

Logan shrugged. "There was probably some kind of avoidance thread within the spell. It would've kept everyone away. But Derek lost control over the spell—and you—when I tackled him, and I guess the avoidance aspect stopped working then as well. Mr. Green was probably just passing by."

Ms. Park's footsteps sounded in the hallway outside, and Logan dashed back to his own bed. He was still pulling the covers up over himself when she walked through the doorway. "You're both looking better," she said, before checking Logan's pulse and temperature, then mine.

"How much longer do we have to stay here?" Logan asked.

Ms. Park handed him a medicine cup filled with a thick moss-colored liquid. "Until I say so."

Logan drank it, then grimaced. "Couldn't they come up with a better flavor?"

Ms. Park handed me a shot glass-sized cup of the same medicine. "Your turn," she said.

I swallowed it in one quick gulp. It wasn't fast enough to avoid the gritty texture. Or the bitter aftertaste. "Thanks, I guess."

"It'll help with the pain." Ms. Park collected up the cups and our trays and balanced them easily in one arm. "Get some rest, both of you. I'll be waking you periodically during the daylight hours, and Dr. Norlgren will be in to see you first thing tomorrow evening." She switched off the overhead lights on her way out, leaving only one lamp burning.

Logan punched his pillow twice and lay down facing

me. "Goodnight," he said. "If anything happens, wake me, okay?"

"Okay." I tugged the blankets up to my chin. "Goodnight." I closed my eyes, but I knew sleeping wouldn't be easy after everything that had happened. And knowing I had to see Dr. Norlgren when I woke up? That just made me feel worse.

"Logan," I said, opening my eyes to look at him. "I'm glad you're here with me. This would've been so much worse on my own."

Logan's dark eyes glimmered, and a soft smile spread across his face. "I wouldn't have missed it for the world."

***

The next night I woke up feeling surprisingly refreshed. And also guilty. Had anyone told Haven and Cayley what had happened? They must be totally freaking out.

I got out of bed, moving slowly and carefully so I didn't wake Logan, and looked around for my bag. It didn't take long to find it. It had been stashed in the lowest drawer of the night table beside my bed. I quietly pulled it out and rummaged around for my phone.

Crap.

It was full of missed calls and unread messages from Haven and Cayley.

I sat back down on the bed and started a new group message: *I'm so sorry!!! I wasn't able to get to my phone. But I'm okay. And Logan's okay.*

Haven replied immediately: *OMG!!! We were planning on sneaking out to see you guys, but Ms. Emmerson stayed up drinking tea in the common lounge all night. We couldn't get past her.*

Before I could reply, another message came through, this time from Cayley: *I heard they caught the person who did it.*

Haven messaged again: *Who was it? I'll eviscerate them.*

I settled back down on the bed and lay my head against the pillow before answering: *Derek Watson.*

The screen lit up with more messages, but I couldn't respond. Dr. Norlgren walked through the door, a stethoscope slung casually around his neck and a broad smile on his face. "How lovely to see you awake, Emily," he said. "I'm Dr. Norlgren."

My phone fell onto the bed.

I didn't say anything. I could barely even think straight. Just like on the night of the fire, Dr. Norlgren glowed, his green skin bright like sunlight.

I need to touch him.

No.

Something wasn't right. Was this part of Derek's dark magic?

"The spell," I said, forcing my head to turn so I couldn't see him anymore. "Derek's black magic. Is it still … happening?" The doctor's hand came into view, and I lost my train of thought. "The spell—it's not—I can't—"

"Hmmm." Dr. Norlgren bent down and looked into my

eyes. "If I had to guess, I'd say you've still got a bit of a concussion. Let's get you checked out."

He examined me thoroughly, checking my vision, balance, reflexes, and coordination, all while I desperately tried not to look at him. "It seems I was wrong," he said when he was done. He picked up the chart that was hanging on the end of the bed and wrote something down. "I guess there's a first time for everything."

He laughed, but I didn't join in. I just stared at the spotless tiles beneath my feet. "Can I go now?"

I had to get away from him.

I want to be with him forever.

"Well," he said, "your concussion seems a lot better, though you might notice some lingering effects over the next couple of days, and all of your contusions are healed. We'll need to take one more set of X-rays, but it looks like your skull and ribs are almost healed as well. I'd let you go straight away, but—" He paused and hung up the chart. When he spoke again, his voice was soft. "Something's wrong, isn't it?"

I opened my mouth to speak, though I still hadn't decided what to say. "I—you look—" I stopped when Logan yawned loudly.

"What time is it?" he mumbled, his eyes closed.

"Time for your check up," Dr. Norlgren said, again chuckling at his own joke.

"It's too early." Logan struggled to sit. His eyes were hooded, and his hair was sticking up in all directions. "Come back later."

Dr. Norlgren smiled. "Take a few minutes. Wake up slowly. I need to finish up with Emily, anyway."

Logan's focus sharpened, his gaze coming to rest on me. "Hey." He rubbed the back of his hand across his mouth and grimaced. "I'll be back in a minute." He shoved his feet in his shoes and took off out the door.

Dr. Norlgren turned his attention back to me. "Are you able to tell me what's wrong? Is it about the attack? Your injuries?"

I looked at him without meaning to.

"If it's something delicate or uncomfortable," he continued, "I can get Ms. Park to act as a chaperone."

I tried to look away, but I was trapped by something I didn't understand.

What are you?

Dr. Norlgren was tall, with forest-green eyes and a narrow jaw. A long silver ponytail hung halfway down his back, revealing ears that were pointed at the tips. He looked like an elf, but he was something different. Something *more*.

I reached out a hand. "You're luminous."

Dr. Norlgren's eyes widened and he stumbled back. "What did you say?"

"You're glowing," I said.

"No. No, it can't be." He hurried over to the door and locked it. His heart was pounding loudly in his chest, but he wasn't scared, and he wasn't prey. "This is incredible."

"What does it mean?" I said, my voice soft and unreal.

He walked back across the room toward me. "Tell me exactly what you see."

"You're the sun and the moon, glimmering and glowing and changing." I breathed in his beauty, unable to see anything else. It wasn't lust; he was just … exquisite.

"Fascinating," he said, studying me closely, his brow furrowed.

"Can I touch you? Please?" I reached out again. "I just—I need to know what it's like to be so alive."

Dr. Norlgren lowered my hands. "Do you know what this means? This isn't anything to do with Derek's spell. You're the *putere*. You're—" He paused at the sound of the door handle.

"Hello?" Logan called. "Can I come back in?"

The doctor stood and smoothed the wrinkles from the front of his long white coat. "I'll explain everything later. In private. Meet me in my office at the start of dinner and do *not* mention this to anyone. It could be a matter of life and death. Do you understand?"

No.

I was too busy seeing galaxies in his skin.

"I mean it," he said, those dark green eyes boring into mine. "You must come alone."

"Alone," I echoed softly.

I stayed sitting on the bed as he unlocked the door. "My apologies," he said, stepping aside so Logan could come back in. "Now, if you'll excuse me, I have to go." He hurried away, leaving the door wide open behind him.

Logan frowned. "What was that about?"

I gave half a shrug, my head all foggy and strange. Why didn't anything feel real?

"Are you okay?" Logan sat down on the chair beside my bed. His words were cloudy, tinged with smoke and soot and worry. "Did something happen?"

"There was a weird—" I tried to focus on his eyes, so dark and wide with concern. "Dr. Norlgren—" I stopped, my stomach twisting. I couldn't tell him. I couldn't tell anyone.

It could be a matter of life and death.

Logan's jaw twitched, and he straightened. "Did he hurt you?"

"No, it was nothing like that." But as the confusion slowly lifted, I wondered if he was planning to. He'd asked me to come back to his office alone and insisted I tell no one about it. That wasn't normal. "Maybe it's just the concussion."

A nurse came in then, offering breakfast to us both and bringing another Nutriment for me. By the time we were done, I almost felt like I'd never been injured at all.

"Do you think they'll let us out now?" Logan said.

I wiped my fingers on a napkin and looked down at my still-filthy clothes. I was desperate for a shower. And some time to consider everything that had happened. I hadn't forgotten what Dr. Norlgren had called me. *Putere.* What did that mean?

"We can only hope," I said.

I was about to message Haven and Cayley—they'd both been blowing up my phone since I'd told them about Derek—when Ms. Park knocked lightly on the door. "How are you both today?" she asked brightly.

"Much better," I said.

"Fantastic." Logan got to his feet. "Can we go now?"

Ms. Park laughed and retrieved both of our charts. "Dr. Norlgren should be the one to officially discharge you, but he had to run out on urgent business, so I'll see what I can do in the meantime." She opened my chart and tapped her pen against the paper as she scanned it. "All right, Emily, you can go. But you'll need to come back later this week for another round of X-rays. And no classes today—you still need to take it easy."

"Sure."

"What about me?" Logan said. "Do I get the day off classes, too?"

Ms. Park opened his chart, then frowned. "Did the doctor examine you?"

He shook his head.

"How strange." The lines between Ms. Park's eyebrows deepened. "I can check you over now, and if everything looks okay I'll let you go to your dorm, but you'll have to come back later today. Dr. Norlgren needs to sign this off."

Ms. Park closed the curtain between the beds, and I tried not to listen as she examined Logan—it seemed too invasive. I grabbed my bag and my phone, which was still buzzing repeatedly with new messages, then looked around to make sure I hadn't left anything behind. I was on my way to the door when Mr. Green came in.

"Emily," he said, his mouth broadening into a smile. "You're looking a lot better."

I shifted uncomfortably, my clothes stiff against my skin. I'd been close. *So close.* If I'd left two minutes earlier, I would've been halfway to Worthington Hall already. Halfway to the shower and the comfort of my bed. Halfway to a quiet place where I could think and figure out what I wanted to do about Dr. Norlgren.

"Are they releasing you today?" he continued.

I plastered a smile on my face and nodded. "Yep. I was just on my way out."

"Well, I won't keep you, but I wanted to let you know that I'm happy to rearrange my schedule today if you need an appointment."

"I'll be fine until next week," I said. "At least it'll give us something to talk about, right?"

Mr. Green's brow wrinkled like he was trying to figure out if I was serious or not. "I suppose so. Anyway, you know where to find me."

I twisted the strap on my bag, my practiced smile fading. "Thank you. And thank you for rescuing us last night. I don't know what things would be like for me—or for Logan—right now if you hadn't."

"You're more than welcome."

My phone beeped loudly, and I fished it out of my bag to silence it. "Sorry. Haven and Cayley won't stop messaging. I think they're still worried."

Mr. Green nodded. "That's understandable. Two of their closest friends have been through a terrible ordeal. It wouldn't be unusual for them—or for *you*—to feel anxious or scared about the situation."

I swallowed hard and glanced down at the floor. Mr. Green was looking at me closely. Too closely. His words felt like a test, and I knew he was using his werewolf-enhanced senses to evaluate my physical responses—my heartrate, my scent, my breathing—to figure out how I was really feeling.

"Ugh, I'm fine," I said, when I couldn't take his silence any longer. "I'm not going to lie and say this whole thing hasn't thrown me, but I'll deal with it, like I've dealt with everything else."

A soft cough came from the other side of the room, and Ms. Park opened the curtain that had been shielding Logan's examination. "James," she said to Mr. Green, "I didn't realize you'd be stopping by."

"Good evening, Hye-in." Mr. Green inclined his head politely, then looked down at his watch. "I need to get to my first appointment, but I popped in to let these two know they can come and see me anytime."

"Thanks," Logan said.

My phone beeped again. "I'd better go," I said, before I slipped out of the room, sighing with relief as I walked down the corridor and escaped into the night. The cool breeze was soft on my skin as I made my way to Worthington Hall, and I tilted my head back and looked up at the sky. This was exactly what I needed. Fresh air and stars and a moment to think. A moment to breathe.

It didn't last.

It never does.

She came up behind me, pushing me before I had a chance to turn. "What did you do to my boyfriend, you bitch?"

7

I STUMBLED FORWARD, my bag swinging off my shoulder and onto the path. I snatched it up and whirled around. Vanessa was standing so close that the toes of her shiny black ballet flats were touching my sneakers.

"What did you do to him?" she said, her breath hot and angry against my face.

My fingers tightened around the strap of my bag, but I didn't back away. I wouldn't give her the satisfaction.

"Tell me!" she screamed.

Courtney and Danielle walked up behind her, beautiful and terrible and wild, then firmly pulled her back.

"Answer the question, mosquito." Danielle's words were a snarl, her voice straddling a razor-thin line between civilized and deadly.

"We won't hold her back for long," Courtney said.

I looked at the three of them, their faces contorted,

their wolves living just below the surface of their skin, and I knew it wouldn't matter what I said. They'd never believe what had happened. They just wanted someone to blame.

I turned and walked away without saying a single word.

"Derek didn't do anything wrong," Vanessa said, her voice cracking dangerously. "He called me before they took him away. He said it was you and Logan. He caught you doing something sick."

What the hell?

I didn't stop. I didn't look back.

"We know what you did to Logan. And what you let him do to you," Danielle said.

A few people walked by, their expressions curious, and I wanted to stop—I wanted to march right back to Vanessa and Courtney and Danielle, and show them I wasn't their punching bag. But I knew it wouldn't help.

"Why did you blame Derek?" Vanessa screamed at me, the scent of wolf and fur and rotting leaves filling the air between us. "He doesn't deserve this."

"But you do, don't you, Emberlee?" Courtney drawled. "We know what you did. And the alpha will not be pleased."

I slowed, the hunger stirring to life in my veins.

"I'm not part of your pack," I said through gritted teeth. "What your alpha thinks doesn't matter."

"What about what everyone else will think?" Danielle said. "Word spreads quickly in this place. Soon everyone will know about the sex, the mutilation, the damage you both did to each other."

I turned on my heel. "What the hell are you talking about?"

Danielle smiled, a slow menacing lift of her lips, then she looked over at Courtney. Something unspoken crossed between them, and Courtney nodded, her golden hair bouncing around her shoulders.

"Now," she whispered.

They let Vanessa go.

My fangs snapped out as she flew toward me, her hands outstretched and her eyes flashing amber. I planted my feet firmly on the ground, my muscles tightening as I braced for impact in three, two—

"Not today, bitch," I said as I twisted to the side.

Vanessa toppled forward, propelled by her own momentum, and the rough cobblestone path sliced open the skin on her hands and knees. "You'll pay for that," she snarled.

I stood over her and breathed in deep as the scent of her blood drifted up on the breeze. "Do you want to see what these fangs are really capable of?" I said. "Or should I tell you the truth about what happened last night?"

"Screw you, mosquito. He told me you'd lie." Vanessa scrambled to her feet, blood dripping down her legs from her lacerated knees.

Drink it.

Take it.

I licked my lips and forced my gaze higher. "Did Derek

tell you he attacked us? Did he tell you he used back magic?"

The assembled crowd—*where the hell did they come from?*—began to murmur. Anticipation and violence colored the night sky, and I forced my shoulders back and straightened my spine.

"Derek came after us," I said, raising my voice so everyone could hear. "Logan and I didn't do anything wrong. We're the victims in this."

"No." Vanessa paled, her body trembling as she backed away. "Just—no. You're trying to take the attention away from what you both did."

"Would I smell like the truth if I was?"

The murmurs grew louder, and Courtney hurried over to Vanessa and put a protective arm around her shoulders. "The alpha will be hearing about this," she snapped, her voice ice-cold. "He needs to know what Logan's been doing."

"Everyone knows he's crazy," Danielle said. "We've all seen the scars."

"Hey, look!" Someone in the crowd pointed toward the medical center. "It's him."

I turned and watched as Logan made his way down the stairs, his attention on his phone. He didn't acknowledge the crowd, and he didn't acknowledge Courtney or Vanessa or Danielle, though I was certain he'd heard their words. At the last step, he faltered, his gaze locking onto mine.

"Hey," I mouthed, lifting a hand.

A muscle in his jaw twitched, and for a second I thought he might wave back, but he pulled his sleeves down over his hands and turned away.

I'd been so focused on Logan, I hadn't even noticed Mr. Green step out onto the stairs. "Everyone move on," he barked as he surveyed the crowd. "I'm sure you've all got places to be."

The onlookers scattered, but from the curious backward glances, the conversations I couldn't quite hear, and the sheer volume of people on their phones, it was obvious the entire school would know everything in about … well, less than five minutes.

Courtney, Vanessa, and Danielle began to walk off, too, but Mr. Green hurried down the stairs and onto the path. "You three," he said, pointing toward them with an accusing finger. "You're coming with me."

Courtney's hand flew to her chest. "Us? I don't understand? Why?"

"It was her fault." Vanessa whirled to face me, her bloodstained hands curling into fists. "It was her and"— she turned again, her eyes turning wolf-yellow as she caught sight of Logan—"him."

"Now, Vanessa—" Mr. Green began, but she cut him off.

"No," she said hotly. "They're sick. Both of them."

Logan had kept walking away through the entire exchange, his back to us all, but he spun around then, his eyes flashing with what looked like anger and shame.

"What the actual fuck, Vanessa?" he said as he stalked toward her. "What did I ever do to you?"

"You're crazy, you—"

"No." He stopped right in front of her. "I've had enough of the rumors. The threats. The snide remarks."

A trickle of power, warm with the scent of wolf and forest air, swirled around us. But before I could figure out exactly what it meant, it was gone.

"To my office now, ladies," Mr. Green said firmly. "Unless you'd prefer to see Mr. Olaru?"

The three of them shook their heads, and Courtney's eyes shone with a flicker of fear. I tilted my head and studied her more closely. *What else are you afraid of?* It was knowledge that could potentially come in handy one day.

"Logan and Emily," Mr. Green said, breaking into my thoughts. "Go and get some rest. I'll catch up with the two of you later."

He marched back up the stairs to the medical center with Courtney, Vanessa, and Danielle following close behind. Danielle turned to look at us, her green eyes glittering. She mouthed something I couldn't quite catch, then extended a middle finger before stalking into the building. The heavy arched doors slammed shut behind her.

"Bitch," I muttered, my fangs catching on my tongue.

Logan sighed. "I'm sorry."

"That Danielle's a bitch?" I forced my fangs to retract, then smiled, though it wasn't a happy one. "I'm sorry about that, too."

Logan ran a hand through his hair. "I'm sorry you got dragged into this. That you're now associated with me and—and all the—" He shook his head. "I have to go."

And then I was left alone, exhausted and confused, wondering which problem to deal with first.

The heavy doors of Worthington Hall swung open before I even reached for the handle.

"Emily!" Miss Lassila exclaimed, ushering me inside. "You're late. Again. Ms. Park told me you were on your way back some time ago."

"Sorry," I mumbled, following the tiny haltija up the winding staircase.

"What on earth were you doing?" Her kitten heels clicked loudly against the wooden steps. "I do have other matters to attend to, you know."

"There was—" I paused, the shadow of a headache pulsing in my temples. "You know what? Just ask Mr. Green. I'm sure he'll explain. It's complicated."

Ms. Emmerson was waiting for us at the top of the stairs. "Oh, Emily," she said, her arms open wide. "You poor thing." She folded me into a hug, and the scent of peach pie and ice cream washed over me. Unexpected tears sprung up in my eyes.

I pulled away. "I'm sorry," I said, rubbing at my face with my dirty sleeve.

"Hush, now." Ms. Emmerson started off down the hall,

her long woolen skirt swinging around her legs. "There's nothing to be sorry for." She opened the door to my room and waited for me to enter.

"Except for being late," Miss Lassila muttered.

Ms. Emmerson rolled her eyes, her back toward the haltija. "I'll finish up here, Maarika," she said. "You go and finish whatever it was you were doing."

"If you're sure …" She seemed strangely reluctant to leave.

"I'll be fine," I told the two of them. "I just want to take a shower and go to bed."

Ms. Emmerson patted my arm. "I'll have some tea ready when you want it." She shook her head and tutted softly. "This sort of thing just doesn't happen at Mistwood."

"And it won't happen again," Miss Lassila said firmly. "We've checked everyone thoroughly—students *and* staff —and we're confident Derek acted alone. However, security has been increased, and all of the wards have been strengthened. You can rest assured there's nothing more to worry about."

Nothing more to worry about?

Miss Lassila had no idea.

I spent my entire shower worrying. First, about Derek and why he'd been after me. *You have something we want. Who are you? A delivery man.* Second, about Courtney, Vanessa, and Danielle, and the rumors they were spreading. Was I supposed to confront them? Ignore them? Join forces with Logan and take them on together? And third, about Dr. Norlgren. He said he'd explain what was going on. Would I be wrong to trust him?

I padded down the hallway to my room, grateful everyone else was in class. I closed the door behind me and flopped down onto my bed, breathing in the scent of the tea Ms. Emmerson had left on my nightstand. It was a sweetly fragrant blend, a mix of chamomile, linden leaves, and passionflower—apparently designed to aid relaxation, according to the note she'd left beside it—but even after drinking half a cup, I still felt on edge.

I reached for my phone, looking for a way to distract myself, and found a new unread message from Haven.

Went to see you before first period, but Ms. Park said you'd gone back to our room. I must've just missed you? Anyway, look under your pillow. See you soon. xo

Curious, I lifted my pillow and found a small purple box underneath, maybe two inches wide and one inch tall. Written across the top in tiny silver script was a brief command: *open me*. I picked up the box, turned it over and around, and even shook it a little, but I had no idea what was inside. Knowing Haven, it would probably be something … interesting.

I held the box out at arm's length and carefully pulled off the lid. For a second, nothing happened. Then the box transformed, exploding with the noise of a hundred party poppers being blown simultaneously. Balloons and brightly colored confetti rained down on me, and I squealed, partly with surprise and partly with delight.

My ears were still ringing when someone pounded on

my door. "Are you all right in there?" Ms. Emmerson called out.

Shaking confetti out of my hair, I got up to let her in. "Sorry." I stood back so she had a clear view of the disarray. "Haven left me a gift." I grabbed the string of the nearest balloon, a bright pink confection of neon and polka dots, and held it out. "See? It says *get well soon.*"

"Typical Haven, I suppose." Ms. Emmerson sighed, but the smile that touched the corners of her mouth told me she wasn't really annoyed. "Make sure she cleans it up when she gets back. You need to get some rest."

After tying the balloon to the top of my headboard, I got into bed, but I couldn't fall asleep. I lay there for a while, tossing and turning, and trying to ignore the fact that my sheets smelled like the fabric softener my mom always used.

I miss you, Mom.

I breathed in the scent of my past, of my life and my home, and pulled Minikins out from under the blankets. The last nine months had been hard—*beyond* hard—but I'd been slowly getting used to things, adapting to being a supernatural creature. And most days, it was fine. But today? Today I let myself miss all the things I'd lost.

Just this once, I told myself. *Just this once.*

I picked up my phone.

And then I saw him. My brother. Sam. He'd joined pretty much every kind of social media app available when he was eleven or twelve, and I scrolled through three years of comments and pictures, videos and memes, wishing I could see him one more time. Because this wasn't real. And it wasn't enough. I wanted to talk to him. To fight with him over the last slice of pizza. To tell him I was okay.

"Oh, Sam," I whispered.

I paused when I got to the most recent picture he'd uploaded. He looked so much older than I remembered. He was with his friends, laughing at something I'd never get to understand, and my heart splintered at the sight of it.

I missed him so much that it physically hurt.

I tossed the phone down onto the bed and hurled Minikins across the room. What was I doing? I could never go back to my family. I *knew* that. But there'd always be a part of me that didn't want to believe it.

How am I supposed to move on?

I drew in a deep breath, scrubbed the unshed tears from my eyes, and picked up the teacup that still sat on my nightstand. Maybe I just hadn't had enough of it to calm me down. I took one big gulp and almost spat it back out. It was completely cold.

Well, fine. If I couldn't figure out how to move on or calm down, the least I could do was keep myself distracted with something that wasn't memories of my family. I grabbed my laptop off my desk, rescued Minikins from the floor, then sat down at my desk. I shook the tension from my shoulders and opened up a browser in Supenet. It wasn't until I started to type that I realized I couldn't remember the word I was looking for.

What had Dr. Norlgren called me? *Puttear*? *Putener*? Neither brought up any results.

I kept trying and failing, until almost an hour went by and I had to admit defeat. I'd found plenty of references to spells that could make people—and various other things— glow, but none of them resulted in anything like I'd seen with Dr. Norlgren. I'd even done multiple searches on the doctor himself, in case it was something specific to him that had been documented somewhere. But aside from some interviews and a bunch of articles he'd written in some supe medical journals, there was nothing.

I groaned and snapped my laptop shut.

I wished I could remember what he'd called me. I'd recalled it earlier, back in the infirmary, but no matter how hard I tried now I couldn't get it back. I rubbed my temples and tried to focus, but the headache that had been pushing at the edges of my skin all night was getting worse.

"This is ridiculous," I muttered.

Because while I wasn't sure how to deal with Derek and the attack, or the vile rumors that Courtney, Vanessa, and Danielle seemed determined to spread, this was one mystery that could easily be solved.

I was going to go and see Dr. Norlgren.

8

I'd THOUGHT MAKING a decision about the situation would've made things easier. I was wrong. I still had hours to wait until I was supposed to meet with Dr. Norlgren, and I didn't know what I was supposed to do until then.

My skin flushed hot and cold.

I wanted to know what was going on, but also I … didn't. I paced back and forth across the room, tracking a path between the door and my dresser, and confetti sprung up around my feet. It was so bright, so festive, so *fun*, that I couldn't stand it anymore. I pulled a sweater on over my pajamas, then slipped out into the hallway, not even sure where I was going.

"Emily," Ms. Emmerson said, stopping me in my tracks. "What are you up to? You're supposed to be resting."

"Oh, I—" What *was* I doing? "I, um, wanted to get another cup of tea."

Ms. Emmerson took a moment before answering, and when she did her voice was caring yet firm. "I'll make it for you. Let's get you back to bed." She took my arm and silently led me back to my room.

"I don't want to waste your time," I protested as she unlocked the door. "I'm perfectly capable of getting the tea myself."

She didn't move until I was obediently tucked back under the covers.

"How long do I have to stay here?" I asked, hating the whiny note that crept into the words.

"Until I say so."

I sat straight up. "But I'm fine. Really."

Ms. Emmerson's already-wrinkled brow furrowed; the deep lines marked the passage of worries and joys and frustrations on her skin. "You know I can't smell emotions like you can," she said, "but I can still tell when someone's lying to me."

"I'm not—"

She lifted a warning finger. "It's perfectly normal to feel scared or confused or angry after what you've been through. But you can't run from it, and you can't pretend it never happened."

I looked down at my blankets.

"Should I call Mr. Green?"

"No!" My head snapped back up. "I'll be fine."

"You could discuss it with me?"

No way.

Couldn't she see that I didn't want to talk about it? It

was still too raw, too fresh. I'd relive it all with Mr. Green eventually, but it wouldn't be today. I knew it wasn't prudent for predatory supes to bottle things up—it could lead to outbursts and issues with control—but a few days wouldn't hurt. Hopefully.

"I think I'll just rest," I said.

Ms. Emmerson picked up the empty teacup from my nightstand. "If you're sure ..." She left the words hanging between us, the air heavy with expectation.

When I didn't say anything more, she left the room, tutting softly under her breath. I leaned my head back against the headboard and stared up at the ceiling, knowing I'd contributed another wrinkle to Ms. Emmerson's collection.

By the time she came back, holding a tray of tea and cake, I was sitting at my desk, my laptop open in front of me.

"That's not resting," she said sharply. "You shouldn't overdo things. Back in bed, now."

I sighed and rolled my eyes, but I did as she said.

"I know you think I'm being overbearing," she said as she set the tray down on the bed in front of me, "but I've seen and done things you could never imagine. I know the consequences of treating your injuries lightly." She placed her hands on her hips, her cardigan bunching around them. "You will eat, drink, and sleep. And if I see you up and about any time before dinner, I'll have you sent back to the infirmary."

"Yes, ma'am," I said quickly.

By the time I finished the tea and cake my eyelids were drooping. I burrowed beneath the covers, warm and full and uneasy, but not even my worries could keep me awake. Instead, they followed me into my dreams.

"Emily," someone whispered. "Emily, can you—"

"No!" I sat bolt upright, my fangs bared and ready. I wouldn't let him get me. Not this time. I scrambled out of bed, not really seeing anything around me.

"Em, stop. It's us. Haven and Cayley."

The room came into focus and I paused, my heart like thunder in my ears. "What's going on?" I rubbed my eyes and tried to remember how to breathe.

"We came up to see you," Cayley said.

"You weren't answering your messages." Haven pressed a hand to her throat, her eyes wide. "I thought you'd … you know, I thought you were in trouble."

Cayley's lips curled up in a smirk. "I told you she was asleep."

"And sleeping can be dangerous when you have a concussion," Haven retorted.

Cayley folded her arms across her chest.

"She's right," I said. "Sleeping is dangerous when you have a concussion. But I'm fine."

No, you're not. You almost lost control.

I took a deep breath and retracted my fangs, pushing away the remnants of my dreams. They hadn't been pleasant—I'd been taken over by Derek, my body no longer my own—but they weren't as bad as the nightmares I'd had during my time at The Paranormal

Program, the ones that had been manipulated by Kitty. At least I hadn't dreamed about killing my parents or my brother.

"I don't believe you," Haven said, sitting down next to me and enveloping me in a hug. "But since you were attacked, I'll give you a pass."

Cayley leaned against my desk, her arms still folded. She wore a cashmere sweater and black skinny jeans tucked into ankle boots, and though she looked like a dark cloud, she smelled like daisies. Relief.

"I loved the surprise," I said to Haven, turning to pull on the balloon that was still tied to my headboard.

"I knew you would."

"What I don't understand," Cayley said, boosting herself up to sit on my desk, "is why Derek attacked you. He's always been an asshole, but he's never been violent before."

Haven sighed. "I told you before. Logan was the target. It's pack politics."

"Then why bring Emily into it? She's not part of their pack."

"I guess …" I trailed off as the two of them looked at me expectantly. I wasn't sure why, but I didn't want to tell them what Derek had said to me. I didn't understand why he'd called himself a delivery man, but he'd been so serious about it. Like it was a job of some importance. My skin prickled, and I rubbed my arms. "I guess I was in the wrong place at the wrong time."

Cayley arched a brow. "Like you were in the wrong place at the wrong time during the fire?"

"Cayley!" Haven's blue eyes flashed. "Can't you see she's already worried?"

"I'm being realistic," she said. "Derek went after her twice. I don't think that's a coincidence."

Haven chewed her lower lip quietly, her brows drawn down. She wasn't often silent, and when she was the room felt larger, almost hollow. It was like the space she normally took up with words and exaggeration and laughter didn't know what to do with itself. "Maybe you're right," she finally said. "But why would he have done it?"

Cayley shrugged. "Do you know him, Em? I've never heard you mention him before, but were you enemies? Friends?"

"No. I'd never even seen him until last night." Pain inched its way through my skull, my earlier headache attempting a comeback, and I gritted my teeth.

Haven stood. "Research. We need to research." She made her way over to her desk, her vintage green dress swirling around her. "I think Cayley's right—all of this is connected. I mean, I don't *want* it to be connected, because this sort of stuff just doesn't happen at Mistwood. But the fire? The spells? Dr. Norlgren and the weird glow that only you can see? It can't be a coincidence." She turned to me, her eyes sparking. "When you were in the medical center earlier, was Dr. Norlgren still glowing?"

"Yeah, but—"

"We need to find out why." She flipped her laptop open and brought up a Supenet browser, her fingers flying across the keyboard. "The fire wasn't an accident. I overheard two of the teachers discussing it between classes."

Cayley swept across the room and peered over Haven's shoulder. "Do you think—"

"—it was Derek?" Haven's eyes were fixed firmly on the screen.

"Stop interrupting!" Cayley exclaimed. "It's rude."

Haven spun around, her cheeks flushed pink. "But this feels big. Important. Emily and Logan were attacked —*attacked*—on school grounds. We need to know why it happened. And we need to be prepared."

Cayley raised an eyebrow. "Prepared?"

"In case something else happens." Haven turned back to her laptop, the wild scent of magic drifting around her. "Em, can you describe the glow?"

"He was … bright, I guess? Shimmering. But … there's something else. Something I haven't told you."

"What?" Cayley's hazel eyes were curious.

Should I do it?

I leaned forward, my elbows on my knees, too tired to care if I was making a mistake or not. *It could be a matter of life and death.* Then I told them everything.

Haven's mouth dropped open when I was done. "You're going to meet Dr. Norlgren? Alone? After everything you just told us?" Her voice got higher and higher. "Are you insane?"

Maybe?

"At least take one of us with you," Cayley said. "I could wait outside. Dr. Norlgren will never know."

"But he said it was a matter of life and death." I drew a circle in the confetti on the floor with my toes, then scrubbed it out in a mess of color and sharp-edged lines. "Ugh. I shouldn't have told you."

"Yes, you should have," Haven retorted, her attention half on me and half on her laptop screen. "It's too dangerous for you to go alone."

"We don't know that," I said. "Let me do this. You know where I'll be. Give me fifteen minutes, and if I'm not out by then you can … do something?" I sighed and pressed my palms against my forehead. It was cool, as always, but the pain behind it throbbed in time with my pulse.

"What's wrong?" Cayley said.

"Just a headache. I'll be fine."

"We'll go." She tapped Haven on the arm. "You should get some rest."

Haven closed her laptop and stowed it in her bag. "Do you need the doctor? The nurse? Maybe some painkillers?"

I shook my head, regretting it immediately as pain spiked behind my eyes. "I need more sleep." I lay down, and my pillows were soft beneath my head. "But I need to ask you something first."

Haven raised her eyebrows.

"The rumors. About me and Logan. Have you … have you heard them?"

Haven exchanged a glance with Cayley. "We know they're not true. We know you both better than that."

I blinked, struggling to keep my eyes open. "They keep saying Logan's crazy. That he's got scars. What do they mean?"

"That's not our story to tell," Haven said. "But Logan's not crazy. And he's not dangerous."

Cayley's eyes were shadowed. "You're almost asleep. We'll come back and check on you later."

"Text if you need anything," Haven said, creeping toward the door.

My eyes were already closed.

I stared up at the medical center as I finished the double chocolate chip muffin I'd bought from the campus coffee shop. Dr. Norlgren had wanted to meet at the start of dinner, so I hadn't eaten and was starving. It turned out enhanced healing used a lot of energy. Energy that needed to be replenished with food. And no doubt more blood.

After tossing the wrapper in the trash, I wiped my hands on my jeans and wished I was somewhere else. The medical center was more imposing than usual, its gray stone façade heavy and cold in the lamplit dark. A lone chimera patrolled the roof, staring down at me.

An icy shiver crawled up my back.

I took one step forward, then another. I couldn't look at Haven and Cayley, who sat quietly on a bench a few yards away. They'd been there at least half an hour already, but we couldn't be seen together. Dr. Norlgren might be watching, and he had to believe I'd come alone.

I *was* alone.

No one made their way up the stairs to the entrance beside me. No one pushed the heavy door open with me. The hallway that led through the ground floor was empty.

I took a deep breath and held my head high as I walked toward Dr. Norlgren's office. My headache was gone, cured by hours of sleep and as much food as I'd been able to manage quickly, but I still felt like I was making a big mistake.

What if he tries to kill me?

I'd never be able to defend myself. He was too mesmerizing. Too *much*. It was like I lost myself when I looked at him. What if I couldn't find my way back?

My heart in my throat, I stopped outside Dr. Norlgren's office door. His engraved copper nameplate gleamed in the artificial light of the hallway, and I looked away. It reminded me too much of his glimmering skin. With my gaze fixed firmly on the floor, I raised my hand and knocked three times. With my other hand, I found my cell phone in my pocket.

"Come in," Dr. Norlgren called. "The door's unlocked."

I checked my phone, making sure Haven's number was onscreen and ready to call, then pushed the door open before I could change my mind. Still looking at the tiles beneath my feet, I moved slowly into the office.

"Hi. So … um …" What the hell was I supposed to say? "What's this all about?"

"Close the door. I'll explain everything."

The edges of my phone bit into my fingers. *This is a bad idea. A bad, bad idea.* I eased the door shut.

"Is it done?" Dr. Norlgren asked.

I nodded, and my head felt oddly light, like it wasn't quite mine. None of this felt real.

"You'll have to speak up," he said. "I'm behind the screen so as not to enthral you."

Warily, I lifted my gaze, ready to run, but all I saw was an ordinary office. There was a large green desk, a tidy bookshelf overflowing with medical tomes, a tall lamp in the corner, and a couple of chairs. The screen Dr. Norlgren had mentioned was near the back of the room. It was large, almost half the width of the office, and was embellished with images of red flowers and green flowing vines.

"Are you there?" Dr. Norlgren asked.

My phone beeped, and I looked down at the screen. It was a message from Haven. I quickly replied: *everything's fine.* Then I crossed my fingers and hoped it was the truth.

"Emily?"

"I'm here," I told the doctor.

"Are you alone?"

One breath. Two. "Yes."

"Fantastic." Excitement turned his voice high and sharp. "Take a seat. This may be a lot to take in."

I eyed the wooden chair next to me but didn't sit

down. I wanted to be able to get out of there as quickly as possible.

"Are you ready?"

No.

"What are you?" I said. It came out louder than I'd intended, and I rubbed my fingers over my lips. "What am I?"

There was a pause, a moment when everything felt wrong. Then Dr. Norlgren cleared his throat and began. "I am an elf, and you are a vampire, one of us magical and one of us predator, though both of us could become something more. Long ago, there was a prophecy about a creature called the *putere*." He paused, and I heard his heart thumping loudly in his chest. "That creature could be you."

Putere.

It was the word I'd forgotten. The word he'd called me in the infirmary.

"*Could* be," I said, trying to make sense of what he was saying. "What does that mean?"

Dr. Norlgren's shoes came into view under the screen, and I immediately took a step back toward the door. "It means that one day, if the prophecy comes to pass, you could be powerful beyond measure."

"And you?" I said warily, my phone clutched tight in my hands. "What do you have to do with this?"

"I am the *adjutor*—your helper and protector." His feet moved again, the polished brown shoes edging their way toward the end of the screen.

"Wait," I said. "Stop. Don't come any closer."

The neatly-laced leather brogues halted. "My apologies. I was merely retrieving my pen, which I'd left on the end of the bed." His voice softened. "I mean you no harm, Emily. You must believe me. My role—a role that has only been spoken of in incomplete whispers within my clan for hundreds of years—is to assist you in any way necessary."

The fresh smell of mint told me he was telling the truth. I put my phone in my pocket and shook out the cramp that had coiled itself within my fingers. "You said something about a prophecy?"

"Yes, the prophecy of the Sapphire Eclipse. It's an ancient—" He stopped abruptly when the front doors of the medical center banged shut.

I pulled my phone from my pocket again as footsteps drew near. Moving closer to the door, I drew in a breath, sorting through the array of smells that filled the air until I settled on the one that didn't belong.

"It's Mr. Olaru," I whispered.

I heard the scratch of what sounded like pen against paper, then Dr. Norlgren cleared his throat. "Don't look at me," he whispered as one solemn knock heaved against the door. "I'm coming around the screen."

I turned to face the door, my gaze locked on the dull brass knob. It twisted slowly, the trefoil design spinning like a tumbling leaf under the pointed arches of the lock plate.

"Miss Sanderson." Mr. Olaru's expression twisted as if

he'd swallowed something sour. "What a surprise to see you here at this time of night."

"I had an appointment, sir."

Dr. Norlgren came up behind me. "As I'm sure you're aware, Emily's injuries were significant. I needed to make sure she was healing as expected."

The headmaster's lip curled as he swept into the room. The faint smell of mustiness clung to him like a tattered shroud. "And is she as you expected?" he barked.

Dr. Norlgren chuckled softly. "Not entirely."

The headmaster stilled, and it was something both inhuman and shrewd; his predator was never far from the surface.

"Emily is healing better than I anticipated," Dr. Norlgren continued, a small catch in his voice. "Especially for one so young." He held out a folded piece of paper and pressed it into my hands. "This is a slip for the feeding room. You'll need extra feeds for the next few days. Read through the instructions, then give it to the teacher in charge."

I stared down at his hand. The green skin shone like the sun against the moonlit white of my own, and I breathed out a wonderous sigh.

"Off you go," Dr. Norlgren said, pulling his hand away. A light pressure against my back steered me to the door. "Get some rest, and come and see me again before class tomorrow. You'll need one final check, and possibly an X-ray, though I'm sure you'll be completely healed by then."

I let myself be guided into the hallway, barely noticing

when the door closed behind me. After standing outside the doctor's office for far longer than should've been necessary, the world began to come back into focus, and I weaved my way to the exit on feet that didn't fully obey me.

Get it together.

You can't lose control.

I shook my arms out at my sides and focused on everything I could see. The cold stone walls, the tiled floor, the wooden arches of the doors ahead. I was affected by a magic I didn't understand, a magic I was scared would be used to exploit me. I could be forced to do anything.

Why does everyone want to control me?

I stepped out into the night, the cold air a caress against my skin. Mr. Olaru's interruption meant I still had no real understanding of what was going on, but at least I had something to go on. *Putere. Adjutor. The Sapphire Eclipse.*

It all meant something.

And I was going to find out what.

9

"So aside from a couple of terms, you basically learned nothing," Cayley said. She sat cross-legged on the floor in the middle of my room, her fingernails changing color as she trailed them back and forth against the wood.

"It wasn't her fault," Haven said. "Mr. Olaru interrupted them."

"I didn't say it was her fault." Cayley held her hands out in front of herself and inspected her now-purple nails. "I just wish we had more information to work with. Then maybe we could do something."

I leaned back in my chair and frowned at the two of them. "Neither of you will be doing anything. You're not even supposed to know about this."

"Too late," Haven kicked off her boots and flopped down on her bed. "What was it Dr. Norlgren called you? Puttera?"

I shook my head. This time, I still remembered the word. "*Putere.*"

"And he said it's related to a prophecy?" She opened her laptop and started typing. After a few minutes she sat, her legs folded under her and her brows knitted together. "Nothing's coming up. Are you sure that's what he said?"

"Absolutely."

Haven kept searching, her eyes narrowed in concentration. "There should be something. A book. An article. A throwaway line. Anything."

"Try *adjutor*," I said, opening the container of pasta I'd picked up from the dining hall on the way back to our room. "Dr. Norlgren called himself that. It means helper or protector or something."

Haven muttered to herself as she searched, and I ate my pasta. It was a double helping, but it didn't last long, and I grabbed an orange from the fruit bowl. Juice dribbled down my chin, and I wiped it away, wishing I was somewhere else. Somewhere that this wasn't happening. It never would've happened at my old school.

Except … it had. The attack that had turned me, the one back in Michigan, had happened on school grounds. I'd finished packing up after orchestra rehearsal one night and had offered to take some of the extra chairs back to the journalism room. I hadn't seen him in the dark, I hadn't known what was going on.

"You okay?" Cayley asked, watching me closely. "You have some sort of preordained destiny and you don't even know what it is. That's pretty wild."

"It sucks." I picked up the folded slip Dr. Norlgren had given me for the feeding room and turned it over in my hands. The hunger was a quiet hum in my veins, and it filled me with warning and longing. Should I use the slip now?

"It's annoying," Haven said, glaring at her laptop. "I can't find any information."

"Did you look up *Sapphire Eclipse*? Maybe that's—"

"Wait." Cayley stood and held out her hand. "Let me see that note."

"What? This one?" I looked down at it, confused. "It's just a slip for the feeding room."

"There's another note inside it."

The note was tightly folded and there was nothing visible from the outside, but I opened it up and a slip of paper fell out, fluttering to the floor. It was small and cream and covered with spidery black script.

"How did you know that was there?" I asked, bending to pick it up.

Cayley shrugged. "It's a succubus thing. When you have to be able to transform into someone—*anyone*—else, you notice the small things."

"What does it say?" Haven asked, looking up from her laptop. "Is it from Dr. Norlgren?"

I squinted at the words, trying to decipher the thin, sprawling letters, then began to read aloud: "*Emily, do not tell anyone what I have told you tonight. There is too much at stake. There are people who will exploit you and your potential for power. They will not care if they harm anyone in their way.*

I will explain more tomorrow. Come to my office an hour before classes begin. Be discreet. Take care and remain aware of your surroundings. I do not know when they will strike again."

"Shit," Haven said. "That's intense."

Cayley's eyes gleamed. "And intriguing. Maybe that's why Derek was after you. He could've found out about the prophecy somehow." She turned to Haven. "Did you find anything?"

"Nothing." She rubbed her eyes with the heels of her hands, smearing sooty eyeliner across her face. "I'll keep looking."

"I'll help." Cayley sidestepped Haven's boots, which still lay haphazardly on the floor, and crouched in front of her bookshelf. One long midnight-blue fingernail—she'd already changed them again—whispered across the spines. "Which ones do you recommend?"

<hr>

"Dammit!"

I rolled over and almost tipped off the edge of my bed. "What is it?" I said as I pushed myself up to sit. I blinked a few times, trying to dislodge the remnants of sleep from my brain.

"Sorry." Haven sat at her desk, rubbing her fingers. "I didn't mean to wake you. I got my hand caught in the drawer."

"Are you okay?" I couldn't smell any blood. I yawned, then noticed Cayley asleep on the floor, her head propped up on one of my spare pillows. A pile of discarded books lay around her. I yawned again. "What's the time? Did you sleep?"

Haven shook her head. Her hair stood up in messy clumps, with dark roots showing through, and her kohl-smudged eyes were heavy. "I couldn't. There was too much to do." She paused, unusually hesitant. "There's something I need to tell you, and I don't think you'll like it."

I shifted the stack of books I'd fallen asleep over and turned to face her fully. "Yeah?"

"I don't think Dr. Norlgren was telling you the truth. I don't think there's a prophecy."

My skin prickled.

"Are you guys up already?" Cayley's voice was low and husky. She pushed her sleep-tangled hair out of her eyes and sat. "What's going on?"

Dr. Norlgren might be lying.

And I don't hate the idea.

I'd been so busy in the few hours since I'd found out about the prophecy, searching and reading and looking for information, that I hadn't examined the implications of the situation. I hadn't wanted to. Because if the prophecy was real … What did that mean for me? Did I still have any kind of agency in my life? Had I ever?

"I think Dr. Norlgren's lying," Haven said. "Unless either of you found something before you fell asleep."

I shook my head. "Nothing."

Cayley picked up one of the books from the stack

beside her. "I found heaps of stuff about prophecies in this one, but no mention of a *putere* or an *adjutor* or anything called the Sapphire Eclipse."

"There was nothing on Supenet either." Haven sighed. "I searched every major website and academic database. If this prophecy existed, it would be mentioned somewhere." She scratched at the nail polish on her thumb, and tiny red flakes drifted onto her lap. "Something doesn't add up."

"But what would Dr. Norlgren have to gain from lying?" Cayley said.

"I don't know."

"I'll find out when I see him again," I said, rummaging around on my bed for my phone. "I know this whole thing is weird, but … I do think he was telling the truth. It didn't smell like he was lying."

"You can cover up emotions though," Haven said, still scratching at her nail polish.

"Yeah, but—ugh, finally." I pulled my phone out from beneath a thick, leather-bound book called *Prophecies of Ancient Times*. "Crap. I'm late." I leaped off the bed and shoved my feet into the nearest pair of shoes. "I was due there half an hour ago."

"We'll come, too." Cayley stood. Her tangled hair smoothed out, and within moments her clothes had changed both form and color. "We can confront him together."

"No." I was already at the door. "I have to go alone."

"What about—" Cayley started.

"No," I said, firmer this time. "I told you last night—you shouldn't be involved. Logan got hurt because of me. He could've been killed. Don't you understand that? Derek obviously knows what I am. Or what I could be." I ran my hands through my hair and hastily gathered it up into a ponytail. "Dr. Norlgren said people would exploit me and my possible powers. Who knows how many people know?"

"That's even more reason for us to go with you," Haven said.

I opened the door. "Forget it. All of it."

"Emily!" Haven called, but I was already halfway down the corridor.

I should've kept this a secret. What if Haven and Cayley got hurt? Or killed? *I do not know when they'll strike again.* Dr. Norlgren's note had told me more than enough to know I'd made a big mistake. If something happened to my friends, it would be all my fault.

"Slow down, Emily," ordered a voice from behind me on the stairs.

I grabbed the bannister to slow myself down, then turned and found myself face to face with Miss Lassila.

"Whatever it is can wait the extra few minutes it would take to walk." She gave me a steely look. "Classes don't start for another thirty minutes."

"I know." I took the next step slowly, trying to look normal. "I'm late for an appointment."

She raised a pale eyebrow. "Another doctor's appointment? This early?"

I nodded.

"Very well." She gave me a quick up-and-down glance before walking ahead. "But no more running on the stairs. And tie your laces. Dr. Norlgren can wait."

I cursed silently to myself and bent to sort out my shoes. My unbrushed ponytail slipped over my shoulder and I wished, not for the first time, that I had some of Cayley's abilities. Not the way she'd eventually have to feed—in some ways, being a succubus was worse than being a vampire—but the ability to change the way I looked. It could come in handy sometimes.

When I stood back up, Miss Lassila caught my eye— she was talking to someone at the bottom of the stairs—so I walked the rest of the way. I didn't want to draw any more attention to myself. Nervous energy crackled over my skin, and by the time I made it to the medical center I was ready to explode. I pushed through the wooden doors, walked past the nurses' office where Ms. Park was tending to a witch with a bleeding hand, and headed straight to Dr. Norlgren's office.

"Mr. Dufort," I said in surprise as I saw my history teacher striding toward me, a five foot nine paragon of vampiric authority. Everything about him commanded respect, from the tilt of his head to the way the air parted around him as he moved. He was old—not as old as Mr. Olaru, though the years had thinned his deep brown skin into something tinged with gray—but despite his age, his eyes still held the spark of humanity. It gave me hope.

"Emily." He slowed to a stop just past Dr. Norlgren's

office. "I was shocked to hear about what happened to you and Logan." He spoke with the hint of an accent, his soft vowels suggestive of distant times and places that no longer existed. "I trust you are healing well?"

I nodded politely, arranging my features into an expression that hopefully appeared calm, though I couldn't help but glance at the doctor's door.

"I believe Dr. Norlgren has stepped out for a while," he said, following my gaze. "Ms. Park is in her office. She may be able to assist you."

"Okay … um, thanks."

Breathe. Stay calm.

He considered me carefully. "Will I see you during first period today?"

Don't let him smell your fear.

"Sure. I'll be there."

He inclined his head, a movement that was both gracious and genteel, then started off down the hall. He moved with power and grace, something very non-human concealed just below the surface, and a shiver skimmed over my skin.

As soon as he was gone, I rushed over to Dr. Norlgren's door. Maybe Mr. Dufort had been mistaken about him not being there. Dr. Norlgren couldn't have left. Not without telling me everything. This was too important.

I knocked on the door, my heart in competition with my hand. "Dr. Norlgren. Are you there?" I pressed my ear up against the door, just in case, but I already knew the answer—nobody was inside.

What am I supposed to do?

I leaned back against the door, my fingers drumming lightly on the polished wood. Dr. Norlgren's nameplate pressed into my spine, and I straightened when I saw Ms. Park, who was speeding down the hallway toward me, the injured witch I'd seen earlier trailing behind her.

"Dr. Norlgren's not here, Emily," Ms. Park called over her shoulder as she passed. "Try again in an hour."

An hour?

I pulled my phone out of my pocket, ignoring the unread messages from Haven and Cayley, and checked for any missed calls or new emails. Dr. Norlgren had access to my contact details through my school file. Maybe he'd left me instructions?

Nothing.

I gripped my phone tight in my hands and trudged out into the night. If I stayed near the entrance to the medical center, maybe I'd see Dr. Norlgren come back. I found the nearest bench, a wooden monstrosity with uncomfortable slats and swirling metal arms, and sank down into it.

"Hard day?" The seat shifted as Logan vaulted over the back of it. He looked across at me, his dark eyes curious.

"I've had worse," I muttered.

"Same." Logan leaned back, his legs crossed at the ankles. "Although this is almost as bad as fighting Derek."

I shot him a steely glare. "I'm not in the mood for sarcasm right now."

"That wasn't sarcasm."

"Fine. I'm not in the mood for trying to figure you out.

Go away." I waved a hand, directing him somewhere
—*anywhere*—else.

Logan twisted to face me directly. "I was actually
serious."

I tilted my head and looked at him, breathing in the
scent of forest and wolf, mint leaves and truth. I didn't
have to figure him out. Not this time. For once, this was
just Logan, genuine and unfiltered.

"Okay, then," I said slowly. "Yes, I'm having a hard day.
Night. Whatever this is."

His expression softened. "I'm sorry."

"Why?" My predator stirred in my chest. It didn't like
being pitied. Pity made us weak. Pity made us prey.

"Why am I sorry?" Logan's eyebrows dipped. "Because
I'm a decent person?"

I rubbed my hands over my face and pushed the
predator away. "So why is this almost as bad as fighting
Derek? Is it the conversation? Or the bench? Because
it's—"

"It's not the bench."

Logan's gaze hit mine, and something hitched in my
chest.

"I wasn't sure you'd want to talk to me—or be seen
with me—after what happened yesterday." He pulled at a
loose thread on the sleeve of his hoodie. "After what
Vanessa and Courtney and Danielle said."

The words hung between us, stark and real and
vulnerable. I didn't know this boy. He was a stranger, a
friend of a friend, a mystery. But as he pushed his hair

back off his forehead, his eyes wide as he waited for me to respond, I realized I wanted to know more. I wanted to know what he liked, what he hated, what he longed for in those quiet moments when he let himself dream. *If* he let himself dream.

I put a hand on his arm. "Why would I listen to Vanessa or Courtney or Danielle?" I said softly.

Logan didn't move. "Because some people do."

"Those people are idiots."

He tilted his face away, but not before I saw the hint of a smile playing at the edges of his lips.

I didn't fully understand the social dynamics at Mistwood yet—I'd been told that cliques worked differently here than in the human world, and that more predatory supes would sometimes goad each other to see who was strongest—but I knew that listening to Courtney, Vanessa, and Danielle would never tell me anything real about Logan.

I drew in a breath, ready to ask what they meant when they called him crazy and referred to his scars, but he played with the edges of his sleeves, his fingers never still as the scent of soot and daisies—fear and relief—swirled between us, and I knew it would be an intrusion. If he wanted me to know what they'd been talking about, he'd tell me when he was ready.

The campus was getting busier the closer it got to first period, and Mr. Green crossed the path not far from us, his briefcase tucked under his arm. He walked quickly, his forehead creased, and he was clearly deep in thought. He didn't notice us sitting a few feet away.

"Are you going to go see him?" Logan asked, nodding his head in the direction of the psychologist. "About the attack?"

I shrugged. "I have to go and see him every week whether I want to or not. It's compulsory for anyone who gets forcibly turned." I scratched at a faded mark on my jeans and wondered what I'd be doing right then if I'd never become a vampire. *No. Don't even go there.* "I don't talk to him a lot. Not about what matters, anyway. Mostly I use Fred as a distraction."

"He can't help you if you won't let him."

"He's a miniature dragon. He can't help me anyway."

Logan snorted. "I didn't mean Fred."

"I know you didn't. I just don't want to talk about things; I don't see the point. I was turned, and I can't change it."

"You're right. You can't change what happened." Logan's eyelashes cast dark shadows on his cheeks, and for a moment he looked younger. Innocent. Vulnerable. But when he looked up he was pure fire, ablaze in a way I didn't understand. When he spoke again his voice was low. "The only thing you can control is yourself and how you respond."

"Do you really believe that?"

He shrugged and looked away, the fire already gone. "I dunno. Not really, I guess. But I work on it every day."

I didn't know what to say. Because if Haven was wrong

and the prophecy was true, then I really did have no control over anything in my life. Whether that lack of agency extended to my own thoughts, my own responses … Who knew?

"I hope you're right," I finally said, trying to ignore the ice that crept up my spine.

I turned away as I searched through my phone for the Mistwood Academy website. Every staff member had an email address—I just had to find Dr. Norlgren's. Checking over my shoulder to make sure Logan couldn't see, I composed an email, telling the doctor that I'd come to his office whenever he could fit me in.

He has to see me.

He has to explain.

Maybe this was me controlling what I could. And this time, I wouldn't be late.

10

I WALKED through the doors into History and checked my phone for the thousandth time. No new notifications. No missed calls. Nothing. Nothing. Nothing.

"Come on," I muttered, closing the email app and opening it again. I knew I was being unreasonable. It hadn't even been twenty minutes since I'd emailed Dr. Norlgren. I just wanted—no, *needed*—to find out what was going on.

"Get out of my way."

Something sharp pressed into the small of my back and I stepped forward, away from Vanessa and the boxy green bag she held out in front of her like a weapon.

"Learn some manners, asshole," I muttered, just loud enough that I knew she'd be able to hear it.

"What was that?" Courtney stood behind her friend, her hands on her hips, her eyes flashing a challenge.

I didn't answer. I just walked away and took my seat, three rows from the front. Courtney huffed, clearly irritated at being ignored, and tossed her curls over her shoulder before heading to the back row. We didn't have assigned seating, but everyone always sat in the same places. Whether it was due to habit, unspoken social convention, or because we all craved some sort of order in our lives, I didn't know. And right then, I didn't care. I had more important things to think about. Like whether Dr. Norlgren would ever respond to my email.

"She's here," someone in the front row whispered. "See? Behind you."

I placed my phone on the desk in front of me and tried to ignore the looks. They'd all heard about the attack; they'd all heard the rumors. And while some were equal parts curious and sympathetic, others shot me glances that could only be described as derisive. It came as no surprise that those people, the ones who believed Logan and I had hurt each other on purpose, took their seats near Courtney and Vanessa.

Haven and Cayley slipped into class just before the bell. "What's going on?" Haven whispered as she sat in the empty seat beside me. "Did he tell you everything?"

I shook my head. "He wasn't there."

"You should've let us come with you." Haven dropped her bag onto the desk in front of her and pulled out her laptop. "I still don't think we can trust him."

"I won't risk you getting hurt." I checked my emails.

Again. And again. And again. "Why won't he email me back?"

"You should stop by his office again," Cayley said. "We could all go now. Mr. Dufort won't miss us."

"Good evening, students." The history teacher walked through the door, his arms full of books and his gaze full of knowing. He locked eyes with Cayley. "I hope you're all ready to work."

"Damn vampire hearing," Cayley muttered, dropping down into the chair next to Haven. Even slouching, she looked perfect. She'd changed into a black flippy skirt, a wine-colored sweater, sheer black tights, and black Oxford pumps. Yet despite her polished appearance, the undercurrent of unease that followed her around, the one that suggested she'd rather be anywhere but here, pulled at the air around her. It was prickly and electric, and sometimes I wondered what it would be like when it finally ignited. If she'd soar and shine, or if she'd accidentally take us all down with her.

"Phones away." Mr. Dufort set the stack of books he'd been carrying down on his desk. He shrugged out of his coat and arranged it neatly on the back of the chair. When he was done, he stood tall and surveyed the room. He could've been imposing, with his sharply-defined jaw and long steel-gray hair, but he wasn't. He didn't demand obedience like Mr. Olaru did, he earned it.

I checked my phone one last time, then slipped it onto my lap beneath my desk. Hopefully Mr. Dufort wouldn't notice. "Looks like we're stuck here," I whispered to Cayley, though I'd had no intention of skipping class and she knew it.

"So," Mr. Dufort said, "who can tell me where we left off last time?"

One of the boys in the second row, a werewolf, raised his hand. "We were looking at the history of hauntings in America."

"And?"

"And the proliferation of false haunted attractions in the human world," said a girl to my left.

Another girl, a pixie who sat in the second row, raised her hand. "We also looked at how we can tell the difference between real and fraudulent hauntings."

"Excellent." Mr. Dufort set his laptop on a desk at the front of the room and opened up a new presentation. "Today we will be moving on to the history of haunting as metaphor in the human world and how that differs from our experience of hauntings, both real and false, as supernatural citizens."

Mr. Dufort kept talking, and I tried to concentrate, but it was useless. His words were black and white static, a buzzing soundtrack to the thoughts drifting through my mind. *Where's Dr. Norlgren? Why isn't he answering my email? Why wouldn't he—*

"Emily," Haven hissed.

I blinked and looked around. "Sorry, what?" The entire class was staring at me, and someone at the back of the room—Vanessa, probably—laughed. I wanted to slip beneath my desk and disappear.

Mr. Dufort sighed. "I asked your opinion on—"

He was cut off as the door swung open and two boys I'd never seen before burst into the classroom. One was impossibly tall and lanky, with large blue eyes and a shock of messy black hair, while the other was shorter and broader, with blond hair and a wide smile.

"Sorry we're late, sir," the dark-haired one said. "Philip had to finish off some paperwork in the main office."

"Who are they?" I whispered to Cayley, relieved to have a distraction.

"The tall one's Thomas. He's Logan's brother. I dunno about the other guy. He must be new."

"He's cute," Haven whispered. She ran a hand through her hair and tried to smooth down the small tuft that kept sticking up in the back. "Now I wish I'd had more sleep."

"My bad," I said.

She flashed me a grin. "I'd never turn down the chance for research."

"You still should've let us come with you," Cayley said, fidgeting with the necklace that had suddenly appeared around her neck. "You know we don't need protecting, right? We have powers. We can look after ourselves."

"But Logan—" I started.

"Can look after himself, too," Haven said. "Does he know? About the … you know what?"

I shook my head.

"Are you going to tell him?" Cayley asked.

"I don't think I should."

Thomas and Philip squeezed past us to the two empty seats at the end of the row. "Hi, Haven," Thomas said. His voice was resonant and warm, and he smelled like vanilla cookies. "Hey, Cayley." He smiled at me and nodded.

"This is Emily," Haven told him. "She's new. Kind of."

The blond boy smiled. "Nice to know I'm not the only new one here. I'm Philip." I could tell he was a werewolf, but something about his scent seemed slightly off, like weeds growing up through a garden, or spring blossoms in the fall. Maybe it was something to do with whatever pack he was from.

"Quiet!" Mr. Dufort clapped his hands. "Where were we?"

I stopped thinking about Philip and held my breath, praying Mr. Dufort wouldn't call on me again. I had no idea what we'd been discussing for the last half hour. Someone giggled at the back of the room, filling the room with sulfur and spite, and I knew what was coming.

"You'd just asked Emily a question, Mr. Dufort," Courtney said. "You wanted to know her opinion on Maxwell's theory of the phantom as metaphor in contemporary American life."

"Indeed." Mr. Dufort looked straight at me, his pale eyes shrewd, then turned back to Courtney. "And since you were obviously paying such close attention, Miss Beckett, I'm sure you'd be delighted to share your thoughts on the matter with the class."

Courtney stuttered, clearly taken aback, and I tuned out again. I didn't mean to. There was just too much going on in my head and the time was going so slowly, each heavy second stretched and suspended like a swollen balloon.

Why won't he email me back?

And then my phone beeped. I knew the penalty, but it didn't register. I just lifted it and read, my heart like thunder in my ears.

My phone clattered onto the desk.

It wasn't from him.

Mr. Dufort slid a small yellow card toward me. "You know the rules." He held out his hand, and I placed my phone into his broad, lined palm. "Detention, after school. Don't be late."

I went to two more classes after that, Algebra and English, but I didn't take anything in. Dr. Norlgren still hadn't emailed me back, and if I heard one more person talking about me and Logan and our night in the infirmary I was going to scream.

I checked my phone again, then stopped outside the door of my Environmental Sciences class. *Should I?* Wearily, I reached for the door handle. Someone walking by jostled into me, then streaked away without even saying sorry. The hunger whispered in my veins—*take it, take it, take it*—and I leaned my forehead against the door. Then I turned and walked away.

I'd never skipped class before. Not even when I was human. And I didn't know what to do. How not to get caught. Where was I supposed to go?

I wandered aimlessly for a while, then eventually found myself at the entrance to the Music Department. Some part of me had known exactly where I needed to be. Ignoring the hulking chimera that watched me as it paced along the edge of the roof, I slipped quietly through the doors and made my way to the storeroom. Then I let myself into the nearest unoccupied practice room and began to play.

It was an exhale, relief after holding my breath too long. My cello was my lifeline, the thing that helped me keep control more than anything else. When I played, it felt like the warden at The Paranormal Program had been right, that I was strong enough to manage this life.

I played until my fingers hurt, and I didn't want to stop when the knock came on the door. But Mr. Longley called my name, and I knew I had to let him in. I carefully placed my cello on the carpeted floor and tried to think of an excuse for being there. I still didn't have one—not a good one, anyway—by the time I opened the door.

"Marvelous!" Mr. Longley smiled broadly. "You've been working hard today."

"Thank you." I waited for the reprimand I so obviously deserved. Mr. Longley must've known I'd skipped class; no one has that many study periods in a row.

"I realize you're not supposed to be in here right now," he said, his pleasant expression faltering, "but I'm going to let it slide, just this once. You've been through a lot, and music can help with that." He pulled a thin brown folder from his bag and held it out to me. "As you know, we have a concert coming up at the end of semester. I was hoping you'd play a solo for us."

A warm glow ignited in my chest. I took the folder and nodded.

"It's a Prelude by Bach," he said. "Have you played it before?"

I opened the folder and skimmed through the music, the notes playing in my head. "I haven't, but it looks amazing."

"We'll run through it at rehearsal next week." He inclined his head, then turned to go. "Carry on."

I closed the door and thought about practicing some more, but the thoughts that had plagued me, the ever-spinning worries about Dr. Norlgren and the prophecy and Derek and Logan, had finally settled. For the first time in days, I felt like myself. I started packing up my sheet music and was tucking it into my folder when my phone beeped.

It was Haven: *Why weren't you there for Environmental Sciences? And study hall? Why haven't you replied to any of my messages? Where are you??? I have a lead. Finally!!*

My heart leaped into my throat, and I thumped down on the chair, pulling my cello toward me. I held it close, my fingers sketching out fragments of old favorites on the strings, and I exhaled. This was good. A lead was good.

I'd almost finished responding to Haven's message when my phone started ringing. "Hey," I said as her face popped up on the screen.

"We have to go to Adventure Gardens tomorrow night," she said, her tongue tripping over the words.

"What?"

"Adventure Gardens. It's an amusement park about an hour away. Philip and I found it by mistake when we were searching for something to do. Anyway, it's off-campus night tomorrow, so the timing is perfect, and we can all go together, you and me and—"

"Wait," I said, frowning. "What's this got to do with my … situation?"

Haven paused to take a breath. "This," she said, "is where you find out how brilliant I am." She held the phone up to her laptop. "Look at this photo. There's a mural outside the mirror maze. Can you see what's painted at the top?"

I squinted. "No?"

"It's an eclipse. And there's a little bit of script in the corner that says *sapphire*. Somebody there knows something. I have to go, but we'll talk later, okay?"

The screen went black, and I stuffed my phone in my pocket before taking my cello back to the storeroom. I wasn't sure Haven's lead was anything solid at all—the whole thing seemed a bit tenuous—but maybe Dr. Norlgren would have some news.

Five minutes later I was standing outside his office. He didn't answer when I knocked, so I leaned against the door and finished off the apple I'd found in the pocket of my bag. I was debating whether to stay any longer—and risk being late for detention—when Ms. Park walked by.

"Where's Dr. Norlgren?" I said. "I need to see him."

Her eyebrows lowered. "He had to take an unexpected trip. He won't here for the next ten days. I might be able to help, otherwise there's a locum coming in from Seattle later tonight."

I shook my head. "It can wait."

It can't wait.

I rushed off down the corridor and went straight to detention, barely noticing the teacher sitting quietly at the front of the room. My heart was beating fast as I took my seat, and I closed my eyes and tried to remember how to breathe. My life was spinning out of control and the only clue I had was a faded mural in a run-down adventure park.

How could he have gone for ten days? Ten days!

I curled my fingers around the hard edges of the chair, as if it could somehow keep me from falling. I'd never been like this as a human—so ruled by my emotions, always changeable and unsettled. Part of me wished I'd paid more attention in my sessions with Mr. Green. Then maybe I'd be more in control.

Maybe you shouldn't be here.

A chair leg scraped somewhere across the room, and I looked up. It was Logan. He sat awkwardly in his seat, his legs tucked under the desk and his chin in his hands. "You okay?" he mouthed.

I nodded, remembering what he'd said to me earlier. *The only thing you can control is yourself and how you respond.* I didn't know if I believed it. Hell, he'd admitted *he* didn't fully believe it. But maybe I had to try.

"Detention has now begun," the teacher up the front intoned. He was an anaemic-looking witch, with frizzy white hair and tired eyes. "You may work or read or stare into space for the next hour. No talking. And no electronic devices."

Logan grinned and raised his eyebrows at me, then took a book out of his bag. He started to read, and I looked around the room. Everyone else was working or writing or reading, so I let go of the chair, my fingers stiff and cramped, and rummaged around in my bag until I found something that wasn't a hairbrush or an empty candy bar wrapper. I pulled out my History textbook, though I didn't feel like reading, and flipped it open to a random page. The words blurred in front of me.

"Justin, put your phone away," the teacher said.

You can do this. You can stay in control.

I ran my tongue over my teeth, then dropped my shoulders and took a slow, deep breath. And another. And another. And another. When I finally looked up, the knot in my chest had loosened and the blood flowed smoothly in my veins. Logan was staring at me, his expression unreadable.

Fifty long minutes later, the teacher stood. "Your punishment is over for the day. You may go."

I stuffed my textbook back in my bag and pulled out my phone. One new email. *Is it ...?*

"Outside, please," the teacher said.

I stumbled through the door without looking where I was going. I was too busy reading the message. It was from Dr. Norlgren.

11

"SHIT," I muttered as I leaned against the wall and skimmed the email again. Whatever state of calm I'd found was gone.

Dear Emily,

I'm sorry I missed you. I waited as long as I could, but if I'd stayed any longer my transport would have left without me. I cannot say much here, but please, be wary. Tell no one, and trust no one. The attack on you was, in all likelihood, related to what I mentioned last night. I am seeking information and clarification on certain issues and will explain everything upon my return. Stay safe and stay alert.

Warmest regards,

Dr. Norlgren

"But ... why?" I gripped the phone so tight my fingers hurt. "Why couldn't you tell me something useful?"

"You're leaning against Mr. Morrison's door. And he's gonna open it any second."

I looked up and found myself staring at Logan. "What?"

The wall behind me gave way, and I stumbled back.

"You requested useful information." His lips twitched as he watched me. "I gave you useful information."

I moved aside as Mr. Morrison, a Math teacher I didn't know very well, stepped out of his classroom. "Excuse me," he said before hurrying off.

My face flushed hot, and I hugged my messenger bag against me like a shield. I should've heard him coming up behind me, even through the thick wood of the door. And I should've heard Logan before he spoke. It was the third time he'd snuck up on me.

It was just … enhanced senses took some getting used to. When I'd first been turned it had been overwhelming —the sounds, the smells, the constant sensory assault. I'd learned to shut it down, to make it smaller, to use it only when I wanted to. But maybe I'd gone too far.

Stay safe and stay alert.

I had to do better.

"Do you need anything else?" Logan cocked his head to the side. "Or was that useful enough?"

"I could do with some patience," I muttered.

Logan's lips twitched again. "I don't think I can help with that. Patience isn't one of my strong suits."

Me neither.

I glanced down at my phone one last time, then locked the screen, wishing I could throw it against the wall. It wouldn't give me any answers, but it might make me feel better.

"So," Logan said. "You got any plans for the rest of the night?"

I shrugged. "I should probably do some practice. Mr. Longley gave me a new piece today to learn for the concert and ..." *I need to play because it's one of the only things that keeps me in control.* "I don't want to let him down," I finished, my voice hollow.

Logan started walking. "Come on. I want to show you something."

"Why? What is it?"

"You'll see."

I followed him outside and down the path toward the library, a magnificent old building with a creaky wooden door and decorative trim around the gables. Inside, there were endless stacks of shelves and sturdy communal tables; the entire building smelled like comfort and knowledge, firelit nights and ink. But—

"I've been in the library before," I said to Logan, who flashed me a sparkling grin.

"Everyone's been in the library," he said as he led me down the path at the side of the building. We made our way past it, beside manicured lawns and strange shaped hedges, then he turned to me, his arms spread wide. "But have you ever been here?"

He stepped aside and I saw it—a tiny enclosed court-yard with spindly trees and moss growing up through cracked cobblestones and a rickety old bench at the far end. It was neglected and private and peaceful.

"I come here sometimes when I need to get away for a bit." He made his way over to the bench and sat. "No one else ever comes here."

"Why not?"

"Because it's technically out of bounds."

I sat down next to him, perched on the very edge of the seat. "Because?"

Logan shrugged. "Not sure."

We sat there for a while in silence, and I breathed in the scent of the night. It was sweet and serene, filled with florals and grass, creatures and mystery. I looked up at the stars twinkling faintly above us, and the knot in my stomach began to ease.

"Are you ever afraid of losing control?" I said.

Logan's breath hitched, though his pulse remained steady. "Yes," he said quietly.

"So am I."

A passing cloud filtered out the stars, casting shadows on my mind. "Sometimes it feels like I'm one wrong move away from ruining everything. There are things—things that—" *No. He can't know that Derek's attack was because of me.* "Never mind. It's nothing."

Logan moved closer; our legs were almost touching. "It's not nothing."

"You're right. It's an opportunity. An opportunity to practice all those things Mr. Green has been trying to teach me."

Logan snorted. "I hear you on that."

I turned to look at him, surprised. "Do you see him, too? Like, outside of talking about the attack?"

He nodded, unashamed.

Maybe that was why Vanessa and the others called him crazy. It didn't make it right, but they were predators, cruel enough to do anything to assert their superiority. My chest burned. Sometimes I hated it here.

"Does it get better?" I asked. "Easier?"

He took his time before answering, and when he did, his voice was low. "It does, a bit. Though I think we're talking about different things."

"Probably." I stood slowly, stretching the kinks from my limbs. "I'd better get back to my room. I've got home-work to do before dinner."

We walked together toward Worthington Hall, talking about classes and orchestra, anything that was light and easy, though there was a part of me that wanted to tell Logan what was really going on. I had a feeling he'd understand. But he didn't deserve to be put in any more danger. Hell, it was probably bad enough we were walking together. That was all it had taken last time.

"Are you coming to Adventure Gardens tomorrow?" he asked when we stopped outside Worthington Hall.

"I—uh—I don't know." I bit my lower lip, frowning. "Why?"

"Because it's the only night juniors are allowed off campus all month and it sounds like fun?"

Does it, though? I mean, the only reason we were going

was because Haven had apparently found some sort of clue. And it didn't even seem like a *good* clue. It was just an old mural. A coincidence.

"They have cotton candy." Logan's dark eyes were hopeful.

"It sounds tempting, but ..." If we could be attacked on campus, with security and wards and chimera, we could definitely be attacked off campus. And what about all the humans? They'd be everywhere, their blood a never ending temptation. What if I couldn't resist? What if I hurt someone? "I dunno. I've never been off campus before."

Logan considered me carefully when I didn't say anything else. "You won't hurt anyone," he said softly.

I took a step back. "What do you mean?"

Am I really that obvious?

Logan glanced around. A couple of girls walked past, but he didn't speak until they'd gone inside. "I smelled your fear spike. I figured you were either nervous about losing control or about rollercoasters." He smiled like nothing was wrong, and he smelled calm, like an ocean breeze, though understanding flickered in his eyes. "Or maybe you're scared of gardens, though the possibility of that seems a lot slimmer."

"What?"

"Why do you think they call it *Adventure Gardens?*"

I didn't answer.

"Look, if you don't want to come, that's fine. But if you

do decide to make an appearance, you'll be among friends. You never know, you might enjoy it."

"I'll think about it." I turned and walked up the stairs, my bag weighing heavily on my shoulder. When I got to the top, I looked back at him. "See you at dinner?" I asked.

He nodded, his hands in his pockets. "I wouldn't miss it."

I wasn't sure why, but something about the way he said those words filled me with a warm glow. It wasn't enough to dispel the worries that still whirled around my head, but as I sat doing homework, my earbuds in to block out the noise of Haven practicing magic, I found myself thinking about dark brown hair, a soft low voice, and warm lips against mine.

The next day, I woke up late. The sky was already a deep, star-clustered black, and I blinked away the remnants of my dreams.

"Finally!" Haven tossed aside the book she'd been reading and leaped out of bed. "I've been waiting for you to wake up for hours."

"Real-time hours or Haven hours?" I said, yawning.

She rolled her eyes. "We have to hurry. There's only one bus that comes through here, and if we miss it we're screwed." She opened her closet door and started pulling out clothes. "You are coming, right? We have to check out that mural."

I nudged Minikins out of the way with my elbow and dragged myself into a sitting position. "Yeah, I'll come." I'd spent a long time thinking about it before I'd fallen asleep just before dawn, and I knew I had to go for two very different reasons. One: I had to find out if the mural was connected to the Sapphire Eclipse. And two: I had to challenge my fear of losing control. Had I lost control before? Yes. But I'd never actually hurt anyone because of it. I'd been making what Mr. Green might call cognitive errors —I'd accepted my worries as absolute truth instead of the automatic thoughts that they were.

"I knew you'd come," Haven said. She threw some shirts and dresses onto her bed, then went back to rummaging through the closet. "Anyway, regardless of whether the mural is important or not, I need you there with me. Philip's coming, and you have to make sure I don't do anything stupid."

"Stupid like investigating a mystery? Or stupid like falling for the new guy?"

Haven turned and her arms were overflowing with a tangle of clothes and hangers. "Both?"

At dinner last night, she and Philip had been so absorbed in each other they'd ignored the rest of us for the entire meal—and the few hours after. I didn't know where they'd gone, but she'd barely made it back to our room in time for curfew.

"I just need you to make sure I'm not too *me*," she said.

"Haven—" I started.

She tossed the pile of clothes onto her bed with the

others and held up a hand. "I'm not totally oblivious. I know I can be too loud. Too energetic. Too overwhelming. I believe my mother routinely describes me to her friends and acquaintances as *an intelligent but excitable child who is liable to destroy her future career prospects and the family name with her capriciousness and idiosyncrasies.*"

"Oh. Ouch."

Haven shrugged. "It could be worse. You should hear what she says about my grandmother."

"Haven, you're honest and kind and loyal, and you're the smartest person I know. Has your mom even met you?"

"Barely," she muttered, and I knew she didn't believe me when the clouded scent of carnations swirled over her skin.

"Ignore her," I said emphatically. "You shouldn't have to change who you are for anyone. Not for your mother. And not for Philip. If he can't see how amazing you are, then it's his loss, not yours." I got out of bed and made my way across the room, the floor cold under my bare feet. "I'm serious. There's nothing wrong with you."

Haven's blue eyes flickered. "I know."

I quickly got dressed, throwing on jeans and a T-shirt, while Haven tried on various combinations of almost everything she owned. Finally, she threw down the last option in disgust.

"We're going to be late, and it's all my fault!" she exclaimed.

Cayley knocked on the door, and I let her in before

going back to my dresser and grabbing my hairbrush. "You guys aren't ready?" she said, perfect in blue skinny jeans and a gray T-shirt, her brown hair loose around her shoulders. "The bus leaves in an hour and we still have to get breakfast."

"I have nothing to wear!" Haven said. "Why didn't you guys tell me my entire wardrobe's ridiculous?"

Five minutes later, we had her ready to go. She looked in the mirror one last time, wrinkling her nose as she considered what we'd chosen—a yellow tank top, black bat-print leggings, and purple Dr. Martens. "You don't think it's too much?"

"Too much?" Cayley raised one perfectly-shaped eyebrow. "This is understated for you."

"You really like him, don't you?" I said.

Haven reached for her lip gloss and sighed. "Maybe. We went for a walk after dinner last night, and he was just so … kind? Not like the guys I usually end up with. I don't want to ruin this before it's even begun."

"You won't," I said. "But if Philip doesn't like you because of your clothes, then he's not the guy for you."

Cayley snorted. "If Philip doesn't like you because of your clothes, then he's not the guy for anyone."

We went down to breakfast, and the others ate quickly while I paid a visit to the feeding room. There were six of us going to Adventure Gardens: me, Haven, Cayley, Logan, Thomas, and Philip. Everyone was buzzing and the excitement was contagious, but when I saw the school gates, I hesitated.

Thomas stopped beside me. "The first time's always the hardest," he whispered.

"What?" I looked up at him sharply.

"I used to be human."

The night stretched around me, elastic and fluid. I didn't know what I'd expected him to say, but it wasn't that. "How long?" I finally managed to ask.

"How long since I was turned?"

I nodded, strangely numb.

"I was eleven. Still a kid." Thomas shrugged his angular shoulders; his body was skeletal and sharp, but his face was gentle. "Logan's family found me and took me in. They helped me through it. I've been one of them ever since."

He led me toward the elaborately-carved steel gates, and we showed our ID cards to the lion-faced chimera who sat to the side of them and nodded us through. My stomach was in knots.

I can't do this.

I'll lose control.

"Are you sure it gets easier?" I whispered to Thomas.

He nodded once. "Without a doubt."

I wanted to talk to him more. I had so many questions. Where was he from? How was he turned? Did he miss being human? But we caught up with the others and the moment was lost.

"Everything okay?" Logan said, falling into step beside me.

I swallowed past the lump in my throat and felt the

cool night air on my face and my arms. I was out with my friends. I was leaving Mistwood. And the earth was still solid and familiar beneath my feet.

"It is," I said, my lips curving into a smile.

We arrived at the bus stop at the end of the long, gravel-lined street with only minutes to spare. Haven was telling a story about accidentally stopping a rollercoaster with a burst of fear-induced childhood magic—she'd been nine years old and hadn't been on a rollercoaster since—when the bus turned up. It was a battered old beast with dirt-covered windows and a sputtering tailpipe, and it was surrounded by clouds of diesel exhaust.

"This bus looks older than my grandmother," Philip said as he covered his nose with his arm.

"There aren't a lot of options for transport around here," Thomas said. "They put the worst bus on this route because no one ever uses it."

We clambered up the dirt-stained steps and the driver glared, his dark eyebrows as ragged as the upholstery on the seats. "No food or drinks," he barked. "No smoking. And no making babies."

"No making babies?" I muttered as I paid my fare. "What do people *do* on buses around here?"

"It takes an hour to get to the city," Logan whispered in my ear as we walked down the aisle to the seats at the back. "People have to entertain themselves somehow."

The bus started moving before we'd even sat. Haven, Philip, Cayley, and Thomas spread out along the back row, so I sat down on the right, directly in front of Haven and Philip. Logan sat next to me, and Haven thrust an open packet of chips between us. They smelled like sea salt and freedom.

"Want one?" she asked, her mouth already full.

I took a handful. Logan shook his head.

"I told you people have to entertain themselves," he said, bumping his knee against mine. "Though I didn't realize we were so boring you'd have to start straight away, Haven."

She smacked him on the shoulder with the chip packet. "It's just a snack. You're such a dick sometimes, Logan."

He grinned, his teeth shining white. "Takes one to know one."

We fell into an easy rhythm, talking and laughing as the bus bumped along the quiet roads, the driver swearing every time we got too loud. I hadn't forgotten about Dr. Norlgren and the prophecy, or Derek and the attack, or Haven's possible clue, but it wasn't consuming me as it usually did. Instead, I focused on the dust-filtered world that rushed past the window, and I saw all of it—the trees, the grass, the fences, and eventually the traffic. Even the smell of diesel didn't bother me. It was all so real, so human. So *alive*. And so was I.

Logan touched my arm, and I jumped. "Haven wants to know if you'll go on the bumper cars with her."

"Everyone else thinks they're boring." She leaned forward and rested her arms over the back of my seat. "I keep telling them they're wrong, but they won't listen."

"Of course I'll go with you," I said, flashing her a grin. "Bumper cars are *not* boring."

Haven thrust her arms in the air. "See! You're all wrong! Emily says so."

"Still not doing it," Cayley said.

Logan held his hands up in surrender. "Maybe I'll join you. You can show me what I'm missing."

His voice was low, and my stomach filled with butterflies. "I won't go easy on you," I said, swallowing hard.

Logan grinned. "I wouldn't have it any other way."

"We're here." Cayley pulled the yellow woven cord above the window and a dull chime sounded. The driver slowed to a stop.

"Good fucking riddance," he muttered as we clambered out the back door, not realizing most of us could hear him.

I laughed as the bus pulled away, and two minutes later we were standing at the entrance to Adventure Gardens. Bright lights and noise streamed through the gates, and the scent of popcorn and cotton candy filled the cold night air. People—*so many people*—were milling around, some waiting to get in, others on their way out, their faces flushed with adrenaline. This was the world. The real world.

And I still belonged in it.

"Okay, I'll admit it," Logan said as he climbed out of his bumper car. "That was actually fun."

"I knew it!" Haven twirled around, both arms raised in the air, and the bats on her leggings flashed silver and gold under the bright indoor lights. "I told you bumper cars aren't boring."

Logan sighed and looked at me. "She'll never let me forget this."

"Neither will I." I gave him a shameless grin.

"You can tell a lot about a person by the way they drive a bumper car," Haven said, her gaze shifting between us. "Em, you're clearly tenacious. And, Logan, you need some driving lessons."

Logan scoffed, and I reached into my pocket and pulled out the brightly-colored map I'd been given at the entry booth. "Where to now?"

"Somewhere you can't cause any more bruises." Logan rubbed his knee and shot me a mock glare.

"Whoops," I said brightly.

Haven led us outside, bouncing past the queue of people waiting to get in. "We've already done the tilt-a-whirl, the rollercoaster, the log flume, and the bumper cars," she said, listing them off on her fingers. "I don't know about you, but I need a break from things that move. And Logan obviously needs something less combative."

He flipped her the bird, then peered at the map over my shoulder, his body warm behind me. "What about—" he started, but Haven was already racing forward.

"Philip!" she squealed, her face brightening as he approached. Cayley and Thomas trailed a few steps behind. "You guys survived the terror drop!"

"—the house of mirrors?" Logan finished.

My stomach fluttered. *There's a mural outside the mirror maze. Somebody there knows something.*

"You should've come with us." Philip hooked an arm around Haven's shoulder and pulled her close. "It was awesome."

"It wasn't that great," Cayley said, her rose-colored lipstick darkening until it was almost black. "Too many assholes."

Beside her, Thomas glowered.

Haven didn't notice—she was too busy staring at Philip. "I could barely handle the rollercoaster," she said. "You know I'd never manage the terror drop."

"But I would've looked after you." Philip's lips brushed against her hair. "What if we went back there. Gave it another go?"

Thomas crossed his arms over his chest. "Let's do something else. Something we'll *all* enjoy."

"Right," Logan said, and a wisp of heat swirled around his skin. It was power and wolf, heady and strong and commanding, and it smelled like a forest breeze. "The house of mirrors it is."

We started off down the path, all of us together, but something had changed, and the easy camaraderie from the beginning of the night had gone. Haven's gaze flicked to mine, her blue eyes serious, and she looked like she was about to speak, but Philip pulled her ahead and the moment was gone. His arm snaked around her waist, his hand settling low on her hip, and the scent of tobacco, possessiveness, filled the air.

Thomas growled, quiet and low in the back of his throat.

"Shit," Logan muttered. The heat around him grew stronger, and I reached out and touched his arm.

"What's the matter?" I said.

His gaze darted to the side, to Thomas, and he shook his head. "Just give us a minute, okay?"

I had no idea what was going on, but I slowed, pretending to tie my shoe as I gave them some distance. Cayley hung back beside me.

"What happened?" I asked when they were far enough away that they wouldn't hear us. "Did something go wrong on the terror drop?"

"You could say that."

I frowned when she didn't say anything more. "Are you going to elaborate? Or do I have to guess? You hate it when Haven does this."

She sighed. "Fine. What do you think of Philip?"

"I don't know. I've hardly spoken to him. But Haven's obviously smitten."

"She shouldn't be. He's a dick."

I looked at her, my eyebrows high. "Because?"

"Because he made it exceedingly clear to us both, right before the terror drop fell, that Haven was his and his alone." She straightened the hem of her T-shirt, her lipstick turning a deep blood-red as she met my gaze. "He had some interesting suggestions regarding what might happen if either of us tried anything."

"Oh," I said, as the meaning of Cayley's words became slightly less murky. "So Thomas likes Haven? And you like Haven?"

She shrugged. "We both did, in junior high. I moved on. Thomas never did."

I looked over at him, where he walked beside Logan, his head bent low and his shoulders folded forward. He was submissive, cowed, but there was still something wild in him, and as he turned his face to the side I saw his eyes flash amber. Wolf.

"Does Haven know?" I asked.

"About me? Yes. About Thomas? No."

"He's never told her? Since junior high? And she's never suspected?"

Cayley shrugged. The colored lights strung up along the fence on the other side of the path cast violent streaks of red and blue across her face. "I asked him about it once, and he said it was pointless. That she'd never be into a guy like him." Her gaze lingered on Thomas' back, and a telltale note of wistfulness softened her hazel eyes. "It's true—he's not really her type. I don't know why. He'd treat her a lot better than Marcus, her last boyfriend. Or Philip, it seems."

Her voice was quiet, and she reached for the necklace that hung beneath her T-shirt. She was sea spray and soot, vanilla and roses, and I knew what I'd seen in her eyes was true. Cayley had feelings for Thomas.

"Does he know how you feel?" I asked, though I wasn't sure if I should.

Cayley looked down at her feet. "He knows."

"Oh."

"It's fine." She said it quickly, the two words almost merging into one. "I'm a succubus. We're not built for relationships."

I didn't believe her, but the tightness in her jaw told me not to take it any further. "Philip didn't hurt you guys, though, right?"

She shook her head. "Not this time."

We fell quiet as we came to the house of mirrors. Haven and Philip had already gone in, but Logan and Thomas were waiting beside the door. Thomas didn't speak. "Ready?" Logan said, forcing a smile. It was almost convincing.

"Sure." Cayley shrugged. "Why not?"

I studied the mural that covered the wall by the entrance. It was old and faded, a paint-flaked scene of a midnight-blue sky hanging low over a darkened forest. The moon in the corner was full, yellowed with age and dirt, and it was covered with the half-shadow of a still progressing eclipse. Beside it, in thin black script, was the word *sapphire*.

I moved closer, my heart pounding in my ears.

Is it a message? A clue? A trap?

I ran my hand across the wall, the paint rough against my fingertips, and I stopped when I got to the moon. *The prophecy of the Sapphire Eclipse.* That's what Dr. Norlgren had called it. But what the hell did it mean?

"You coming?" Logan said, looking at me curiously.

Yes.

No.

Maybe?

My phone buzzed with a new message from Haven: *Did you see the mural? I'm looking for more clues inside. Talk to you when we're out.*

I took one last look at the faded scene. "I guess I'm coming," I said, pocketing my phone as I walked slowly back to the door.

My heart pounded in my ears.

There was no queue, and no attendant, so we walked

straight in through the dark, narrow doorway—Logan, Thomas, Cayley, then me. The entire building was silent.

I swallowed hard.

We emerged into a room made entirely of mirrors—the walls, the ceiling, the floor. They were shiny and polished, almost hyper-real, and I tilted my head as I watched the four of us in duplicate, trying to figure out the illusion.

Haven and Philip were nowhere to be seen.

"Let's split up," Cayley said, pointing out the four mirrored doorways that blended in along the back wall.

"Not a chance, Rodriguez." Logan's grin, genuine this time, was reflected back infinitely. "We stick together on this one. Right?" He glanced at me, his eyebrows raised.

"Definitely," I said.

Thomas grunted.

We followed Cayley into another mirror-lined room, and the door slammed shut behind us. A moment later, ominous moans filled the air, and I found myself standing closer and closer to Logan, goosebumps rising on my skin.

"Which way now?" Cayley asked.

I turned around slowly. It was difficult to make out where the walls ended and the floor began. The room was irregularly shaped, the ceiling hanging low over our heads, and all I could see was the four of us, reflected over and over in every direction. This time, there was no obvious exit.

"Do you think it's a puzzle?" I reached toward the ceiling, my fingers grazing the glassy surface. "Can you see any clues?"

Will it tell me what I am?

Thomas finally spoke, and his voice was low and rough. "I can't see anything except us."

"You say that like it's a bad thing," Logan said, putting a hand on his brother's shoulder.

Thomas shrugged him away. "Isn't it though?" He stepped forward until he was toe to toe with his reflection, his dark-lashed eyes staring back at him. His lip curled up in disgust, and I wanted to look away, but I couldn't. Everywhere I turned I saw him, caught in a scene of intimate self-loathing. His face even shone up at us from the mirrored floor.

Logan stared at Thomas' reflection, his dark eyes worried, then he straightened his shoulders and whispered something in his brother's ear, so low I couldn't hear it. The two of them retreated to the farthest corner of the room, Thomas a caged animal, Logan his keeper.

I didn't know where to look. I wanted to give them privacy, but everywhere I turned I could see it all. The flash of amber in Thomas' eyes. The firm set of Logan's jaw. The way they faced each other down, Thomas looking away first, blinking rapidly as he stared at his own reflection. The entire space burned with them, hot and wild and fierce. The air was electric with power and wolf.

My vampire was close beneath my skin.

I wasn't sure whether I was predator or prey.

My fangs were a tingle beneath my gums, ready to

come through, and I closed my eyes and willed them away. Then everything shifted. The room became cooler, sweeter, calmer. When I finally looked up, Thomas' face was flushed.

"Shall we continue?" Logan said, standing shoulder to shoulder with his brother.

I tapped the wall beside me. "No door, remember?"

None of us mentioned what had happened. It had been a moment of private pain, and it was easier to pretend that it had never occurred. Pain meant weakness, and weakness meant prey, and it was wrong and it was stupid, but I couldn't change the way I felt when I smelled Thomas' fear, and I couldn't change the way I felt when I smelled Logan's power.

"Pick a wall," Cayley said, crossing the room and moving us on with decisive speed. "We'll go clockwise. Check every mirror until you find the way out."

"And if we don't?" Thomas said, his expression still serious.

"This is an amusement park, not a dungeon." She pressed her hands against the glass, her hair smoothing itself back into a ponytail as she worked. "They're not going to trap us forever."

I started checking mirrored panels, running my fingers over them, whispering under my breath. *"Putere. Adjutor. The Sapphire Eclipse."*

Nothing happened, and for the first time, I wished I could do magic. Maybe there was a spell that would reveal the door. Or the prophecy. A spell that would save me from wondering what the hell was going on. But vampires couldn't do magic. Magic was the domain of witches—and witches only.

Wait.

Something stirred in my chest. A flicker of memory. Of a person. Of something that was mine but … wasn't.

"Nothing over here," Logan said, and I turned, the feeling already gone.

"I've got nothing either," Cayley said. "Em?"

I quickly checked the rest of the mirrors on my side, then shook my head. "Nothing." I reached forward one last time and touched the glass in front of me again. It was smooth and cold, cognizant of nothing, but static prickled over the back of my neck. "Do you think someone's watching us right now?"

Logan shrugged. "They must have cameras, but—"

A scream filled the room, high pitched and piercing. I stumbled back, covering my ears with my hands. I closed my eyes and willed it to stop, but it kept getting louder and louder until it found its way inside me, vibrating through my skull and blood until I was convinced my ears were bleeding.

Then, just as I was beginning to think I couldn't take it anymore, it stopped.

I blinked carefully. Once, then twice. The room came into focus around me and I straightened. I didn't even realize I'd been bent double, my hands still over my ears.

"There's a door." I saw Thomas' mouth move, but I could barely hear the words over the ringing in my ears.

He pointed and I turned. One of the mirrors had turned black, a gaping mouth ready to swallow us whole.

Cayley touched my arm, and I jumped. "Let's go," she said.

I followed her through the doorway, stumbling as I walked, and she gripped my hands, steadying me. The next room was larger than the others, hexagonal, and brightly lit by hundreds of hanging lamps. This time the doors were obvious. There were two of them, on opposite sides of the room.

"Which way?" Thomas asked, pointing at one door, then the other.

I leaned against one of the mirrors and looked up at the ceiling, waiting for my hearing to return. "I don't think it matters," I said.

Putere.

Putere.

Putere.

Was I ever going to find out what I was?

"This one'll do," Logan said, heading for the farthest. "You coming, Em?"

I glanced at the mirrors as I followed the rest of them across the room. They were oddly shaped, some concave and some convex, and all of them made us distorted. I stopped, tilting my head as I examined my reflection more closely. Was this what I was now? Monstrous? Grotesque? Was this what hid behind the illusion of humanity?

The scent of lemon, sour and sharp, filled the air

around me, and I looked up at Logan, confused. "Can you smell the lie?" I whispered.

And is it the human? Or the vampire?

"I think we need to hurry," he said, holding out his hand.

My heart was a hammer in my chest, but I took his hand and went into the next room with the others. Unlike the rest of the chambers we'd been in, this room wasn't empty. Three young girls, maybe twelve or thirteen years old, were in there, making faces at themselves and giggling loudly. They were dressed in floral party dresses, and they must have bathed in scented body spray, because I couldn't smell anything else. One of them turned to look at us, still laughing, a gummy bear in her hand.

"Let's keep going," Logan said.

There was only one door, so we headed straight for it. Thomas got there first and opened it quickly, but it slammed right back in his face.

"What the hell?" he said, stepping back onto Cayley's foot.

"Ow!" she yelped.

"Shit." He covered his mouth with his hand. "I didn't know you were behind me."

"Well, I was," she retorted.

The girls' laughter intensified, transforming into something dark, filled with hunger and malice. It was the sound of every nightmare I'd ever had, and I thought of Kitty, and how she'd almost destroyed everything. She'd never been completely real.

I drew in a breath.

There was blood, slow and cold, and a scent I didn't recognize, mostly hidden beneath the artificial smell of fragrance and candy.

They're not human.

"Do you know the way out?" Logan asked them, and I gripped his hand tighter.

They just kept cackling.

Another door swung open. "Come on," I said, dragging Logan behind me. "Hurry, before it shuts."

We made it into the other room.

Cayley and Thomas didn't.

"This place is fucked up," Logan said, turning around in a circle as he gazed at the reflective walls around us.

I ran my hands over the mirror—the door—in front of me. There had to be a handle somewhere. A safety latch. A way to let Cayley and Thomas through. "Open the door," I yelled when my search proved futile. I pounded my fists against the glass, my reflected eyes wild and wide. "Come on. This isn't funny anymore!"

Logan gently pulled my hands away. "Stop. You'll break the glass."

"I don't care."

"But—"

"Those girls aren't human," I said, stumbling toward the center of the room. "I don't know what they are, but Cayley and Thomas are trapped in there with them, and I don't know how to get them out."

Logan paled. "What do you mean? They were creepy, but they didn't—"

"Shhhh." I closed my eyes and held up a hand, then drew in a deep breath. I let it sit in my nose and my lungs, searching until I found it. One tiny thread, delicate and wispy, almost hidden behind the magnified scents of people and junk food, glass cleaner and fake-wood floors. "Magic," I whispered.

Logan went still. I could feel the change in the space between us. He pushed out with his power, his eyes flickering with a hint of amber. "It's not necessarily a bad thing," he said. "Haven might've done a spell to find the door. Or the owner of Adventure Gardens could be a witch. They could've used their powers to amplify the effects of the mirrors."

"You're wrong." I pulled my phone out of my pocket. "We're not safe here. I can feel it." Fingers shaking, I tried to call Cayley, but my phone wasn't working. "Crap. There's no service."

Logan looked at his phone, his forehead creasing. "That's weird. My battery's dead. I swear I charged it before we left."

I raised my arm, holding my phone above my head as I walked around the room. "If I could just get—"

The lights went out, plunging us into absolute darkness.

No.

I jabbed at my phone, trying to get the screen to light up, but it was dead. And I couldn't see. *Why can't I see?* I was a predator, I should've been able to see something, *anything*, in the dark.

"Logan?" I said, my voice higher than usual.

He breathed in sharply. Once. Twice. A breath in two parts. "Yeah?"

"Can you see anything?"

"Nope."

A hand gripped my arm, and I screamed.

"Relax," Logan said, close to my ear, his voice calm and soothing. "It's only me."

I couldn't relax, but I leaned against him, listening carefully in the dark. Heartbeats. Breath. Blood moving through veins. There was nothing unexpected, but nothing useful either. Nothing until—

"There's someone in here," I whispered, stiffening.

Logan straightened. "I know."

My fangs slid out and the hunger flared to life beneath my skin, sharp-edged and ready. *Focus.* Footsteps padded toward us, inching closer and closer. I paused. Held my breath. Then I pushed Logan out of the way.

"What the hell?" he said.

I leaped to the side.

Something crashed into the empty space between us, and the weight of a body, warm and angry, brushed against the side of my leg. I breathed in slowly, searching for the person—the creature?—but I couldn't tell what it was. It was earthy and sweet, not human, but not something I recognized either.

"Incoming," Logan said as the body moved again.

I darted out of the way, and something flashed bright in one of the mirrors. Cat eyes? A flame? I looked up as a chandelier burst to life above me, filled with flickering candles.

"Who are you?" I yelled, spinning around.

But there was no one there.

Not even Logan.

"Logan?" I said, ice skimming over my skin. "Are you—"

The floor dropped out from under me.

I screamed as my body slid down what felt like a rough, vinyl-lined chute. When I got to the bottom, I fell to my knees, my heart in my throat. My hands were pressed against a checkerboard floor, the black and white tiles shiny and cold.

It's a game. It's all just a game.

I stood, realizing everyone was watching me. Logan, Haven, Philip, Cayley, Thomas, and the three strange girls in the party dresses. One of the girls, a thin-lipped blonde with crooked teeth and a dusting of freckles, stepped forward and grinned. "Thanks for playing!" she said. "Come again any time. Invite all your friends."

She ushered us out the final door, her bright smile frozen in place, but when she looked at me her eyes transformed. The lids disappeared and the pupils elongated into vertical slits. Scales erupted over her skin.

"*Putere,*" she whispered.

Then she slammed the door in my face.

THE WEEK after the trip to Adventure Gardens was strangely normal. There were no more attacks, no mention of prophecies, and no strange serpent girls who looked like they wanted to devour me. We'd never found out why they'd been part of the house of mirrors, and I still didn't know how they knew what I was—no, what I *could* be—but none of us had wanted to stay at the park any longer. We'd gone straight back home to Mistwood.

I was sure the entire thing had been a trap.

It had also been a wakeup call. A reminder not to be complacent. Because while the girls hadn't hurt us, they easily could have. And I still didn't know what they wanted with me. So I did as Dr. Norlgren had suggested— I stayed alert. I did nothing out of the ordinary. I went to class, I did my homework, and I made sure I was in my room well before curfew. I practiced my piece for the concert until it was perfect. I had extra sessions with Mr.

Green, and I stopped resisting his help. I went nowhere alone.

And sometimes I secretly checked for emails that never came.

Every time I found myself spiraling, wondering when the next attack would come, or fearing the possibility of a life where none of my decisions were my own, I let myself worry for five minutes, as Mr. Green had suggested, and then I did something else. Apparently I had anxiety as a result of the attacks, including the first one back in Michigan that had left me a vampire, but with hard work and time it would hopefully get better.

No, it *would* get better.

"I've been looking into the history of Adventure Gardens," Haven said on Saturday night, exactly one week after our ill-planned adventure. "But I still can't find out who owns it. It's part of an Anonymous Trust. I mean, I could ask my mom—I'm sure someone owes her a favor— but I don't want to deal with her questions."

I shut my laptop and turned around in my chair. "What does your mom do?"

"It's better not to ask."

I leaned my chin on my hands and watched as Haven got ready for her date with Philip. I still didn't trust him. He'd apologized to Cayley and Thomas the night after we'd been to Adventure Gardens, but it seemed a little too rehearsed to be real. He'd told them the whole thing had been a misunderstanding, a joke, an attempt to subvert the notion of the possessive boyfriend. But he hadn't subverted it—he'd just reinforced it. And while Haven knew my concerns, she didn't agree. So I watched and waited and hoped with everything I had that she didn't get hurt.

"Do I look okay?" she asked as she laced up her boots.

"You look great." And she did. She wore a pink polka dot dress, a lemon-yellow cardigan, and her trademark heavy boots. Her hair had been carefully tousled, and a row of rose gold studs glittered in each ear. "Are you—um —are you sure you should—"

She held up a hand, her expression hardening. "We've talked about this. Philip's a good guy. You just need to spend more time with him."

"Okay, I will, but—"

"You don't know him like I do. Anyway, you should be more concerned about yourself. We still don't know how those girls in the mirror maze knew what you are."

"What I *could* be," I said quickly.

"Fine. What you *could* be." She stood and assessed herself in the mirror, straightening her cardigan and smoothing down the non-existent wrinkles in her dress. "I have to go. Cayley should be here in a minute. You're both staying in tonight, right?"

I shook my head. "Cayley's going out. And I'm going running."

Her eyes narrowed. "Since when?"

"Since I decided to earlier this evening?"

She sighed and leaned against her dresser, her arms folded over her chest. "Are you going alone?"

"How could I? None of you let me go anywhere by myself." Cayley and Haven made sure someone was always with me, and I didn't know what they'd said to Logan and Thomas, but they wouldn't let me be alone either.

"It's for your safety. And only until we find out more about what's going on." She pulled her phone out of her purse and scrolled through it, frowning. "Why didn't anyone tell me about the change of plans?"

"Because I want half an hour to myself. I'm in our room, in a well-warded dorm, with Ms. Emmerson and Miss Lassila downstairs. Just give me this. Please."

Haven pursed her lips, but eventually she nodded. "Who's running with you? Thomas or Logan?"

"Logan."

She nodded slowly and crossed the room, turning when she got to the door. "You like him, don't you?"

My face was too warm, and I pressed the backs of my hands to my cheeks.

"You like him!" Haven bounced up and down, her lips curving into a smile. "I knew it! This is the fourth time you've gone running together this week."

"Because you won't let me go anywhere alone!"

Her smile widened, and she closed the door behind her.

I flopped down onto my bed and closed my eyes. Haven was right—I *did* like Logan. The trouble was, he was so hard to read sometimes that I wasn't sure if he liked me back. I mean, sometimes he held my hand, and he seemed to like spending time with me. But did he like me as a friend? Or as something more?

Why can't I smell it on his skin?

He hid so much of himself away. But I wanted to know him. I wanted to *know* him.

I squeezed my eyes shut and groaned. Nothing about Mistwood Academy was what I'd expected, including Logan Adams.

My phone beeped, jerking me out of my head, and I swiped the screen to see the message: *You ready?*

I looked down at my clothes—pajama pants, a sweater, and socks. Not ideal running attire. I messaged back: *Give me two minutes.* Then I threw the phone down on my bed and set about searching my room for something clean to wear.

Five minutes later, the floor was a mess, but I was dressed in a pink tank top, shiny black leggings, and white running shoes. I managed to coax my hair into some sort of messy bun as I ran down the stairs.

"Ready?" Logan said when I got outside. He was bouncing up and down on the balls of his feet, clearly ready to go. At times, he seemed to run for nothing more than the joy of it, but I suspected he was more serious about it than he let on. He ran almost daily, whatever the weather, sometimes twice a day, and I was surprised he let me tag along. It was obvious I was holding him back.

I lifted a hand and attempted to fix my hair. "As ready as I'll ever be, I guess."

We made our way across the grounds to the track by

the gym. It was the only place we'd run together, though I knew some of the kids and teachers, especially the were-animals, liked to run in the woods. Unlike the sprawling expanse of natural forest, the track was large and oval, the surface brick red with crisply painted lanes. It smelled of faded sunshine and rubber, and it was simultaneously inviting and revolting.

Logan and I did a quick warm up on the grassy area between the track and the gym, then we started to jog, slowly at first, then increasing in speed until we were running faster than any human ever could. It was strange —I'd never really exercised in my old life, but the wind whipping across my skin, biting cold against burning muscle, was changing me. Molding me into something different. I was awake and alive in a way I'd rarely experienced before; music was the only thing that compared.

Logan glanced at me as we ran. "How was your day?"

I met his gaze, and the intensity there made everything else fall away. For a moment, there was only us, running side by side, strides matching, hearts beating in unison. The world was ripe with possibilities.

Then Logan grinned, his teeth straight and shining, and surged ahead into the night.

I pumped my arms and legs, catching him easily. "My day was fine. How about yours?"

"It was okay." Another glance. Another grin. "Better now you're here."

He pulled ahead again, and this time I didn't try to catch up. I watched him run faster, his body moving with grace and strength, and I almost stumbled over my own feet. He looked back over his shoulder and flashed me that sparkling grin.

"Catch me if you can," he called.

I allowed myself once last glance at his speeding form, then pulled my thoughts back to the task at hand. I focused on closing the distance between us, and my lungs burned like fire in my chest.

"You can do it!" Logan called.

"How'd you get so quick?" I asked when I finally caught up, gasping for air between each word.

"Practice." Logan slowed down a little, and I knew he was only doing it for me. "I've been running like this for years. It gets easier."

"Sure it does." I sucked air into my lungs and tried to look normal.

We slowed even more, then ran for another half hour, sometimes talking, other times moving together in silence. When we finally stopped I was aching and exhausted, though I knew my accelerated healing abilities meant I wouldn't be feeling it for long.

We walked around the oval to cool down, and Logan stretched his arms over his head. "You really pushed your-self today."

I glanced at him out the corner of my eye. "*You* really pushed me today."

"You did the work. Being a vampire gives you strength and speed, but having the internal fortitude to improve on that is what gives you character." His screwed up his nose, and his voice turned bitter. "At least, that's the sort of thing my dad always says."

"Um …" I wasn't sure how to respond. "Okay?"

"Sorry." Logan stopped and turned to face me. "My dad's kind of a dick. But I do think you're amazing." The color on his exercise-flushed cheeks deepened. "I mean, I think what you're doing is amazing."

I scuffed the toe of my sneaker against the track. "It was Mr. Green's idea."

"It was for me, too."

Neither of us moved.

"Do you think it helps?" Logan asked, the words stark in the still night air.

"Yeah."

"I think it does, too."

We left the track and made our way across campus to the dorms. The night was clear and cool, and stars glittered above in the cloudless sky. The scent of the woods, heady and thick, filled the spaces between us. This life, this strange new life, felt so full of promise, like a dream or a story or a song.

It was beautiful.

"Crap," said Logan.

"What?" And then I noticed the sickly sweet scent of chemicals and wolf. "Oh, no. Not again."

"Hi, Logan," Courtney said as she walked toward us, accompanied, as usual, by Vanessa and Danielle. "What's up?"

She ignored me with both her words and her gaze, and

so did Vanessa, but Danielle caught my eye and sneered, her lips twisting cruelly. *Don't give in. Don't look away.* I bared my teeth in an expression that felt somewhere between a promise and a threat, but she just stared harder.

My fangs snapped out.

"Bitch," she muttered, but she looked away first.

Courtney stepped closer to Logan and put a hand on his chest. "Maybe *we* could work out together," she said. "I have a lot of … stamina."

"Sorry." Logan smiled politely through gritted teeth. "My schedule's full."

Courtney finally glanced at me, and her eyes narrowed into sharp pools of gray. Her lips parted slightly, then she turned back to Logan, dismissing me with a flick of her honey-blonde curls. "It's so nice of you to take on a charity case," she said to him, her voice sickly sweet. "But your father would want me to remind you what matters the most." She leaned forward and her eyes flashed amber; it was a split-second of heat, just enough to remind us what she truly was. "Family. Pack. Obligations."

Logan's back straightened, his spine lengthening until he stood his full five foot eleven. "You know my views on this, Courtney." Power, warm and sharply-spiced, drifted around him, and he put an arm around my shoulders and steered me down the path.

"Nice shirt, Logan," Vanessa called as we walked away.

Danielle sniggered. "Long sleeves are totally in fashion right now."

"Practical too." Vanessa dissolved into giggles. "So no one can see—"

Logan turned, his raised voice cutting her off. "Heard from Derek lately? Oh, wait. I forgot."

Her face paled.

Logan's power flared, his palm burning into my arm. "Now leave us the fuck alone."

There was a sharp intake of breath, but I didn't look back.

"Fuck," Logan muttered under his breath.

As soon as we were out of earshot, I slowed and looked up at him. "What's going on?" I said, pushing my hair back from my face. "Why do they treat you like crap? I know things are different here, and predators challenge each other, but Courtney likes you. I can smell it on her. She obviously wants a relationship, or *something*, with you. So why is she such a bitch?"

He sighed, and was silent for a long moment before answering. "You're right in that some of it's because we're predators. The repeated challenges are a way to gauge who's strong, who's 'worthy' to be around. But I think some of it's also frustration. There are a lot of good things about being a werewolf, but our pack structure isn't one of them. Women have no real authority within the system —they can never be alpha and they only hold status through family lines. Courtney knows I'm the best chance of increasing her ranking."

"Okay, but ... how?"

Logan looked away. "Through marriage."

"Through marriage? But that's ridiculous. You're seventeen. You can't be thinking about—"

"My dad and Courtney's dad made some sort of deal when we were children. It's not set in stone, but there are certain expectations." He ran a hand through his hair, and for once I could smell the emotions pouring off him. The frustration, the anger, the hopelessness. "The system is fucked. And some of us think it needs to change. I just don't know how yet."

"What about when you're alpha? Couldn't you—"

"No." Logan cut me off. His veins were singing with blood and bile. "I'm never going to be alpha."

"Why not?" I stopped walking. "It sounds like you could make a real difference."

Logan paused, then simply said, "This." He shoved up the left sleeve of his shirt and thrust his arm toward me. "This is why I'm not fit to be alpha."

It took me a moment to figure out what I was seeing. Scars. Dozens of them, silver lines that slashed their way across his flesh from one side to the other. Some were long, some were short, but all carried the memory of pain, of suffering etched deeply into his skin.

"I thought … Did you …" The words dried up in my mouth. This was what Vanessa and the others had meant when they'd mentioned his scars.

"I shouldn't have shown you." He rolled down his sleeve, his head turned away.

I did the only thing I could think of. I took his hand and said, "Come with me."

We walked down the path into the woods, Logan following a half-step behind me, until the trees dwarfed us on both sides and the campus felt a long way away.

"Why are we here?" Logan asked.

I shrugged. "Philosophers have been asking that for thousands of years. I'm pretty sure none of them have ever come up with a decent answer."

It was enough to raise the ghost of a smile on Logan's lips. "You know what I meant."

"Of course I know what you meant."

"Then why did you bring me here? To the woods? Especially after what I showed you."

I shrugged again. "Why wouldn't I?" In truth, I didn't know why I'd led us there. There was just something about it, something in those trees, in that darkness, the dirt. It smelled like wildness, and it reminded me of Logan.

"I know where we can go," Logan said. His heart hadn't stopped hammering since he'd bared his arm. I could hear it, taste it, feel it in the touch of his skin against mine. He hadn't pulled it back or covered it up, though I knew he probably could. "It's one of my favorite places."

We moved off the path, and Logan took the lead. I held onto his hand as we dodged underbrush and leaves and moths, before the greenery parted and we came to a large clearing. The moon was high above, bathing the glade in a soft, diffused light, and the scent of evening primrose was warm in the air.

We lowered ourselves onto the long damp grass, and

Logan stretched out beside me, his gaze focused on the sky. "This place reminds me of home," he said. "But only the good things—the trees, the smell of the deer and the rabbits, the possibility of more. Of doing what I want with my life. Of being who *I* want to be." He looked over at me, his eyes almost black, unreadable. "Do you think I'm crazy?"

I lay down beside him, my eyes never leaving his. "For wanting to choose your own destiny? That's not crazy at all."

He blinked, a long slow movement, then looked back up at the sky. "Everyone thinks I am. They think I'm unstable." A pause. A long breath, catching in his throat. "I can never be alpha. I can never do what's expected of me, *be* what's expected of me, because of the things I've done. Because of what I showed you." He swallowed hard. "Because of other things."

"And what do you want to be?"

He turned his head, his dark eyes on fire, flames eating him from within. "Unafraid."

I touched his arm and he sat, so sudden it was almost violent, and covered his face with his hands. "This is ridiculous. What the hell was I thinking, telling you this, showing you—"

"No," I said, sitting up beside him. "It's not ridiculous. It's brave. *You're* brave."

"Brave? *Brave?*" He lowered his hands and laughed, the sound splintering through the clearing. "I'm scared. Do you know that? All the fucking time. I'm not brave. I've never been brave. I'm a fucking coward." The last words were the most biting, razor-edged and jagged, meant more for himself than for me.

"Well, I think you're incredible. I don't know what you've been through, but you're here and you're strong and you're really fucking brave—infinitely, impossibly brave—and I won't let you say anything otherwise."

His eyebrow twitched. "You won't *let* me?"

"I've heard your heart, Logan. I know you're stronger than you think."

His inhaled sharply, fear and shame flitting across his face. "You're wrong. I'm not whatever you think I am. It's … it's more than just the cutting. Everyone knows about that—I didn't even try and hide it when things were bad— but no one knows what I'm going to tell you now. Well, no one except my family and Haven and Mr. Green. But I have … I have obsessive compulsive disorder." He throat moved up and down as he swallowed. "OCD."

I'd heard the term before, mostly from memes and weird little internet quizzes, but I didn't really know what it meant. "I—"

"*Putere!*" It was shriek, echoing around the glade. I couldn't escape it. It was around me, *in* me, pulsing through my limbs.

I stood, shockwaves spreading down my skin.

Something moved in the woods behind us. Branches snapped and cracked.

Logan stood and I grabbed his hand.

And then we ran.

14

Blood pounded through veins. Branches bounced off faces and bodies. Muscles burned, burned, burned. My stomach ached from the effort, but I barely noticed. All that mattered was that someone had found me. *There are people who will exploit you and your potential for power. They will not care if they harm anyone in their way.* I had to get somewhere safe. I had to get *Logan* somewhere safe.

"Why are we running?" Logan said as he glanced at me over his shoulder. "Who was that?"

"I don't know." My hair whipped around me in the dark, and I pushed it out of my eyes. "But they're dangerous. I can feel it."

A twig snapped under Logan's feet. "Did you hear what they said? Put-something?"

I pressed my lips together and focused on dodging a low-hanging branch. I couldn't lie to Logan, and not just because he'd be able to smell it. He'd told me his deepest secret, a truth he kept hidden from almost everyone he knew. He'd trusted me. And I'd put him in danger. Again.

"*Putere!*" It was farther away this time, but the sound still found its way to us, snaking through the trees and echoing until it was all I could hear.

"*Putere?*" Logan's brow furrowed. "What does that mean?"

Again, I didn't answer. I just plunged ahead, bursting through the trees, my shins sore, my feet aching. *We have to get to safety. We have to get away from the voice.* I pushed harder and harder, but it didn't feel like it was enough.

We ran.

We ran.

We ran.

Pain speared through my side, but I didn't slow down. I just massaged the stitch and hoped it would go away. I didn't know how long we'd been running—it could've been minutes, it could've been hours—but time didn't matter. It was suspended. Unimportant. The only thing that mattered was distance.

But now I had no idea where we were.

"Logan?" I risked a glance behind me, my chest burning with every breath. "How far are we from—?"

I stopped.

He wasn't there.

Then something hit me—or maybe I hit it—and I bounced backward, stumbling over my feet. My skin buzzed with electricity.

"What the hell?" I shook out my hands, trying to quell

the continuing pull on my muscle and bone.

Is this another attack?

I looked around wildly, my vision closing in, then I spotted a handful of thin brown sticks that stood knee-high in the dirt. Boundary markers. I must've run right past them and smacked into the wards—the invisible protections that kept us in and humans out.

No one had ever told me they hurt so much.

"Logan?" I said again, rubbing my shoulder where the impact had been the worst. Pain sparked beneath my fingertips, and I bit back a gasp.

Shit.

I reached out with my senses, opening up the connection between myself and everything around me, searching for Logan's pulse, his breath, his blood. He had to be there. He had to. But there were so many sounds, and so many scents, and I couldn't figure out how to sort through them. Sensation slammed into me—*too dark, too loud, too much*—and the predator flared to life in my chest.

Blood.

I need it.

I want it.

My fangs slipped out and I fell to my knees, the dirt rough and uneven beneath me. There had to be something, someone I could—

No.

I didn't need to feed. I'd had plenty of food, and blood from a willing and well-compensated donor. I needed to find Logan.

Logan.

The thought of him was enough to shift the predator within me. I wrenched back my fangs and fought my way up to the surface, struggling past the hunger, past the instinct to feed, until I was back in control. Me. Emily. The human.

I stayed on my knees and placed my hands on the dirt, fingers spread, my body grounded by the earth. I shook off the strange whisper of familiarity that made no sense, a kind of déjà vu for something that had never happened, and then I began to search. I sifted through worms and insects, trees and grass, through the days-old scent of werewolf and rabbit, and then I pressed out farther.

The predator wavered at the edges of my mind.

It was close.

So close.

But—

Logan was alive. He was alive and I'd found him. He was out there in the woods, bright and vital and moving. And he wasn't the only one. There were others in the dark —a group of werewolves and a lone werejaguar, an incubus and an elf, a couple of dryads somewhere nearby. But I couldn't identify the owner of the voice. The one who'd called to me. It could have been any of them. Or none of them.

I stood, reaching for my phone. But it wasn't in my pocket. "Shit." Had I left it on my bed?

I wasn't sure what to do.

Then three chimes rang out, piercing and off key, and

a crackling voice intoned a message. "Please evacuate the woods. This is not a drill. Please evacuate the woods."

I didn't listen. Instead, I headed toward Logan, moving slowly and carefully through the undergrowth, avoiding the group of werewolves who were hunting in animal form, and giving the werejaguar a wide berth. She seemed to be doing nothing more than taking a moonlit stroll, but I couldn't be certain she wasn't the voice.

Tell no one, and trust no one.

My stomach churned and I quickened my pace. What if whoever had screamed wasn't discernible at all? What if they'd hidden themselves with magic? They could be anywhere. If something had happened to Logan … If he'd been attacked again because of me …

And then I saw him. He was standing alone between two tall pine trees, gesticulating wildly as he spoke into his phone. "Yes, a locator spell," he said, exasperation seeping into the words. "Can you hear me? Haven? Haven?"

I stepped through the trees without thinking. "Logan? Are you okay? Did they find you? Did they hurt you?"

His gaze met mine, and the relief that lay stark on his face stopped me in my tracks. "Emily? I—" He rushed forward, so fast I could barely understand what was happening, and then his arms were around me.

"I thought you'd been attacked again," I whispered against his chest. "I thought they'd found you."

Logan's arms tightened, pulling me closer. "I thought they'd found *you*. You took off so suddenly, and I started running after you, but Mr. Collins saw me and told me to stop. By the time he let me go, you were gone."

"Who's Mr. Collins?" It came out muffled, but I didn't care. I wasn't moving my face away from Logan's chest. He was warm and comforting, a light in the dark.

The chimes rang out again. "Please evacuate the woods. This is not a drill. Please evacuate the woods."

Logan ignored them. "He teaches chemistry. He was out on patrol when he heard the scream. He escorted me back to the path and told me to go back to Emberfield." His chin rested gently on top of my head. "Once he'd left, I sneaked back in to track you, but I wasn't fast enough, so I called Haven to get her to do a locator spell. In hindsight, I probably should've just kept tracking. But I—" His voice lowered to a whisper. "I thought something had happened to you."

I pulled back, just enough to look up at him. His face was veiled in shadow, cloaking his eyes in darkness, but something inside him burned so fierce and bright that I couldn't look away. "Logan, I—"

"Can I kiss you?"

"What?"

He pressed his lips together. "Sorry, I shouldn't have …"

"No." My mouth went dry. My body was too small, too big, too *much*. I didn't know what to do with my hands or where to look or how to breathe. "You should."

He raised his eyebrows, and I nodded.

He brought his lips down to mine, gentle and soft, and

for a moment there was nothing else. We were hands on faces, warm skin on cold, breath against breath against breath. I rose up on my tiptoes, bringing us closer, but—

"Ow," Logan said, holding a hand up to his mouth.

I took a step back. "You're bleeding."

"It's fine."

"No, it's—" My tongue brushed something sharp as I spoke, and my stomach turned to lead. "I didn't—I mean, I—"

Logan reached for me, but I turned, my face flaming hot.

My fangs were out.

My fangs were out.

"We should go," I said quickly, making my way to the nearest path and hoping the earth would swallow me whole.

Logan hurried to catch up, but his phone rang, loud and metallic, and he fumbled to answer it. "Hello? Are you there?"

I slowed when I heard Haven's voice through the speaker.

"She's with me," Logan said. "We'll be there in a minute."

I turned onto the path and forced my fangs to retract. I could do this. I could pretend to be normal. I'd never kiss anyone again, but I could pretend to be normal.

"That was Haven." Logan was suddenly beside me, warm and real and smelling of blood. "She said she'd—"

"Meet us at the main entrance to the woods," I

finished, increasing my speed. "I know. I heard."

We carried on in silence. Well, I was silent. Logan kept clearing his throat, his fingers tapping against the back of his phone. And the awkwardness was broken only by more chimes and another exhortation to evacuate the woods.

As soon as I saw Haven, I put on a burst of speed. "What are you doing here?" I said, giving her a quick hug before nodding at Philip, who was standing beside her.

"Checking up on you guys. We heard they were evacuating the woods."

Philip put an arm around Haven, holding her tight. "Never a dull moment around here, huh?"

Haven twisted to look up at him, but he held her closer to his chest. "It's not normally like this," she said. "I think they're just being careful after what happened with Derek."

Logan was silent, his fingers still tapping against the back of his phone.

Haven's eyebrows twitched.

He slipped his phone into his pocket. "We should—"

"Wait, there's blood on your lip." Haven reached forward, but Philip tensed and she lowered her hand. "What happened?"

"Nothing." Logan shrugged. "A minor mishap."

I lost control of my fangs, and I didn't even notice.

"We should go," I said, scuffing a trail in the dirt with my shoes. "We did a lot of running and I'm tired." It wasn't entirely true. I was tired, but it wasn't because of the running—my muscles had already recovered. I was tired because of the voice, because of the prophecy, because I still had no idea what was going on. Because I'd almost lost control.

Because I was tired of being a vampire.

"Do you wanna swing by Coffee and Cake?" Haven asked. "We could get brownies. Or ice cream. Or cinnamon buns. I know how much you love them."

She was right. I did love them. But I didn't want desert. I wanted to kiss the boy I liked without causing him injury. I wanted to know I could control myself. I wanted to know I'd never be sent back to a cell at the Paranormal Program.

"They have a two-for-the-price-of-one special tonight," Haven said.

Logan looked at me expectantly.

Philip looked bored.

Haven looked worried.

"You guys go," I said, mustering a smile. "I'm gonna head up to my room."

Haven's gaze flicked between me and Logan, then she extricated herself from Philip's grip. "I'll come with you. We can call Cayley. Make it a girls' night."

Philip's hand lingered on her arm. "What about our date? It wasn't over."

"Emily needs me right now." She pulled his face close to hers for a kiss, and his hand slid lower on her hip.

"What about me?" he said. "I need you, too."

I looked away as he thrust his tongue into her mouth.

"You need a cold shower," I muttered under my breath.

Logan snorted.

"Hey," Philip said, shooting me a glare. "Just because you're not getting any …"

Haven slapped him lightly on the arm. "Don't be so mean! Or you won't be getting any either." She slipped out of his embrace and took my hand. "Let's go."

I felt Logan's gaze on my back as we walked away.

Haven didn't ask me anything until we were up in our room. But as soon as the door clicked shut, she whirled around to face me, her forehead furrowed. "What happened out there?"

"Well, uh, there was a voice, and it—"

"No! Not that. I mean, we'll get to it, and you do need to know that I'm planning on strengthening the wards in our room as soon as I can. But first, what happened between you and Logan?"

I flopped down onto my bed, face first. "I can't tell you. It's too embarrassing." I rolled over and stared at the ceiling. "But the voice thing was bad. For a secret, ancient prophecy that we can't find any information on, a hell of a lot of people seem to know about it."

"What?" The bed bounced as Haven dropped down next to me. "Logan didn't say it was linked to the prophecy. He just said there was a weird scream and that you guys had gotten separated."

"Because he doesn't know about the prophecy!"

"Okay, sure, you may have a point there. Tell me what happened."

I quickly filled her in on everything that had taken place—leaving out the kiss, because no way was I explaining that—and by the time I was done, her face had turned pale.

"I feel like we should tell someone," I said, grabbing Minikins and hugging him close. "Like, an adult who can fix things. I just ... I don't know who to trust."

Haven rolled onto her side and propped her head up on her hand. "When does Dr. Norlgren get back?"

"Three days." I covered my eyes with my arm and groaned. "What am I supposed to do? I've emailed him a couple of times, but other than that first reply, I haven't heard back." My phone beeped and I reached out automatically to grab it, but it wasn't on the bed.

"Over there." Haven pointed. "On your desk. Maybe it's Dr. Norlgren."

I tossed Minikins aside and sat, frowning. "Did you move it?"

"Why would I move it?"

"But I left it on the bed."

"You know I'd never touch your phone." Haven's nose wrinkled. "What's wrong? You look kinda weird."

Something inside me twisted, and all of the fear I'd been trying to conceal erupted in my chest. Adrenaline surged through me and I held it close, my predator transforming it into anger. Because anger felt better than being lost, felt better than being confused, felt better than being weak.

"What's wrong?" I spat, storming across the room.

"Someone's after me and I don't know why, I've totally messed things up with Logan, and now apparently I look weird, too. That's what's fucking wrong." I picked up my phone, and its plastic frame creaked in my too-tight grip.

This isn't right.

Haven ignored my sudden ire and leaned forward, her eyes narrowing. "How exactly did you mess things up with Logan?"

Breathe.

You're losing control.

All I could smell was rotting leaves and soot, the scent of anger and fear like perfume on my skin, but I swallowed it down and loosened my grip on my phone, breathing past the pain. My predator was wrong—my fear wasn't weak. It wasn't pleasant, but it would never be weak.

"I kissed—oh," I said, glancing down at my phone as it beeped again. "It's him."

The messages were short and to the point: *Can we talk? Please?*

"You kissed?" Haven said, her voice rising three octaves. "But how did you mess everything up?"

"Hold on." I started replying to Logan's messages, but the words didn't sound right, so I deleted them and started again. I was halfway through my third attempt when a pillow hit me on the side of the head. "Haven!" I picked up the offending object and threw it back at her. "What the hell? Did you really think that was a good idea?"

"I want to know what's going on between my two best friends!"

"I'll let you know if I ever figure it out." I set the phone down on my desk, and it rang immediately. "Oh, crap." I picked it back up. My heart pounded in my ears. "What do I do?"

"Answer it."

"But—"

"Answer it."

I closed my eyes and swiped the screen before I could lose my nerve. "Hello?"

"Hey." Logan paused. "Are you busy?"

"No."

"Can we talk? In person?"

I took a deep breath. "Sure."

Suddenly, Haven screamed.

My eyes flew open and I whirled around, my fangs already out. "What's wrong?"

Then I saw what she was holding. I dropped my phone on the desk, or maybe the floor. I didn't know which, and it didn't really matter. "Where—?"

"It was sticking out from under your pillow," Haven whispered.

"But how?" I took it from her shaking hands. It was an envelope, thin and white and ordinary. It could've come from anywhere. Yet the word on the front, one word, inscribed in swirling dark script, was anything but ordinary.

Putere.

15

I HELD the envelope out in front of me, my fingers curled gingerly around the edges. I held it like it could hurt me. I held it like it was a weapon. Like it could ruin everything.

Something about this is wrong.

Haven stood by my side. "Are you going to open it?"

I stared at the envelope like it wasn't real. There were only two options. One: Open the envelope. Two: *Don't* open the envelope. Neither one appealed.

I ran my fingers across the word on the front. *Putere.* It was written in smooth black ink, the penmanship elegant and refined, and it was somehow both a promise and a threat.

It could be the answer to all of my questions about the prophecy.

Or it could be the start of something terrible.

Haven held out her hand. "Shall I?"

I almost gave it to her. It would've been so easy to give in, to place it in her hand and walk away. But the easy route isn't always the right one, no matter how much you want it to be, so I turned the envelope over and lifted the seal.

My fingers were trembling, my blood frozen under my skin.

"What's in it?" Haven said, her voice low and intense. "Is it a letter? A picture?"

The world moved both too fast and too slow. There was a pause, a space in between knowing and not knowing, and I didn't want it to end. It was safe. A refuge.

"It's—" I took a deep breath and looked inside. "Shit. No. *No*. It can't—"

Carefully, breathlessly, I pulled out the lock of turquoise hair that had been nestled inside the envelope. It was tied at the end with a black rubber band, the strands sticking out like bristles on a paintbrush. They flickered faintly, a whisper of frailty and dread.

Haven stilled. "Is that Dr. Norlgren's hair?"

She couldn't see the shimmer. She couldn't see how each hair was lit from within, sparkling weakly, the last gasps of a dying star.

My knees threatened to give way.

"I think—I think he's dying." I had no proof. I mean, maybe the magic leaked away once his hair was removed from his body. He could be safe and sound, unaware that someone had left a lock of his hair in an envelope under my pillow. But … I didn't think so. I knew what I saw, and I knew what I felt. And none of it was good.

"Is there anything else?" Haven lifted the envelope off the floor and peered inside; I hadn't even realized I'd dropped it. "It's empty. There's no note. No address. Nothing."

I gazed at the fading strands of Dr. Norlgren's hair, my stomach twisting. "Logan mentioned something about a locator spell. Do you think you could do one? To find Dr. Norlgren?" I wasn't sure it would help—I didn't even know what city he was in or how we'd get to him. But I had to try. I couldn't just sit and watch his glow fade to nothing.

Haven nodded. "They're easy. I did one earlier to find you."

As Haven rummaged around in the trunk at the end of her bed, I checked every inch of our room. I couldn't smell anyone who shouldn't be there. I couldn't hear errant heartbeats or sense blood flowing through intruding veins. But I still looked under the beds and in the closets. I didn't know as much about the supernatural world as almost everyone else at Mistwood, but I'd learned that people could cloak themselves with magic—dark magic—and I had to be certain that whoever had left the envelope had gone.

But there was nothing. Not even a forgotten dust bunny.

"You smell like Philip," I said to Haven when I stood, pushing my hair back from my face.

"Of course I do." She closed the trunk, then placed four candles on the floor in the center of the room—one each for North, South, East, and West. "Give me your phone. I'm almost out of battery."

I unlocked the screen and handed it over, my mind whirling. "How do you think someone got in here? There are locks, spells, wards, chimera. People are always in the corridor—going in and out of their rooms. And Ms. Emmerson and Miss Lassila are usually close by. Nobody should've been able to get in undetected. Even if they were cloaking their scent."

Haven shrugged. "I don't know. Let's just take this one thing at a time." She brought up the maps application on my phone, zoomed out as far as she could, then placed it between the unlit candles on the floor. "You ready?"

My heart pounded against my ribs, and I swallowed past the lump in my throat. Dr. Norlgren's hair was a dim flicker in my hand. I looked away; it didn't mesmerize me anymore. "You have to be quick. I don't think there's much time."

Haven took the lock of hair and set it down on the floor beside my phone. She lit the candles and sat, her knees beneath her, her back straight and ready. She began to chant, quietly at first, then gradually increasing in volume until her words filled the room. It was rhythmic, quick, and repetitive, and I didn't understand a word of it. She held a single pendulum, a pale pink crystal on a string, over my phone and it began to spin.

I stood silent, watching, desperately wanting to do

something, *anything*, to help. I clenched my fists, my fangs tingling, and dread crawled beneath my skin, pressing like thousands of pinpricks from the inside out. This was taking too long. I couldn't do this. I couldn't wait—

The pendulum dropped.

Haven leaned over the phone, zooming in on the map. "He's here." Her gaze met mine, her eyes pale in the flickering light. "He's at Mistwood."

"What?" My heart stuttered. "Where?"

"The medical center." Haven blew out the candles, then stood, tossing my phone at me. "Let's go."

I scooped up the lock of Dr. Norlgren's hair—I didn't feel right about leaving it behind—then practically flew down the corridor. A few people watched, curious, as I ran down the stairs and across the foyer, but I didn't care what they thought.

"Excuse me," I said, pushing past a girl with long brown hair.

"Hey!" She glared dangerously, but I was already out the door.

I sprinted down to the path, Haven somewhere far behind me, and Logan fell in step at my side. "Where are you going?" he said.

"Medical center."

When I didn't say anything else, he glanced back at Haven, who was puffing loudly. "It's complicated," she called, her hands flying up as she lurched forward, her foot slipping on an uneven cobblestone. "I'm okay! I'm okay! I'll catch up with you guys in a minute."

It didn't take long to get to the medical center. Still, each step felt like a fight against gravity, like it was holding me back, like I needed to move *faster, faster, faster.* The light had gone out and I needed to *run.* The lock of hair in my hand barely glimmered at all.

"What's going on?" Logan said as I heaved open the door at the entrance.

"I don't know. I can't—" I ran down the wide, empty hall to Dr. Norlgren's office and skidded to a stop in front of his door, holding onto the handle for balance. "Dr. Norlgren! Dr. Norlgren are you in there?" I rattled the door handle, then banged against the wood with my fist. "Dr. Norlgren!"

One of the nurses, a witch I'd never seen before, darted out from the nurses' office. "The doctor's not in right now," he said as he hurried toward us, his voice low with disapproval. "You need to make an appointment with the locum."

My hand stilled. "I—"

"It's my fault, Mr. Lopez," Logan cut in. "I was hoping to see Dr. Norlgren this evening. When will he be back?"

The nurse's mouth was a thin line. "Not for a couple of days."

"I can wait." He walked toward Mr. Lopez, smooth and calm and steady. "Could you set up an appointment for me at the office?"

"I suppose so. I—"

"Great." Logan slowed, then looked at me over his shoulder. "You coming, Em?"

I almost said yes. I'd believed every word he'd said. But then I realized what he was doing, and I paused. A small part of me was appalled by the way he'd manipulated the situation with such ease—*he doesn't even smell like a lie*—but mostly I was impressed.

"I don't have all night," the nurse snapped.

"Okay, I'll just be a minute," I said. "I—um—have to—you know. Use the bathroom."

Logan's lips twitched, only noticeable because I was looking for it, then he pulled it back, the polite mask slipping over his features before he turned back to Mr. Lopez. "Will Dr. Norlgren be back by Friday?" he asked, continuing down the corridor toward the office.

Mr. Lopez nodded, but he watched me, his dark brown eyes boring holes into my skin, until I entered the student bathroom down the hall. I closed the door quickly, my hands shaking, and counted to two hundred. Would that be long enough?

I pressed my ear against the smooth, hard wood and listened. I couldn't hear anyone outside, so I eased the door open and peered out into the corridor. The coast was clear.

I was back outside Dr. Norlgren's office in less than ten seconds. "Dr. Norlgren," I said quietly, tapping my knuckles against the door. "It's Emily. Let me in." I glanced down at the lock of hair. The shimmer had almost faded completely.

"Hey! You there! What are you doing?" Mr. Lopez strode toward me, his face contorted with anger. Logan and Haven hurried behind him. "I knew you were up to something."

"I'm not. I promise," I said, curling my hand tightly around the hair. I couldn't let him see it—there was no logical explanation for its presence. "It was just … I heard something in there when I was coming back from the bathroom."

Mr. Lopez pinched the bridge of his nose, clearly out of whatever small amount of patience he possessed. "You kids get worse every year," he said, fixing me with a glare. "What were you really doing? Looking for money? Drugs?"

"Open the door and check," I said. "*Please.*"

It was probably a stupid move. I didn't want anyone else involved, not until we knew what was going on with the prophecy, and I didn't know who to trust. *It could be a matter of life and death. Tell no one, and trust no one.* Dr. Norlgren's warnings echoed around my head, but I couldn't open the door, and he was possibly injured or dying or—

"Fine," Mr. Lopez said sharply. "I'll have to go and get the master key. You all better be here when I get back, or I'll have to call Mr. Olaru." He strode off, shaking his head.

"I'm sorry," Haven whispered, putting a hand on my arm. "He cornered me as soon as I entered the building."

"He totally bought my story about wanting an appointment." Logan shrugged a shoulder. "But it didn't take very long. And I couldn't keep him talking."

"Maybe it's a good thing," I said, glancing down at the lock of hair. "At least he can let us in."

I just hope we're not too late.

"Is anybody gonna tell me what's going on?" Logan said. "I heard you both over the phone. Haven screamed and then the call just ended. What the hell happened?"

"It's comp—" Haven started.

"No. Don't tell me it's complicated." He ran a hand through his hair, his eyebrows dipping low. "We've been friends for how long, Haven? Ten years? Don't I deserve—"

"It's not my place to tell you," Haven said, shooting me a meaningful look.

Logan paused. "Oh."

The smoky smell that had surrounded him disappeared as he pulled everything back. He was shutting down, hiding behind neutrality, and I stared down at my shoes, my skin suddenly hot. Logan had told me his deepest secret, and I hadn't told him anything. But … that didn't mean I owed him an explanation. Not before I was ready. Not if I wanted to keep him safe.

"You should go," I said.

He regarded me carefully. "Is that—"

"I'm surprised to see you all still here," Mr. Lopez said as he strode back toward us, holding a large brass keyring in his hands. He stopped in front of the door and examined the keys slowly, checking each one individually until he found the one he wanted. It was long and spindly, with a decorative bow at the end that echoed the trefoil design of the lock plate on the door, and its teeth were blunt and uneven, the metal scratched from years of use.

Hurry up. Hurry up.

"Hello?" Mr. Lopez knocked loudly on the door. "Dr. Norlgren? It's Francisco Lopez. Are you in there?" He paused, his head tilted. When there was no reply, he called, "I'm coming in now." He inserted the key in the lock with painstaking precision.

Faster. Faster. Faster.

The door swung open and the room beyond was shadowed, lit only by a single lamp that glowed dimly in the corner. Mr. Lopez entered first, and it took every bit of self-restraint I possessed not to push past him.

"Dr. Norlgren?" Mr. Lopez flicked on the overhead lights, bathing the office in a dense yellow glow. "Elias? Are you here?"

There was a cough, a rasping intake of breath, thick and wet.

The entire room smelled like blood.

I didn't wait any longer. Pushing past Mr. Lopez, I ran to the back of the room, following the trail of thick, dark liquid that had spilled across the floor. The hunger didn't even stir within me.

"Dr. Norlgren?" I pushed the broken privacy screen out of my way. "Are you—" I stopped, the unfinished question suspended between us. There was no point asking—the doctor was clearly not okay. He was scrunched up awkwardly on the narrow bed that took up most of the back wall, his skin and clothes stained with blood. He barely glimmered at all.

"Emily." One word, scraped out through thin, dry lips. "You—need to—"

"Elias!" Mr. Lopez rushed past, sharp and focused. "What happened?"

"I need—to speak—to Emily," he rasped. "Not much—time." He coughed and his body curled in on itself like it was about to split apart. Blood trailed down his chin.

"I'm here." I slipped past Mr. Lopez to the head of the bed, then pressed myself against the wall, trying to take up as little space as possible while the nurse worked on Dr. Norlgren. "Who did this to you? Who hurt you?"

"Didn't—didn't see. You need—" Dr. Norlgren paused to cough again, his thin body shuddering. "The—the blade." He met my eyes and smiled weakly, an incongruous expression given the circumstances. "Find it."

"Where?" I leaned forward. "Where do I find it?"

"Get back," Mr. Lopez said sharply. He swept out an arm, his impatient displeasure reaching Haven and Logan, who'd gathered at the end of the bed. "You need to leave. All of you. Find Ms. Park. Find Dr. Patterson, the locum. I need help here." He grabbed a pair of latex gloves from a box on the wall and thrust his hands inside.

"I'll do it," I said. "I'll help you. Tell me what you need."

Mr. Lopez glowered, but I squared my shoulders. Something in Dr. Norlgren's pale turquoise gaze told me I needed to stay.

Logan was the first to move. "We'll go get the others."

"As quick as we can," Haven added.

They rushed from the room, and Mr. Lopez pointed at the box of latex gloves. "Put some on. Quickly. And if you get in my way again, you're out of here. Do you understand?"

I nodded.

Dr. Norlgren coughed. "I—I'm—sorry," he whispered, wiping the blood from his chin with shaking fingers.

"This isn't your fault." I stuffed the lock of hair in the pocket of my leggings, then snapped on a pair of gloves. "You were attacked, right?"

Dr. Norlgren nodded, a small shift of his head that left him wincing. "The—prophecy. I was—supposed—to protect. To—stop. They know." He coughed again. "You—must—not trust—"

"Concentrate," Mr. Lopez barked at me. He placed a folded white towel in my hands, then pointed to a large, bloody wound on the side of Dr. Norlgren's torso. I hadn't even noticed it. I hadn't wanted to. "This one's the worst. You need to put pressure on it."

I set the towel on top of the dimly flickering skin and pressed as gently as I could. Dr. Norlgren's lips twisted with pain.

"Harder," Mr. Lopez said. He ducked down to grab another towel from the shelves beside the bed, muttering under his breath.

I did as he said, but my eyes burned and I gulped past the lump in my throat. "I'm so sorry," I whispered.

"I—would've—liked," Dr. Norlgren began, "to see—to

see you—" He stopped and drew in a noisy breath, his entire chest sucking inward. Blood dribbled down his face and dripped onto the bed; the drops were pure and bright against the white, wrinkled fabric.

"It's okay," I whispered. "It's okay." But it wasn't, and I was glad he couldn't smell the lie. His shirt lay open from where Mr. Lopez had peeled it open, and his body beneath was covered in wounds. Some were only scratches, the barest whisper of violence, while others were gaping mouths, and I couldn't do anything to fix their horror.

"I was—supposed to have—" Dr. Norlgren said, his voice a quiet rasp. "To have—protected—stopped—the prophecy—"

The door burst open and his words were lost in the sudden flurry of activity. I found myself pressed up against the wall, while Ms. Park and a small blonde woman I assumed was Dr. Patterson crowded around the bed.

"All students need to leave," the doctor said, her words as clipped and efficient as the gaze she shot in my direction. She turned her attention to Dr. Norlgren, examining him with shrewd eyes and careful hands. "You need to be transferred to the operating room. I can—"

"No." Dr. Norlgren struggled to sit. "I have to—find—I need to—"

Ms. Park stepped forward. "This will help," she said as she injected something into his upper arm. She smiled at him gently, then turned to Dr. Patterson. "Are we ready for transfer?"

"I've got the stretcher," Mr. Lopez said, hurrying back into the room.

Had I even noticed him leave?

"Emily, you shouldn't be here." Ms. Park touched my arm, and I almost jumped out of my skin. She told me to put my bloodstained gloves in the trash, then guided me to the door, nodding at Haven and Logan who were in the hallway outside. "Go and take a seat out front. Someone will come and check on you later."

I clung to Haven's arm as Dr. Norglren was wheeled out into the hallway.

"Emily!" The doctor sat, bursting open the restraint that had been clipped across his chest, his eyes wild and bright. Too bright. He beckoned me with a shaking finger.

"Lie down, Elias." Mr. Lopez brought the stretcher to a stop and put a hand on Dr. Norlgren's shoulder, but he quickly shrugged it off, swinging his legs around in an attempt to stand.

"There's a—letter. It will—explain." He paused, his body shuddering as he gasped for air. "You—you must —find it."

"Shhh," Ms. Park said, slipping another needle into his arm. "You can talk to Emily later."

Dr. Norlgren cried out, his fingers splaying as he scrambled to find purchase, his eyes rolling back in his head. He slumped back against the bed, limp and boneless, and Mr. Lopez refastened the restraints, tighter this time, then nodded to Ms. Park.

"Let's go," she said briskly.

Dr. Patterson had already disappeared down the corridor.

No one else spoke.

We just stood and watched them go.

16

TWENTY MINUTES LATER, we were sitting outside the medical center, and we still had no idea what was going on. I'd washed my hands and arms three times in the bathroom sink after Dr. Norlgren had been taken away, watching as the blood swirled down the drain, but the scent was still there, sharp and metallic, somewhere below the surface. Somewhere I couldn't see. It was a reminder of everything I'd lost, of everything I could never be, but for once I didn't want to drink. The hunger lingered as it always did, as a faint buzz beneath my skin, but Dr. Norlgren's blood wasn't mine to take.

Please be okay. Please be okay. Please be okay.

I clutched the lock of his hair in my hands and repeated the words, over and over in my head, like a prayer or a hope or a wish. I didn't really know Dr. Norlgren, but I didn't want him to die. And not just because he hadn't given me any answers about what I was or what I could be. I didn't want him to die because he was a living being who didn't deserve this. Any of this.

This is all my fault.

Would they come for me next? For my friends? My teachers?

"We need to find the letter." Haven couldn't sit still. One leg bounced up and down, shaking the small wooden bench we all sat on, and she kept folding and unfolding her arms. "You know, the one Dr. Norlgren mentioned. He said it would explain things."

"What things?" Logan said. "I don't understand what's going on."

I stood, and the space between us felt enormous. "We don't even know where the letter is," I said, looking up at the medical center so I didn't have to look at Logan.

"We'll start with his office." Haven jumped up, her dress flaring out around her. "It's the last place he was— it's probably in there."

"And if someone catches us?"

Haven ran a finger along the row of shiny rose gold studs in her ear. "I'll drop one of these as soon as we're through the door. That way, when I say we were looking for my earring, it's not technically a lie. No chance of anyone catching us out."

"What if whoever did that to Dr. Norlgren comes back?" Logan said.

"We run or we fight." Haven lifted her chin. "You coming?"

We followed her back into the medical center, but each

step felt heavy. Labored. I didn't want to search Dr. Norlgren's office. I didn't want to find out everything from a letter. I wanted to hear it from Dr. Norlgren himself. The whole situation felt too big, too intense to experience without a direct explanation. What if I had questions? What if—

"Hurry up," Haven hissed, easing open the door to the doctor's office.

I guess no one had bothered to lock it in all the commotion.

We all went through, and it was like going from one world to another. When we crossed the threshold we slipped into a place of violence and horror, where pain was written in streaks on the walls and on the floor.

Bile rose in my throat.

Haven shivered, then dropped an earring on the tiled floor. "There," she said, bending to retrieve it. "Our excuse is sorted. Let's find the letter and get out of here."

Logan surveyed the room, his expression dark. "Where do we even start?"

The office, which had once been so tidy, was in disarray. Books spilled from the bookshelf, papers were flung out across the surface of the desk, and the lamp in the corner had been knocked askew, its shade digging a deep groove into the wall. The screen at the back of the room no longer provided privacy; it lay on the floor from when I'd pushed it earlier. A great gaping hole split the fabric in two, and smears of blood peered out from the tiles beneath.

"I'll take the desk," Haven said, crossing the room. "Logan, you check the bookshelf. Emily, you do whatever's left."

I was crouched down low, searching through a filing cabinet hidden in a back corner of the room, when Logan spoke. "What exactly are we looking for again?" he asked.

"A letter," Haven said. "You know, a written thing, a piece of paper with words on it. Usually addressed to a specific person."

Logan shifted one book, then another. "Helpful. Really helpful."

"We don't have any details," I said carefully. "But it might be addressed to me. Maybe." I opened the bottom drawer of the filing cabinet. Empty. "I'll come and help with the bookshelf."

"I'm done." Logan stood. "There's no letter in here. Just books."

"Okay. Haven?" I turned to where she was still searching through Dr. Norlgren's desk. "What about you?"

She held up a bunch of papers. "There are tons of letters, but none relating to—" Her eyes cut to Logan. "You know. Stuff that's about you."

Logan's brow wrinkled. "This would be a lot easier if you'd just—"

"There's a prophecy, okay?" I said quickly. "Look for anything that relates to me or a prophecy."

His eyes widened, just a little, but he didn't say anything more.

I didn't know why I felt so weird about telling him. It

wasn't even safety-related anymore. He'd gotten himself involved, whether I liked it or not. *What if he thinks you're a freak? What if he thinks you shouldn't be here?* I swallowed hard, ignoring the questions in my head. I looked around the room for somewhere else to search, when—

"Wait." My fangs slid out, but I forced them back in. I couldn't even think about losing control. This was too important. "There's something over there."

Haven moved forward to look, but I was already kneeling beside the bed that still held the imprint of Dr. Norlgren's bleeding, crumpled body. It wasn't the bed I was interested in, though—it was what was inside it. Three large drawers had been built into its wooden-framed base, and a thin edge of blood-soaked paper, the barest tip of a page, peeked out from the highest one. I slid the drawer open slowly.

I wanted to know.

I didn't want to know.

I pulled it out. It was thin and tacky, an ordinary object turned grim. My name was written on it in slanted black scrawl.

"Is it—?" Haven asked.

I nodded. "Let's go."

I didn't breathe again until we were outside, crushed together on the wooden bench, Logan on my left, Haven on my right.

"Are you going to read it?" she asked.

I traced a finger along the folded edge of the letter. "I guess I should." Slowly, I unfolded the letter, a simple gesture that somehow felt colossal. There was so much riding on this. Whatever the prophecy was, it was obviously something important. Important enough for people to get hurt over. Important enough for people to potentially be killed over.

"What does it say?" Haven said, leaning closer.

I pressed my lips together, but I didn't read the words. I couldn't. Not yet. Instead, I breathed in the scent of wolf and witch, of discipline and wildness, and I paused for a moment, knowing I wasn't alone.

When Haven nudged my side for the fifth time, I knew it was time to read.

Dear Emily,

I have failed to protect you, and for that I am deeply sorry. There is so much I need to tell you, though I suspect I will not be able to. For now, know this: the putere *will come to power on the night of the Sapphire Eclipse. As the power ascends, a darkness will rise, and with it will come the destruction of our world.*

There is a book called Putere: Prophecy and Destiny. *Find it and read it. You must learn everything you can, because you will be*

"That's it?" said Haven, who'd been reading over my shoulder. "You will be ... what?"

I shrugged, my stomach churning. *I'm going to cause the destruction of our world?* "I don't know. I guess we ask Dr. Norlgren if—no, *when* he gets better. And for now, we should try and find a copy of that book."

Haven was already searching Supenet on her phone.

"Don't bother," Logan said quietly. "I have a copy."

"You?" Haven leaned around me to stare at Logan, her face glowing bright from the light of her phone. "*You* somehow have a copy of the specific book we need? A book I've never heard of, even though I'm intimately acquainted with every single book the library has on prophecies. How? Why?"

Logan produced a thin, gray-covered volume from somewhere beside him. "I swiped it from Dr. Norlgren's office."

I reached for it gingerly, then drew my hand back. "I can't. There's blood on my hand from the letter. I'll ruin the pages."

"We could just leave," Logan said. "One of the teachers or nurses will come and find us if they need us."

I glanced at the letter one more time, then put it in my pocket. I didn't know what to do. Nothing in my old life, my human life, had prepared me for this. *The destruction of our world.* What the hell did that even mean?

Haven glanced over at me. "Are we staying or going?"

In the end, the choice was made for us in the form of Ms. Park, who was making her way slowly toward the bench where we sat. She looked physically fine, with all of her usual features and limbs, but something about her was wrong. Something was missing. When she finally stood in front of us, her hands clasped together, fingers wound, I realized what it was. She was broken, and though she was trying her best to hold it together, the bitter scent of anger and grief that drifted from her was unmistakable.

Logan stood. Haven and I quickly followed suit.

"Is Dr. Norlgren okay?" Haven asked.

Ms. Park shook her head, her dark eyes shiny. "I'm afraid he—" She swallowed hard, her throat moving up and down. "The wounds were too great. We couldn't save him."

Haven's hand slipped into mine. "You couldn't—?"

Ms. Park shook her head again. Her usually neatly-bound hair was coming loose, and deep black strands clung to her cheeks.

She didn't look real.

Nothing looked real.

I squeezed Haven's hand, then reached out for Logan, who looked at me for a moment like I was something odd or unknown. Then his eyes cleared and his fingers touched mine; his pulse skipped fast through his veins. I was anchored between the two of them, the witch and the werewolf, my best friend and my newest friend. I bit back a sob, and Ms. Park turned her sad, kind, hurting eyes my way.

"Whoever did this will be caught," she said. "The SCC have already been called. They'll be here soon."

"What do we do in the meantime?" Haven asked, uncharacteristically tentative. "How do we know we're safe? I mean, we're the ones who found Dr. Norlgren. What if …?" She trailed off, the rest of her question left unsaid.

Logan squeezed my hand, his grip so tight it almost hurt.

Ms. Park offered us an imitation of a smile. "Your

safety—and the safety of all students and staff—is our top priority. We're going into an official lockdown. No one will be allowed in or out of school grounds, barring SCC officials. For now, go straight to your dorms. Extra wards are being applied to them, and to the school perimeter, as we speak." She glanced at her watch. "You should have just enough time to get yourselves cleaned up before dawn. We haven't disclosed the reason for the lockdown, so please be discreet—we don't want to cause unnecessary panic."

A stab of fear found me through Logan's warm skin. "And tomorrow?" he asked. "What happens then?"

Ms. Park's cell phone rang, and she glanced at the screen and grimaced. "I have to take this. Tomorrow you'll need to give a statement to the SCC regarding what you saw and what you did." Her phone stopped ringing, then immediately started again. "Excuse me."

"I guess we should go," Logan said when Ms. Park moved away to answer the call.

Dawn was close. I could feel it singing in my bones, but I didn't want to leave when I still needed answers. I needed to read that book.

Haven tapped my arm. "You coming?"

The same off-key chimes that had announced the evacuation of the woods rang out. "Mistwood Academy is now on lockdown. All students must stay in their dormitories. Mistwood Academy is now on lockdown. All students must stay in their dormitories."

"Come on," Haven said. "We need to get cleaned up."

The school grounds were empty. Eerie. Curfew had come and gone while we'd been sitting, suspended in time, on the bench outside the medical center.

"Something about this feels wrong," Logan said, pulling his sleeves down low over his hands.

We hurried over the cobblestone paths, dozens of chimera watching us from the top of the buildings we passed. They paced slowly, great toes curling as they moved, their faces grave. I should have felt comforted by their presence—they were there to protect us—but they were too imposing. Too strange.

Haven shivered.

We were almost at Worthington Hall when I smelled someone coming up behind us. Someone I recognized.

"I was hoping I'd catch you," Mr. Green said, his long strides eating up the ground beneath him. "I heard about what happened."

None of us spoke.

Mr. Green brushed a hand over his close-cropped hair. "You shouldn't have been left alone. Someone should have accompanied you back to your dorms. We're on lockdown."

Logan shrugged and pointed skyward. "We're not alone."

The nearest chimera, a strange amalgamation of eagle, goat, and snake, tilted its head and stared down at us, beak open wide.

"Be that as it may," Mr. Green said, "someone should be with you until you're inside your dorms." His gaze skipped over us, then caught, his eyes lingering on the pilfered book that Logan still held in his one clean hand.

I froze.

It was the only thing I had that might tell me about the prophecy. About who I was, about who I could be. About what I might *do*. I couldn't lose it. I couldn't.

I held my breath.

The chimera paced.

Logan shifted his weight from one leg to the other, then held out his hand—the one covered in blood from holding mine. "I'd like to go," he said quietly. "I need to get cleaned up."

Mr. Green nodded, the movement quick and sharp. "Of course."

We walked on together to Worthington Hall. Mr. Green didn't mention the book. He didn't even look at it again. But it didn't change the fact that he'd recognized it. I'd seen it in his eyes, that spark of familiarity. Had he read it? Did he know about the prophecy?

Haven touched my arm, drawing me away from my thoughts. "What are they saying?" she whispered.

I looked to where Mr. Green stood at the door, talking quietly to Miss Lassila. I reached out with my senses, but I couldn't make out anything beyond "Dr. Norlgren" and "discreet." I glanced back at Haven and shrugged.

"They're saying something they don't want us to hear." Logan sighed. He looked exhausted, like he'd aged fifty years in the last few hours.

Without thinking, I went up on my toes and kissed

him. *Shit.* "Sorry," I said, stepping quickly back. "This isn't the time or ... "

As the power ascends, a darkness will rise, and with it will come the destruction of our world.

My stomach pitched.

"I don't mind," Logan whispered.

Mr. Green cleared his throat and I looked up sharply. He raised his eyebrows, then gestured for Haven and I to go inside. "I'll see you two tomorrow," he said. "Until then, try and get some sleep."

"Yes, sir," Haven said.

He turned his attention to Logan. "Come on, let's get you down to Emberfield. You've had a hell of a night."

17

"COME IN, QUICKLY." Miss Lassila ushered us inside. "I've heard about what happened."

"I—it was—" I stopped, the words stuck in my throat. There were so many things I could've said, so many things I *wanted* to say, but none of them could undo what had happened. None of them could make it make sense.

Haven muttered something in Latin under her breath, and bright lights sparked across the windows and walls. They were almost beautiful, electric and yellow, like magical fairy lights.

"*Consisto*," Miss Lassila said, waving a hand.

The lights went out.

"Oh, crap." Haven turned pale. "I wasn't thinking. I shouldn't have—"

"It's fine," Miss Lassila said, wrapping a blue knitted blanket around Haven's shoulders. "Just don't do it again."

She took another blanket, burgundy this time, from the desk by the front door, and started toward me.

"I don't need a blanket," I said, and my voice sounded odd, like an imitation of a voice, far away and unexpected. "I'm not cold."

"But you're a vampire." Haven pulled the blue blanket around herself like a cocoon and shivered. "You're always cold."

"No I'm not." I wasn't cold. I wasn't anything. I was blank. Empty.

Am I even real?

"We need to cover you up," Miss Lassila said as she arranged the blanket around me. "We can't risk anyone seeing you like this."

"But they need to know. They need to see what I am." I struggled against her, shrugging off the blanket, then I stumbled toward the door. "*As the power ascends, a darkness will rise, and with it will come the destruction of our world.*" Laughter bubbled up in my throat, desperate and hysterical. "Do you know what I am? What I could be? What I'm going to *do*?"

Haven coughed and shot me a warning glance. "We should go get cleaned up. Now."

"But the proph—" I started.

"It's been a long night," Haven said, turning to Miss Lassila. "Can we go upstairs?"

"Of course." The housemistress led us up the stairs and down the corridor, stopping outside the bathroom. "Everything you need is already in there."

"Thank you." Haven leaned against the wall, her cheeks hollow and her eyelids heavy. She was close enough to grab me if I did something stupid.

And I wanted to do something stupid. I wanted to scream. And run. And fight. I wanted to tell Miss Lassila about the prophecy so I didn't have to worry about it anymore.

I wanted to cry.

Because I was numb, yet somehow I felt *everything*.

"Don't take too long," Miss Lassila said, her eyes narrowing as she studied our faces. Her lips parted as if she was about to say something else, but her phone let out a loud beep and she sighed. "Ms. Emmerson's on her tea break, but I'll be in my office if you need me."

I followed Haven into the bathroom, every step, every breath, every movement a lie. *I* was a lie. A dangerous secret that got people hurt and killed. I didn't deserve to be here. I should be locked up, sequestered away in the penitentiary cells at the Paranormal Program, like Michael Miller and Kitty and all of the others who couldn't control their powers.

Would I destroy the world if I wasn't a part of it?

Suddenly I whirled, smashing my hands into the wall beside me. Over and over and over, until my skin burned and I couldn't breathe. When I finally stopped, Haven put her arms around me, and we slid to the floor together.

"It's going to be okay," she said. "We can fix this."

I wanted to believe her. I wanted to believe her because everything hurt—breathing, sitting, remembering. I wanted to believe her because I couldn't bring him back. *He's still alive. He has to be.* And I wanted to believe her because of what I was destined to do.

"Em?" Haven said quietly.

Why am I the darkness?

I sat, pulling away from her like the dried blood pulled at my skin. "I don't understand," I said. "I could see his life just … fading away. And for what? A prophecy? About me?"

"This isn't your fault."

The coming dawn was an itch in my veins, drawing me forward, shutting me down. It wouldn't kill me, but it would force me to sleep. And I couldn't sleep here. I stood, my legs shaking, and drew the letter from my pocket.

Haven got to her feet beside me. "We'll deal with that tomorrow."

"But it says—"

"No." She plucked the paper from my hands. "Go get cleaned up."

I tried to snatch the letter back and almost slipped on a patch of water. "I have to know what it means. I need to—"

"Tomorrow," she said firmly. She pocketed the letter and spun me around to face the showers. "Go. Unless you want to fall asleep like that."

I looked down at my clothes. There was so much blood. It had soaked right through the fabric and onto my skin. *Into* my skin. "I don't know what to do with this," I whispered, pulling my shirt away from my body.

"We'll wash it. Or trash it. Whatever you want."

"And this?" I picked up the blanket, which lay in a heap on the tiled floor. "It's school property and it's ruined. There's blood. See?" I thrust it toward her, and my fangs tingled in my gums.

"We'll buy the school a new one."

"But I don't want to!" I threw the blanket as hard as I could onto the wooden bench behind us. "Someone died because of me! Don't you get that? And it's only going to get worse. I'm supposed to destroy everything!" My fangs slid down before I could stop them.

"It's going to be okay." Haven's voice was calm, and the space between us filled with the scent of orange blossoms. Trust. "Now go have a shower. Get some sleep. And we'll face this together tomorrow. Okay?"

I wasn't sure why, but I actually listened. I left my clothes in a pile on the floor and locked myself in one of the stalls, letting the burning hot water pour over me. I used half a bottle of body wash and scrubbed until my skin was raw and broken, but eventually the pull of the sun became too much to ignore.

Will I smell like blood forever?

Haven rubbed a towel over her water-flattened hair. Her eyes were bloodshot, the skin beneath them purple and bruised, but she attempted a smile. "It's almost dawn."

"I know." I'd spend the rest of my life knowing. Knowing and fearing and hiding.

"You go. I'll clean this up."

I didn't have the energy to argue.

The next day, straight after breakfast, I found myself sitting at a table in a tiny room near the school's main office.

"One last question," said Rogerson, the grouchier of the two SCC agents who sat opposite me. He was a vampire, with pale white skin and hair as dark as his designer suit, and though he looked no more than eighteen, I was pretty sure he was at least two hundred, at least if the offhand comment his partner had made about his upcoming birthday was anything to go by.

"Are you ready, Emily?" McKinney, the good cop to Rogerson's bad one, smiled encouragingly at me, her brown eyes friendly.

I folded my hands in front of me. "Go ahead." We'd been doing this for half an hour already, and I hadn't told a single lie. I'd merely danced selectively around the truth, a skill I was improving at every day. Maybe I could've told them about the prophecy—they were supernatural law enforcement, after all. Maybe they could've helped. But Dr. Norlgren's warnings kept coming back to me: *It could be a matter of life and death. Tell no one, and trust no one.*

And he'd been right.

It *was* a matter of life and death.

Rogerson narrowed his eyes. "Have you omitted any information in your testimony today?"

Shit.

I exhaled slowly, trying to keep my reactions—my

scent, my mind, my body—under control. Though I couldn't take back the extra thump my traitorous heart had already given. I knew they'd both heard it—Rogerson's gaze cut to McKinney, his mouth tightening at the corners—but I plastered a neutral expression on my face and straightened my spine.

"Possibly," I said, my voice loud and clear.

Rogerson's nostrils flared. "Explain."

I ran my fingers across the tabletop. It was smooth and slick, almost over-polished. "Memories are fallible. They're reconstructions of events, not photographs. Maybe I forgot to tell you that I'd gone to the bathroom. Maybe I remembered a smell that wasn't really there." My fingers stilled. "One of those things may end up being important. Hence my answer."

Rogerson leaned forward. "Stop wasting my time. Tell me what I—"

McKinney stopped him with a glance. She smelled like wolf, though her scent was different to Logan's. While he was made of trees and wildness and power, she was drier, yellow and hot, like the desert. "Is there anything else you'd like to tell us?" she asked.

I shook my head. "Nothing."

It wasn't a lie.

McKinney smiled, and her teeth looked very white against her dark brown skin. "You may go."

Rogerson slammed a hand against the table. "What about—"

"She answered everything we asked," McKinney said.

"She's only seventeen, and she clearly didn't murder the doctor. Let her go."

I stood before Rogerson could resume his rant.

"Call me if you remember anything else," McKinney said to me, sliding a small piece of card across the table. It was the color of oatmeal, and when I picked it up I realized it was a business card, with her name and cell phone number printed in the center.

"Thanks," I said, slipping it into my pocket. I lifted my chin and glared at Rogerson. "Enjoy your birthday. Maybe you'll learn compassion by the time you're two hundred and fifty."

My legs were shaking as I shut the door behind me.

Why did I say that? What the hell is wrong with me?

I leaned my head against the wall and let out a quiet string of curses. If Rogerson wasn't gunning for me before, he would be now. *Stupid. Stupid. Stupid.* Whatever happened to keeping my head down and doing what I was supposed to?

"Are they ready for me?"

I jumped and turned to look at Logan, who was sitting on a bench seat a short way down the corridor.

"They want to see me next." Logan seemed distant, his expression arranged in the polite way expected of acquaintances and businessmen. His crisp blue button-down and polished brown shoes completed the picture. "Should I knock? Or do you think they'll come out?"

I frowned. This wasn't the Logan I knew.

"No talking," said the bald-headed man sitting next to

him. He must've taken over from the woman who'd waited with me. "This is a murder investigation."

The door to the interview room swung open. "Who even cares anymore, Smith?" Rogerson snapped, stepping out into the corridor. "This whole thing's been a colossal cock-up from start to finish. They didn't separate the girls last night. Or put any of them under observation. Who knows what kind of story they concocted together?"

"Hey," I said, heat flaring in my chest. "Nobody *concocted* anything. I answered every single one of your stupid questions. And you know I was telling the truth when I said I didn't murder Dr. Norlgren. My scent doesn't lie!"

"Fine," Rogerson said, his face contorted with anger. "But you still know more about this situation than you're letting on."

Logan stood. "All we did was find Dr. Norlgren. There's no need to treat us like criminals."

A vein twitched in Rogerson's temple. "Your father won't be pleased to hear about your involvement in this, Adams."

"He won't be pleased that I found an injured man and went to get help?" It was a question that should've sounded sarcastic, but Logan somehow made it polite. I was beginning to realize that this persona was practiced, polished through years of use. So much of who he was seemed to be centered around his life as the son of an alpha—he was civil to adults in power, powerful when dealing with challenges from Courtney and the others, and charming whenever he needed to be. It was impressive, and chameleonic, yet I couldn't help thinking he'd be happier if he had the freedom to be himself.

"People talk, Adams," Rogerson snapped, sweat beading on his forehead. "This will get back to him, no matter what you think."

"He won't be concerned. Perhaps you don't know him very well. I can set up a meeting with him if you like. He's really very personable." Logan tilted his head, clearly assessing the much older vampire, though his composure never slipped. "When he wants to be."

McKinney appeared at the door beside Rogerson. "Come in now, Logan," she said.

He nodded politely, then glanced back at me one last time. There was nothing in his gaze that suggested we were friends. There was nothing left of the boy who'd kissed me the night before. Of the boy who'd rushed to help before he even knew what was wrong. I wanted to say something, to call back the Logan who'd held my hand in the dark, but I couldn't. Not when he was like this, all cool power and political games. He said he wasn't fit to be alpha, but he played the role to perfection.

The door closed behind him, and I didn't move. I stared at the dark polished wood that stood between us and wondered what he'd say to Rogerson and McKinney. Would he give away my secret? *No, he's not like that.* But what if he was? What if they threatened him with real-world consequences, the kind that would impact his alpha, his father, his pack?

Goosebumps prickled on my skin.

"You need to leave," commanded Smith, the bald-headed man who'd been sitting next to Logan.

"Why?"

Smith's lip curled. "Because I said so."

My teeth snapped together. I knew this dance. I'd been learning it from the moment I'd opened my eyes at The Paranormal Program. It was a routine performance of intimidation and threats, most of them never spoken aloud; it was a fight for dominance in a competition I was expected to lose. But I would never give in to Smith, or anyone like him.

No one will have that kind of power over me.

"Go on." Smith hadn't even bothered to stand. He just glared from his perch on the bench, chin tilted up and legs spread wide in a blatant display of machismo.

"Are all SCC agents expected to be rude?" I said snappishly. "Or just the ones they send to Mistwood Academy?"

Smith leaned forward, his lips parting in a terrible smile.

"I'm not scared," I said, squaring my shoulders as I studied his face and willed my body not to betray me. I needed to stay in control. I needed him to believe I meant what I said. "I've dealt with creatures worse than you."

Smith stood. He was tall and broad, his neck corded with muscle. "You haven't seen what I'm capable of yet, girly," he said, stalking toward me.

"Girly?" I pushed away all of my fear and let annoyance

rise to the top. "Are you serious? I'm going to track down your supervisor at the SCC and lodge a complaint." I stepped forward, baring my teeth so he could see my fangs. "And for the record, you're not even half as intimidating as a mara. Or an out of control newly-turned wolf. Or the warden."

He stopped in front of me, and the air between us flashed hot.

I pulled my phone out of my pocket. "What's your supervisor's name?"

"None of your fucking business," he snarled, leaning close enough that his breath hit my face. "Why don't you get the hell out of here before I—"

He stopped.

"Before you what?" I said, already searching the SCC website on my phone.

A high-pitched yapping sounded from the end of the corridor, and Smith flinched. The scent of smoke swirled around him like a beacon.

Fear.

I lowered my phone and turned to look.

"FRED?" I frowned at the tiny blue dragon who was hurtling down the corridor toward us. "What are you doing here?"

Smith's jaw twitched.

And why is Smith afraid of a miniature dragon?

Mr. Green strode out into the hallway. "Fred, come," he commanded, tapping his leg.

The dragon stopped, but didn't turn around. Twin ribbons of smoke rose from his nostrils, and his head bobbed up and down. A quiet growl rumbled up from his throat.

"Fred." Mr. Green's voice held a note of warning, and he tapped his leg again. "Come. Now."

The dragon stared at Smith and shook his wings, his whole body flattening. He extended his tongue and let out a loud hiss, then turned and trotted back toward Mr. Green. His tail whipped back and forth behind him like a violent pendulum. *What the hell is going on?* I'd never seen Fred act this way before.

I stole a glance at Smith. He was standing perfectly still, his back against the wall. His previously blue eyes, pinched in a permanent glare, glowed amber. It was like watching an incoming storm. He was about to break, and I couldn't do anything to stop it.

"What are you looking at?" he muttered under his breath.

A monumental asshole who thinks it's okay to intimidate seventeen-year-old girls.

I didn't say it out loud.

Mr. Green walked toward us. "What's going on here?" he said, bending briefly to clip a lead to the collar around Fred's neck. "Is everything all right?"

I stepped toward him. "No, it's not."

Mr. Green raised his eyebrows. "Smith? Would you like to explain?"

"No, sir." His hands curled into fists at his sides, the skin on his knuckles stretched and white.

"Then I'd like you to leave." Mr. Green's voice was calm, quiet with well-practiced restraint. "I can escort you to the gate myself, or we can both wait here until Rogerson and McKinney are done."

Smith grunted. "Fine." His teeth were clenched so hard his jaw hardly moved. "I'll go with you."

"I thought you would." Mr. Green smiled, and everything about him changed. His perpetually steady demeanor dropped away, and for the first time, I saw a different side to him. A cold, hard smile. A steely gaze. He was sharp and authoritarian, and it was deeply unnerving. "Let's go."

I blinked, trying to understand what was going on beneath the surface. There was a silent threat in Mr. Green's words, a whisper of danger, yet it wasn't violent. Not quite. It was almost disciplinary, like he was a parent or teacher, reprimanding Smith for making bad choices.

Are they friends? Acquaintances? Pack mates?

Fred growled again.

Regardless of how they knew each other, Fred clearly didn't like him, and I couldn't help but agree with the dragon's assessment.

"Emily," said Mr. Green, silencing Fred with a look, "come and see me third period tomorrow. There are a few things we need to discuss."

I nodded, mostly because there wasn't anything else I could do, and watched them go. I half-expected Smith to turn and take a swipe at me, but he didn't. He just walked heavily, one step behind Mr. Green, his shoulders tight, his fists still clenched at his sides.

I glared at his back. "What's your problem?" I muttered under my breath.

A single word, infused with venom, drifted back to me. "*Putere.*"

My heart stopped.

He knew.

Smith *knew.*

And Mr. Green hadn't reacted. Did he know what the word meant?

I paced the corridor aimlessly, barely noticing what I was doing, the walls a faded backdrop to my thoughts. I was faintly aware of my body, like it was something that belonged to someone else. The ice-cold skin, the veins that were frozen with fear—those were happening outside of me, not to me. I didn't feel like Emily. I didn't feel real.

Did Smith know who killed Dr. Norlgren?

I raised a hand, ready to knock on the interview room door. I could tell Rogerson and McKinney. I wouldn't be responsible anymore. But—

I paused. Dragged a breath into my screaming lungs.

I couldn't tell them. I'd decided that already. *Tell no one, and trust no one.* Smith already knew what I was. And he was SCC. Maybe Rogerson and McKinney knew too. I leaned my head against the door and wished it wasn't soundproof. What was Logan telling them in there? Why had I let so people many know what I was? What I might be? It was the one thing Dr. Norlgren had been warning me about from the beginning. And I'd failed at it, again and again and again.

Maybe I hadn't truly believed it.

Or maybe I just couldn't make a decision and stick to it.

But enough was enough. This whole thing was too big, too monumental, to keep hiding from. Someone had died because of me. *Someone had died because of me.* I couldn't keep messing around or changing my mind. I spun on my heel and walked slowly down the corridor, resolve hardening in my chest. I would learn everything I could about the prophecy. And hopefully I'd figure out how to stop it.

I swung open the door and strode out into the night, leaving the sterile interview room and probing SCC agents behind. I didn't need them. I could deal with this. I was a vampire. I was fast and strong and fearless. I was—

"Emily, wait up!"

—suddenly annoyed.

"Sorry, Philip." I glanced at him over my shoulder, but didn't stop walking. "I'm in a hurry."

"It won't take long." He lengthened his stride. "I'm just—"

"Ow!" I stumbled away from the trashcan I'd collided with at the side of the path. I'd been so preoccupied with outpacing Philip that I hadn't even noticed it. "Dammit!" I could already feel the bruises blooming where the ornate filigreed edges had struck me.

"Are you okay?"

I rubbed my hip and kept walking. "I'm fine."

"Are you sure?"

"I have to go." I had research to do. Plans to make.

"Come on, Emily," he said. "This won't take long. It's about Haven."

I froze. I didn't like Philip. Not since that night at Adventure Gardens. He was possessive and spoiled, entitled and rude. But now he sounded different. There was a tremble in his breath and a crack in his voice.

"Is she okay?" I said, turning.

"That's what I wanted to ask you."

"Why?" I pulled my phone out of my pocket, but I didn't have any messages. Nothing from Haven. Nothing from Cayley. "What makes you think something's wrong?"

"She's been avoiding my calls," he said, staring down at his hands. "And she's not texting me back."

I hadn't seen Haven since she'd emerged from her SCC interview, just before I went in. She'd been somber, dressed all in black, but she hadn't mentioned Philip. She'd just squeezed my hand as she'd passed and wished me luck. "Maybe she's got more important things on her mind," I said, wishing I could take the words back before I'd even finished saying them.

The scent of rotting leaves swirled between us. Philip's carefully curated worry was fraying at the edges. His pupils were dilated, and something feral sat just below the surface, waiting to be unleashed. He smelled wrong. Like wolf mixed with something I couldn't identify.

"I know something happened last night," he said, leaning forward. "Someone at Emberfield said Mr. Olaru was murdered."

I didn't move. Didn't think. Didn't breathe. I couldn't afford to give anything away.

Philip moved even closer. "Someone else said it was the doctor."

I swallowed hard.

"Do you know what happened? They said you did it. You and Logan and Haven."

My phone slipped from my hand and clattered to the ground. *Shit.* "That's ridiculous."

"Is it, though?"

I backed away. "Of course it's ridiculous. We're not murderers."

Philip bent down and picked up my phone. "But you think someone *was* murdered?"

I took back my phone and carefully brushed the dirt from the case. I didn't know what to say, so I concentrated on the feel of my fingers on hard plastic, of the small crack in the corner of the case catching on my skin. "I guess the faculty will address the rumors when they're ready," I finally said.

"And Haven?" Philip asked.

"I'll tell her you're looking for her." *And that you're a menacing asshole.* I put my phone in my pocket and turned to go, relieved to be getting away from him, but a strange thought struck me and I paused. "Did whoever told you we'd killed someone tell you why they thought we were involved?"

Philip crossed his arms over his chest and regarded me carefully. "Someone saw you outside the medical center with blood on your clothes."

I shivered. The smell of it was still there, just beyond my skin, the broken bitter odor of violence and death. My fingertips moved silently over my palms and my wrists, up onto my arms, searching for something leftover, a speck that hadn't washed away.

Philip's gaze followed my movements. "Did it hurt when you were turned?" he said, a slow smile building.

I forced my fingers to stop. "I'll tell Haven to call you."

I could feel his eyes on me as I walked away, but I didn't look back. And I didn't look up. I could hear the whispers from every group I passed. *Did you hear what she did? She's a murderer. Why haven't they locked her up already?*

By the time I got back to my room, I was barely holding it together. I'd had breakfast before my meeting with the SCC, including an extra session with a Nutriment specifically so I wouldn't lose control due to the stress of it all, but the hunger still whispered beneath my skin.

"Em?" Haven said, looking up from her laptop. "What's wrong?"

I needed my cello. Why didn't I keep it in my room? It was my lifeline. The only thing that kept me under control.

I slammed the door behind me. "Everyone thinks we did it," I said, hurling myself onto my bed.

Haven's eyes were wide. "The SCC thinks we killed Dr. Norlgren?"

Cayley dragged a sneaker-clad foot along the floor, and my desk chair spun to a stop beneath her. "Couldn't they smell the truth on you?"

"I'm not talking about the SCC," I said impatiently. "It's everyone else. The rumors started last night."

Haven frowned. "Why?"

"Because someone saw us!" I covered my face with my

hands and tried to hold on to the thin ribbon of control that was close to spiraling away. "They saw us last night. Outside the medical center. They saw us, and they saw the blood, and I don't know how but they found out that Dr. Norlgren is dead."

"Why didn't you tell them you didn't do it?"

Cayley's question was irritatingly logical. I dragged my hands away from my face and scowled. "It's easy enough when you're not the one being accused of murder!"

"Fine." She stood. "I'll go out and tell everyone you're all innocent."

"Who was it?" Haven said, ignoring Cayley's suggestion. "Who saw us?"

I shrugged, helpless and annoyed. "I dunno. But you need to call Philip—who's an asshole, by the way—because he's the one who told me about it."

Haven's gaze hit me with the force of a slap. "You promised me you'd try and get on with him."

"He was intimidating me!" My fangs slid out, and I forced them back in. There were too many emotions simmering inside me, and a fight with Haven would only make things worse.

"What did he do?" Cayley asked.

"He got all up in my face. And he—" I broke off, trying to remember exactly what he'd said. But … was it actually his fault? Or mine? I'd snapped at him first. If he was stressed out and worried about Haven, maybe his control had just slipped. Like mine was doing now.

"And he what?" Haven said.

I shook my head. "It was nothing."

Haven frowned at me, then picked up her phone. "He's sent so many messages." She put her elbows on her knees and scrolled through them all, occasionally stopping to read one out loud. "*I just want to make sure you're okay,*" she said. "*I heard about what happened. I'm worried. Are you safe? Are you hurt? Call me. Please.*"

"Are you going to?" Cayley asked. She'd gone back to spinning around in my chair, her face tilted up to the ceiling.

Haven sighed. "I don't know what to say. I can't lie to him. But I can't tell him the truth either." She turned to me, her expression worried. "Not without giving up your secret."

"You can't—" I started.

"I'd never," Haven said. "Not without your permission. It's just … I really care about Philip. And I know I haven't known him long, and I know you guys don't like him much, but when I'm with him, everything feels good. It feels *right*. And I know he feels it, too."

I chewed on my lower lip, breathing in the clouded watercolor scent of baking and mint leaves. Worry and happiness and truth. Haven did genuinely care about Philip. And part of me suspected he actually cared about her, too. It was why I'd stopped to talk to him in the first place. He hadn't faked the break in his voice, or the quavering breath, or the anger he'd felt when I'd suggested he wasn't important to Haven.

"Why don't you just give him an edited version of what

happened?" I suggested. "You don't have to tell him everything."

"You told me everything," Cayley said, tapping the edge of my desk as she spun past it again and again.

"You don't count." I grabbed a pear from the fruit bowl and took a bite. "Anyway, we have bigger things to worry about right now. Smith knows what I am."

Haven sat bolt upright. "Smith? Who's Smith? And how does he know about you?"

"He's an SCC agent. He was waiting outside the interview room with Logan." I swallowed past the lump in my throat, then tossed the rest of the pear in the trash. "And I have no idea how he knows. Or what he might do. Which is why we have to find out everything we can about the prophecy. Fast."

Haven stood. "I still have the letter."

"Good. We can start there, then—"

Three loud taps rattled the window above my desk. "It's me," called a familiar voice. "Can I come in?"

I unlatched the window and Logan swept in, his long legs carrying him easily over the desk and into the room. He was still wearing the blue button-down from earlier, but creases had found their way into the previously pristine fabric, and scuffs had appeared on the toes of his black leather shoes. The polished heir was gone, leaving behind a Logan who seemed so much more vulnerable. Real.

"Hey," I said softly.

Cayley regarded him with curiosity. "How was it?"

"Terrible." Logan ran a hand through his hair, but it flopped right back down above his eyes, which were hooded from lack of sleep. His shoulders slumped, and it seemed like the fatigue had engraved itself deep into his soul. "Rogerson is a dick."

"I know." Haven walked over to her trunk and opened it. "Here," she said, holding out a piece of paper she removed from under the lid. "This is yours."

I rubbed my hands on my jeans, then took it, closing my fingers gingerly around the bloodstained page. It looked worse than I remembered.

"Is that the letter from Dr. Norlgren?" Cayley asked.

Haven clearly *had* told her everything.

I unfolded the letter and read the words, again and again and again. "This isn't enough," I said, frustration prickling under my skin. "We need—"

"This?" Logan held up the thin, gray book he'd taken from Dr. Norlgren's office.

Yes.

It was exactly what we needed.

"Did you read it?" Haven asked, her head tilting to the side as she peered curiously at the pocket-sized volume.

Logan shook his head and passed the book to me. "I thought Emily should read it first since the prophecy's about her."

I sat down cross-legged on the floor and ran my hand over the cover. It was leather, weightier than I'd expected, and it smelled like grass and vanilla, shot through with a faint streak of mustiness. *Grave. Somber. Old.* It was all of those things, but it was also so much more. It was going to tell me everything I needed to know.

I hoped.

"Do you guys want to know what it says?" I asked, tracing the outline of the title with a shaking finger. "Because it's not too late to back out. You can go back to your normal lives. Pretend you never met me."

"Not a chance," Logan said.

"Never," Haven added.

Cayley raised an eyebrow. "Why would we want to do that?"

"Okay, fine. Here goes." I took a deep breath and opened the front cover as the three of them sat down around me. To my surprise, the text inside was hand-written, the ink thin and faded on brittle yellowed pages.

"Holy shit," Cayley breathed, leaning closer to get a better view. "That thing's ancient."

Haven's eyes were wide. "Stop. You need gloves or something." She went over to her trunk, then tossed me a pair of white cotton gloves that she'd pulled out from its depths. "They're not archival quality, but they're better than nothing."

I set the book down carefully on the floor and pulled on the gloves. "Better?" I said, turning to Haven.

She nodded.

"Okay, let's try this again." I opened the book again and skimmed the first few lines, then swore under my breath. "So, um ... This is going to be a lot harder than we thought."

HAVEN'S FOREHEAD WRINKLED. "What's wrong?"

"I can't read it." I looked down at the pages and cursed again. "It isn't in English."

Haven scooted closer and held out a hand. "May I?"

I took off the cotton gloves, then passed them and the book to her and watched anxiously as she flipped through the pages. My fate was written there, etched into parchment in words I couldn't understand. It was so close, yet a million miles away, an uncorrected error of space and time and perception. But I needed to know. I needed to understand.

Too much was at stake if I didn't.

Dr. Norlgren's letter lay in my lap, burning a hole in my consciousness with the words I so badly wanted to be false: *The* putere *will come to power on the night of the Sapphire Eclipse. As the power ascends, a darkness will rise, and with it will come the destruction of our world.*

I was the *putere*. Dr. Norlgren had been convinced of it. But … what if I wasn't? Because underneath it all, beneath the fangs and the hunger and the strange new abilities, I was still just a girl from suburban Michigan. I couldn't destroy the world. Could I?

My chest tightened.

Without saying a word, Logan took my hand. The fingers that curled around mine were warm and comforting and real. I gripped them like I never wanted to let them go.

"Can you read it?" Cayley said, nudging Haven's knee with her foot. "What does it say?"

"Shhh, I'm concentrating." Haven skimmed a few more pages, focusing on the words in front of her with her entire being.

Cayley nudged Haven's knee again. "What do you expect us to do?"

Haven looked up, her expression annoyed. "Can you read Elven? No? Then be quiet and wait."

"Sorry." Cayley's tone walked the line between sincerity and sarcasm. "I'm just—"

"Shhh," Haven said again.

Cayley fell silent, though she couldn't keep still. She crossed her legs and uncrossed them; her hair lengthened slowly until the ends of it hung past her waist; she altered her sweater five times—blue, red, green, pink, black.

Logan and I sat silent, our fingers still entwined.

Finally, Haven looked up. "I think I've found the bit about you," she said.

Cayley leaned forward, her hair—blonde and chin-length now—swinging over her shoulders. One side was curled, the other straight. Impatiently, she pushed it back, and it fell down past her shoulders in its usual brown waves.

"What does it say?" she asked, folding her hands carefully in her lap.

"A lot," Haven said. "It basically explains how the original *putere* came to be. And how another might be created." She turned to me with an expression usually reserved for adults—the grim sort of look they get when they're about to tell you something unpleasant. "Are you ready?"

No. Yes. Maybe.

Logan's fingers tightened around mine. I sighed. This information was everything I'd been waiting for. "Go on," I said. "Do it."

"Okay." She looked back down at the book. "I can't translate everything exactly, so I'll have to paraphrase, okay?"

I nodded.

And then she began.

"Thousands of years ago," Haven said, her voice quiet but steady, "in a country that no longer exists, there lived a warlock. He wasn't wealthy, or famous, and his name has long since been forgotten, but he was strong. And he was evil. On the night of the Sapphire Eclipse, he went out into the woods to perform a sacrificial ritual for … something or someone I don't know how to translate."

"What was he sacrificing?" Cayley asked. "Animal or human?"

"Human. But there was something special about her. She possessed a rare talent, one so unusual there has only been one other documented case. She could ..." Haven looked up at the ceiling and muttered to herself. "Borrow? No, that's wrong. It's steal. She could steal the powers of anyone she touched."

"That doesn't sound good," Logan muttered.

"It's not." Haven stared back down at the book. "The warlock wanted that power, desired it over everything, so on the night of the Sapphire Eclipse, he sacrificed the woman, hoping to steal her ability. He tied her to a tree, performed the spell, then sliced her wrists with something called The Impure Blade."

A memory, anxious and muddled, hovered at the edges of my mind. But I couldn't bring it into focus. It was hazy. Hidden. And the more I tried to grasp it, the more it slipped away.

Haven cleared her throat. "When the Sapphire Eclipse reached its peak," she continued, "he began to drink."

"Drink?" Cayley said.

"Yeah." Haven's nose wrinkled with blatant disgust. "He drank her blood. But something went wrong. As she lay dying, she cursed the warlock. She put a weakness in his spell. He plunged the Impure Blade into her heart in a final act of violence, but it was already too late. The damage was done. The warlock began to wither, and the blood turned thick in ..." She paused, obviously trying to find the right words. "In a throat that could no longer swallow."

All I could hear was the pounding of my heart. "And what does this have to do with me?"

"The warlock wasn't finished," Haven said, lifting the book closer to her face. "He forced down as much of the blood as he could. It transferred enough of the woman's powers for him to survive, but it wasn't enough for the spell to work correctly. When he discovered he couldn't steal anyone's powers, he flew into a rage. He did some really terrible things and eventually discovered he *could* take people's abilities, but not the way she had. Not by touch. He had to kill them and drink from them."

Cayley's eyes widened. "And he discovered this, how?"

Haven shook her head. "You don't want to know."

My breath stopped in my chest. Hunger, sharp and urgent, twisted in my stomach and my fangs slid free.

Shit.

Logan moved closer, but it wasn't enough. My skin didn't fit right. I didn't know how—

"Breathe," he whispered, his lips so close I could almost feel them.

I gripped his hand and exhaled slowly, trying to focus.

I couldn't lose control.

Haven placed the book down gently on the floor in front of her. "Do you want to take a break? We can come back to this later."

"No. Finish it." The words came out brittle and raw, but I embraced the darkness, let it fill my veins for one beat, two, then I pushed it away. I thought of my cello, of hard wood and strings, of music that flowed through my fingers. I'd been scared for so long that the warden had got it wrong. That I should never have been sent here. I'd been terrified that I'd end up like Michael, scared and broken and lost. But I'd been through so much since the night of the fire. And I still hadn't lost control. *I can do this. The warden was right.*

My fangs slid away.

"Okay," Haven said as she carefully flipped through the pages. "So, once the warlock figured out what he could do, he traveled around and gathered up as many abilities as he could. He called himself the *putere*, and was callous and brutal and so very, very feared. He returned home, powerful beyond measure, but … familiarity, I think it says, made him careless. One night, the local elven population managed to catch him. They restrained him, though they couldn't kill him—he'd amassed so many powers he was essentially immortal. After—"

"Oh, crap," Logan said, just before someone knocked on the door.

Haven shot me a look of sympathy.

The knocking didn't stop.

"Maybe they'll go away," I said. But I knew who it was, and I knew that they wouldn't.

"We know you're in there," Courtney called. "You can't hide forever."

"Should I let them in?" Cayley asked as we all got to our feet. "Or should I tell them to go f—"

"We know what you did," Vanessa said, her voice sharp and spiky, even through the thick wood of the door.

Haven rolled her eyes. "Great. Just great." She stuffed the gloves in her pocket, opened my closet door, and gestured toward Logan. "You know the drill."

Logan didn't look happy about it, but somehow he wedged himself in between my jackets and shoes, closing the door seconds before Courtney called out again.

"I'm not comfortable living next door to *murderers*!" she yelled, pounding even harder on the door.

"What the hell, Courtney?" I pulled the door open so quickly she almost fell. "We're not murderers and you know it."

"Do I though?" She grabbed onto the doorframe, obviously trying to be casual about it, but failing. She straightened, her cheeks flushing pink. "You're clearly depraved enough."

"Oh, shut up already," Cayley said. "Don't you ever get tired of the sound of your own voice?"

Danielle sneered. "Not as tired as I get of yours."

"Do you actually want something?" Haven said, coming over to stand beside me. "Or did you just come over to cause a scene?"

"Would you like us to cause a scene?" Courtney asked. Her sudden smile was overly sweet, a practiced concoction of sugar and intemperance.

I stepped forward, fists clenching, but Haven just raised an eyebrow.

"I know Logan's in there," Courtney continued, all

syrup and sprinkles. "I can smell him. Your protection spells don't work when the door's open, Haven." She leaned into the room, her honeyed curls gleaming. "Come out, Logan. Unless you want your dad to find out what's been going on."

The closet door opened. "He already knows." Logan's tone was even, though a flash of irritation sparked beneath the surface of his skin. "But I appreciate the threat. I haven't had enough of those lately."

Courtney's jaw snapped shut.

"It's time you left," I said, swinging the door slowly forward. "And don't—"

"Wait." Vanessa held out a paper bag. "We have something for you. We found it by the steps outside."

I didn't take it straight away like she'd obviously expected.

"Don't you want it?" she said, confused.

I stared at the paper bag and frowned. It was small and brown, the top folded over, and my name was written across the front in bold, block letters. It seemed innocuous. The sort of thing you'd never expect to hurt you. Which was precisely why I *didn't* want to take it.

"What's in it?" Logan asked.

Vanessa shrugged, but her gaze cut to the left.

"You're lying." Cayley moved closer, her body prowling elegantly through the room, beautiful and powerful and deadly. "What's in the bag?"

Vanessa's lips twisted strangely. Her earlier venom had

gone, leaving only this hollow attempt, like a costume that didn't fit right. "Why don't you check for yourselves?"

I took the bag, not because I wanted to, but because there was something in there I needed to see. I didn't know what it was, and I couldn't tell from the weight of the bag, or the size, or the shape. But whatever it was had scared Vanessa. And that meant it was important.

Courtney and Danielle watched and glowered.

I didn't open the bag.

Not with them there.

"We took a risk bringing this here," Courtney finally said in a huff. "The least you could do is thank us."

"I told you we should've given it to Miss Lassila," Danielle said.

Cayley leaned against the doorframe, uncomfortably close to Courtney. "Why didn't you?"

Courtney glanced at Logan, then looked away. "We don't owe you an explanation."

My fangs tingled and my fist tightened around the bag. "Fine," I said. I'd had enough. "Thank you for the mystery bag. I'll be sure to—"

Vanessa suddenly paled. "Ms. Emmerson's coming."

Courtney gave Logan once last look, then flicked her long hair over her shoulders. It was an artfully careless action, one that suggested she cared all too much. "Let's go," she said to the others.

The three of them strode off and I started to close the door, but Ms. Emmerson called out. I plastered a polite smile on my lips, then reached behind the door to slip the paper bag onto the nearest shelf.

Logan headed back toward the closet.

"Is everything all right in here?" Ms. Emmerson said when she got to the door. She peered into the room, her eyes narrowing. "No unexpected visitors?"

"What do you mean?" I said, my voice higher than usual. "Logan hasn't been in here since his first day back." It was a blatant lie, but I was tired, drained from … well, from everything that had happened. Anyway, it didn't matter. She was a witch. She wouldn't be able to smell the sour scent that coated my skin.

She frowned as she stepped past us into the room. "Would your answer still be the same if I gave you a truth potion?"

"Absolutely," Haven said, following her over to the open trunk at the end of her bed. She lowered the lid and smiled. "Sorry. I shouldn't have left that open. Witchcraft 101. *Always keep your accoutrements secure.*"

Ms. Emmerson lifted a hand and muttered a spell under her breath. The walls lit up with electricity, and the air swirled with a sudden burst of red smoke. "More unapproved spell work, Haven?"

"Oh, I—" Haven ducked her head, her gaze coming to rest in the center of the room. "I know I shouldn't have. But I couldn't sleep after finding Dr. Norlgren and I wanted to strengthen the wards. It was only a—"

Ms. Emmerson lifted a hand. "Enough. One wrong incantation could interfere with the already substantial wards placed on your room and on this building. The consequences could be disastrous. You know this. It's been drilled into you since freshman year."

Haven's cheeks flushed red.

"Honestly," Ms. Emmerson continued, her blue eyes flashing. "I expected better from you." She barked out a Latin phrase, and the red smoke disappeared. With a twist of her hand and another few words, the walls stopped sparking.

"I'm sorry," Haven said. "I didn't mean any harm."

"She'd never do anything to hurt us," Cayley added.

Ms. Emmerson's lips were thin. "Misplaced confidence is a danger to us all." Then she turned and stalked away, leaving the scent of magic and disappointment in her wake.

"Well, shit," Cayley said as soon as the doors were shut. "She removed your extra wards."

"I'll put them back before Logan leaves. Otherwise they'll know we've had someone in here as soon as he goes out the window." Haven saw my confused expression and her lips twitched. "It's not the first time I've been busted, and it won't be the last. Ms. Emmerson doesn't give me enough credit. I know what I'm doing—I've been changing the wards in here since I was fourteen."

The closet door opened.

"At least it distracted her from looking for Logan," Haven said.

Logan grinned. "You saved me from potentially dire consequences."

His words were light, an echo of Ms. Emmerson's threat on the day I'd first met him, but it was enough to remind me of a different set of dire consequences. Of the prophecy. Of the danger of being around me. I glanced at the paper bag I'd set down on the shelf, tucked between a bowl filled with crystals and an orb I'd been given by a vampire called Laurence when I was at the Paranormal Program.

"Are you going to open it?" Cayley said, following my gaze.

I shook my head. "Later. Let's hear the rest of *Putere: Prophecy and Destiny* first."

Logan handed the book to Haven—he'd had enough presence of mind to hide it when Ms. Emmerson came to the door—and we all sat back down in the middle of the room.

"Right," Haven said, crossing her legs in front of her. "Where were we?"

"Unimaginable violence," Cayley said. "And elves."

Logan shifted, and his knee came to rest against mine. "Immortality."

"It was a rhetorical question, but okay," Haven said, slipping the gloves back on and flipping gently through the pages. "At least I know you were listening."

She continued looking while the rest of us waited silently. Everything felt different now, more urgent. Like the world or the galaxy or the universe was on edge, waiting with us. Even the air felt fragile, as if it were about the crack into a million pieces.

Or maybe that was just me.

"So the warlock was essentially immortal," Haven began after finding her place, "but that didn't stop the elves from trying to kill him. Not because they were territorial, or violent, or opposed to rehabilitation, but because the warlock had become so far removed from anything that had ever made him human. He'd been swallowed up by dark magic and power. There was no other choice."

That could be me. Dangerous. Inhuman. Willing to destroy the world. Would they lock me up? Or would it be a fight to the death? A fight to—

"Breathe," Logan whispered, threading his fingers through mine.

Haven continued reading. "After realizing that nothing would kill him, the elves devised a different plan. They would remove the spell, and all of his powers, instead." She paused to turn the page, her lips pursed, body tense. "It worked, leaving the warlock weak and dying, as he had been on the night of the Sapphire Eclipse. But there was one last problem—the magic they'd drawn out of him was strong. So strong it needed somewhere to go. It needed a living vessel."

Cayley shifted uncomfortably, her eyeshadow growing smokier as she stretched her legs out in front of her. Again, her gaze cut to the paper bag by the door.

I could open it now. Get it over with.

Logan squeezed my hand and I straightened, trying to concentrate on what Haven was saying.

"The spell kept trying to jump back into the warlock,"

she read, her brow furrowed in concentration. "Somehow he'd bound it to himself, to his very essence. Finally, after a lot of missteps, and more than one casualty, the elves figured out they could send the core of the spell—*without* the powers that had already been stolen—into someone of the warlock's bloodline."

Cayley moved again, restless. Her hair slowly darkened.

"They put the spell into the warlock's youngest child, a boy not much younger than we are now. It recognized elements of the warlock's blood in his ..." Haven frowned, tapping her gloved finger against the page as she searched for the right word. "In his offspring. It went to the boy willingly. It was so willing, in fact, that the elves were able to send it to sleep. They thought it would be dormant forever."

Cayley stood. She walked over to the window and stared outside. She was chaos tethered, electric and dangerous, but she held herself in, and she didn't interrupt.

Haven's eyes shone with sympathy. "I'm almost done. There are only two more things. One: the original spell can be reactivated, as long as certain steps are followed, similar to the original ritual. And two: the prophecy you've already heard, the one on the letter from Dr. Norlgren, was foretold by a local wise woman who was known to, and trusted by, the elves. She came to them, only a few months after they'd sent the spell dormant, and told them what she saw. She said the *putere* would be borne out of hatred, greed, and misery, and would be given its final form by the last living relative of an abominable man."

"What?" I said, staring down at the book though I couldn't read the words. "That doesn't make sense. I have a family. A mom, a dad, a brother. I'm not anybody's last living relative."

The world was set on pause.

I swallowed hard. "I can't be the last," I whispered. "Can I?"

2 0

I GRABBED my phone with shaking hands. Without thinking, without even considering the consequences, I dialed
my mom's cell phone number. It took five attempts to get
it right, to remember the pattern of the number. It took
five attempts to try and connect myself with who I'd been.

There was a pause. A crack through the speaker and a
crack in my heart. But finally—*finally, finally*—I heard
ringing.

"Hello?"

I opened my mouth.

"Hello? Are you there?"

I couldn't speak. It was my mom—and she sounded the
same as she'd always been. Warm. Curious. Comforting.

"Hello?" she said again, and I heard Dad's voice in the
background.

My eyes burned with tears.

They were alive. They were *alive*. And I wasn't the last

living relative of anybody. At least, not yet. Who knew? Maybe the prophecy wouldn't happen for hundreds of years. But … I still couldn't speak to them. They could never know what I was.

Haven gently took the phone from my still-shaking hands. "Sorry," she said, after putting it to her ear. "Wrong number."

When she gave it back to me, the call had been disconnected. "That was my mom," I whispered, sinking down onto the edge of the bed.

"I know," Haven said gently.

"What am I supposed to do now?" I put my phone down beside me and scrubbed my hands over my face. My fangs grazed my lower lip and I pulled them in. I hadn't even noticed they'd slipped out. "There's so much going on right now, and I don't know how to deal with it."

"We'll make a plan," Logan said. "We'll figure something out."

"And if we don't? What then? Another murder? Because that's where we're at. Prophecies and murder and —one day—the end of the world. Because of me." I stood, blood pounding in my temples. "Shall we find out what's in the bag? See what our next disaster's gonna be?"

"Emily—" Haven started, but I didn't listen.

I stalked across the room and snatched the bag from the shelf. A jagged tear slashed through the paper as I ripped it open, but I didn't care. Because none of it mattered. Not really. It was just another crisis to deal with, just another—

"Oh, shit," Logan said as I pulled out the bloodied lock of hair.

—ordinary day at Mistwood Academy.

"Is that what I think it is?" Cayley's nose wrinkled as she stepped forward for a closer look.

I swallowed hard and stared at the green and red strands, still secured at the end with a black rubber band. "Yeah," I said, shoving it back into the ruined bag so I didn't have to look at it anymore. "It's Dr. Norlgren's hair. I guess I dropped it when we found him."

Cayley went back to the window. "At least they didn't get into your room this time." She leaned her forehead against the glass and looked down onto the path below. "Who do you think left it? The whole school's still on lockdown."

Haven lifted her shoulders. "Maybe a friend of Derek's?"

"Or Smith," I said.

Logan frowned. "Smith?" He stood, something in his expression becoming sharp, assessing. "You mean the SCC guy? He knew about the prophecy?"

I screwed the bag up tight in my hands and nodded.

Logan held out a hand. "May I?"

I passed the bag over, the crumpled and torn lines of my once neatly-printed name feeling like a metaphor for my life. Logan hesitated, just for a second, then pulled out the lock of hair. Closing his eyes, he swallowed once, then inhaled deeply, raising the bag, then the lock of hair, to his nose.

I watched silently, my heart in my throat. Why hadn't I thought of doing that? I still had so much to learn, so many things that didn't come as instinctively to me as they did to the others. I was getting better at this whole vampire thing—sometimes, *maybe*—but moments like this reminded me that I'd always be on the back foot, never quite belonging and always scrambling to catch up. Mostly, it didn't matter. But now? When lives were potentially at stake? It mattered all too much.

Logan opened his eyes. "Why did you think it was Smith?" His voice was mild, politely curious, but his body was tense, each muscle beneath his sensible, rumpled clothes alert and ready to act.

I tilted my chin and met his gaze. "Because he knows what I am."

Then before he could ask, I told him everything he'd missed, from the verbal and physical intimidation to Smith's final, menacing whisper.

"Shit." Logan lifted the bag and the hair, and smelled them again. "And Mr. Green was there?"

"Yeah, but ..."

Logan's eyes widened, urging me on. He was a spring wound tight, an animal ready to lunge.

"There was something off about him," I finished. "Something weird. When he found out what had happened, he got really mad. But not like normal mad. More like a sinister, threatening kind of mad."

Haven, who'd been flicking feverishly through the pages of *Putere: Prophecy and Destiny*, looked up. "That doesn't sound like Mr. Green. He's always so nice. And calm."

Cayley paced the room. "I don't trust anyone who spends their time probing into the minds of other people."

"He's a psychologist," Haven said. "It's what they do."

"Doesn't mean I have to trust him."

Logan ignored them and handed the mangled bag and lock of hair back to me. "Smell them."

I didn't want to, but I raised them both and breathed in, frowning when I struggled to draw their scent into me. They smelled wrong, like someone had taken them and watered them down, rendering them lifeless and muted and gray.

"What's wrong with them?" I said.

Logan shrugged a shoulder. "I dunno. Magic? A masking spell that didn't quite work?"

I sniffed them again, slower this time, trying to filter through the muffled strangeness. "Wait," I said, suddenly snapping to attention. "There's a scent … something I recognise."

"Mr. Green," Logan said.

It wasn't a question.

"But why?" I said, ignoring the satisfied smirk on Cayley's face as she rifled through the gemstones in the bowl by the door.

"I don't know." Logan's gaze was troubled. "It doesn't make sense."

"Is this supposed to intimidate me? Taunt me? And why kill Dr. Norlgren? What was the point?"

Cayley stopped. "To remove your protector. To leave you vulnerable."

"But I'm not the last of anyone's line! My family's alive. The prophecy might not even happen for centuries."

Haven's head snapped up. "About that. You don't have centuries. You don't even have a decade." She looked like someone had punched her in the stomach, and when she spoke again, her voice was shaky. "The Sapphire Eclipse is in ten days."

⁂

"I'm not coming out." I leaned my forehead against the cubicle door and wished I was human. "I'm going to stay here until it's over. Then I'll still be me and the world won't be destroyed."

"You have to come out," Haven said. "You'll miss Tuesday's History quiz if you don't."

I slowly opened the door. "That's the main thing you're worried about here? That I'll flunk out of History if I don't … I don't know, try and avoid becoming some sort of power-stealing creature of prophecy who'll destroy the world?"

"Well, when you put it like that." Haven put an arm around my shoulder and steered me toward the sinks. "Take a breath, wash your face, and we'll come up with a plan."

Five minutes later, I was back in my room, nauseous and scared, but willing to try something. I wasn't convinced we'd be able to come up with a workable plan —it sounded like the seer had been pretty certain the prophecy couldn't be stopped—but I couldn't give up. Even if I had no idea where to start.

"I think you should leave Mistwood," Cayley said. "Go into hiding somewhere."

"No." Haven's response was immediate. "She's safest here. There are wards, chimera, the faculty, and I've strengthened—"

"Like those things have done a great job so far." Cayley spun around on my desk chair, one leg folded up beneath her. "Whoever is after her obviously knows she's here. She needs to leave."

Logan gave Haven a small, tight smile. "Cayley might be right."

Irritation flickered through my blood. "Stop talking about me like I'm not here."

"Sorry," Haven said. "What do you think you should do?"

I picked up the small gray book from its place on Haven's bed and ran my fingers over the cover. Its title, so plain and simple, suddenly sparked something within me. "I think," I said, placing the book back down, "I need more information. Is it possible to change your destiny? Do you know?"

Haven sighed. "It's complicated. Once something has been predetermined, it usually—not always, but *usually*— takes place. Not always in the way that's expected, and not always in a way that makes sense. But it usually happens whether you want it to or not."

The spark turned into a flame. "But it doesn't *always* take place, right?"

Haven was already sitting in front of her laptop. "According to the SCC's official page on prophecies and divination, five hundred prophecies have come to pass in the last thousand years." She looked up, and her face was an eerie picture of light and shadow, a portrait of foreboding and regret.

"How many haven't come true?" Cayley asked.

"Three," Haven said, swallowing audibly. "There are only three that haven't."

The flame inside me wavered, but I held it close; I couldn't let it go out. "Well," I said, drawing myself up to my full height, "maybe it's time for a fourth."

I didn't know how I was going to do it, but I had to make sure nothing happened to my family. I had to be certain I wouldn't be the last of my line. I picked up my phone and stared at my mother's number, listed neatly at the top of the row of recent calls. I wanted to call her again, just to hear her voice, to tell her they were all in danger.

"How are you going to stop the prophecy?" Logan asked, his dark eyes worried.

I turned to Haven. "What can you do for my family? Protection spells? Wards? Whoever's after me will be after them. To make sure I'm the last of my line."

Haven's nose wrinkled as she thought. "I might be able

to do some distance work and put some protections on their house and on their vehicles. Maybe on your brother's school, as well."

I nodded. It wasn't perfect, but it was *something*. And maybe I could get them a message anonymously, tell them that—

"Hey," Cayley said suddenly, breaking into my thoughts. "You're from Woodville, aren't you?"

"Yeah. Why?"

"I have a cousin who lives near there." She pulled out her phone, her fingers flying over the screen. "He owes me a favor. Tell me the address and I'll get him and his buddies to watch out for them."

Relief surged through me, an odd sensation that dragged its way up through my stomach and chest, opening small windows of hope in places that had resigned themselves to darkness.

"He won't let anything happen to them," Cayley said, once I'd told her where they lived. "He's a PI. He's had a lot of experience."

"I'll get started on the spells." Haven pulled two large books out of her bookshelf and opened the largest one to the contents page, her finger trailing down the yellowing paper as she skimmed through the text.

"Okay." That was the most important thing sorted, but … "Will that be enough?"

Haven frowned. "The protection spells? And Cayley's cousin? It'll be—"

"No," I said, shaking my head. "I mean, will changing

one thing, making certain I'm not the last of anyone's line, be enough to stop the prophecy from happening?"

Haven's lips thinned. "I don't know."

"What about the ritual?" Logan said. He was calm on the surface, logical and clear, though his heart was a stutter in his chest. "You said the original spell could be reactivated only if certain steps were followed."

I grabbed his arm. "You're a genius. We can disrupt all the steps, come at it from multiple angles. Then it'll be impossible for the prophecy to happen."

"What *are* the steps of the ritual?" Cayley asked. "How many ways can we cause havoc?"

"To the ritual or to life in general?" Haven muttered, retrieving *Putere: Prophecy and Destiny* from her bed. "From what I've read, there aren't a lot of ways to hamper the ritual—it's not that complicated in terms of the actual proceedings—but the best way to avoid it is to either find the Impure Blade, or to stay around others at all times, especially on the night of the Sapphire Eclipse."

"Why?" Logan said.

"Because that's all they need. The magic from the original spell already exists within Emily. All they—whoever *they* are—need to do is wake it up. And for that, they just need Emily, the Impure Blade, and a sacrifice." She turned to me, her eyes darkening. "If you drink the blood of the sacrifice—and don't say you won't, because they'll be able to figure out a way to make that happen—then you'll turn into the *putere*. Easy."

"The Impure Blade," I said. "That's what I couldn't

remember before. When Dr. Norlgren was …" I stopped and swallowed painfully, trying to find a way to say it that didn't make it hurt. That didn't make guilt slice a hole through my chest. "He told me to find the blade. He didn't say anything else about it, but that must be the one he meant—the Impure Blade."

"He didn't happen to mention a location, did he?" Cayley said, though she clearly knew the answer.

"Wait." Logan's eyes widened. "Maybe they're trying to stop the prophecy, too."

"The people who attacked us? Who killed Dr. Norlgren?" I said, my voice rising. "If that's true, then they have a messed up way of going about it."

"Maybe they thought Dr. Norlgren was going to complete the ritual."

Haven shook her head. "That's all wrong. Dr. Norlgren was supposed to *stop* the prophecy from happening. It says so in the book. After the wise woman's warning, the elves nominated themselves to oversee the warlock's line. They wouldn't kill innocents, but they wouldn't let the prophecy happen either. The potential of the power was so great they made sure they had a way to control the *putere*—through the glow you saw on Dr. Norlgren, Em. And it's why they tried to keep the entire thing a secret. They didn't tell anyone in the warlock's line and only passed the knowledge of the spell and the prophecy down to their own descendants."

"Fat lot of good that did," Cayley said archly. "Someone else found out anyway."

"You can't control everything in life," Logan said, his voice low. "No matter how much you want to."

I knew that was true. After everything that had happened to me, I *knew* it with every fiber of my being. I lived it every day. But I couldn't let it stop me from trying. I didn't know how much agency I had over my own life, not anymore—*had I ever?*—but I would do everything in my power to stop that prophecy from happening. I would not let my parents and brother be killed. And I would not cause the destruction of our world.

Haven held up the thin, gray book. It was open to a page filled with foreign words and a single, hand-drawn picture. "We may not be able to control everything," she said, "but we can still find this."

I took the book from her. The paper was thin and desiccated beneath my fingertips, but the image was bright, the ink lines thin and precise and beautiful. "The Impure Blade," I said, studying the illustration of the long slender dagger.

"The one and only." Haven held her hand out for the book.

I ran my fingers across the image, even though I knew I shouldn't, wondering what it would feel like to hold the actual dagger in my hands, wondering if something in me would recognize it or hate it or want it. "I expected it to be more spectacular."

"You're not wearing any gloves," Haven said sharply as she took back the book. "The paper's fragile. And yes, I'll find it for you as soon as I've done the wards for your family. It shouldn't be too hard—just a simple locator spell."

"What about that?" Cayley pointed at the broken paper bag I'd left lying on the floor, the lock of hair still tucked safely inside.

I blew out a breath and shrugged. "I dunno."

Haven glanced at her phone. "Crap, I've missed three calls from Philip. And I don't have all the ingredients I need for the locator spell."

Cayley stood, her hair gathering itself up into a pony-tail and her lips turning red. "Tell me what you need and I'll go to the store." There was a small supply shop on campus, not far from the library. "Go see Philip—and don't tell him *anything*—and we can meet back here in twenty minutes."

Haven chewed her lower lip, then finally nodded. She recited a short list of ingredients and quantities for Cayley, who noted them down in her phone, then the two of them made their way to the door.

"You guys stay here," Haven said firmly. "This won't take long."

"And don't forget about that," Cayley said, nudging the paper bag with her shoe. "You can't trust anyone. It didn't get here on its own."

21

"What do you want to do?" Logan asked.

I picked up the bag and held it to my face. I could still smell Mr. Green, muted and strange, like an illusion or an afterimage. "I don't know."

"We could call him. Or go and see him. It's probably a mistake."

He looked so hopeful, like he could make the words real if he believed in them enough. But I wasn't buying it. I screwed up the bag and let it go; it dropped to the floor, as dismal as my heart.

"I trusted him," I said.

"I know." Logan's pulse sped up, but he didn't try to hide it. "I did, too. Part of me still does."

"Do you think he could've done it?"

Logan shook his head, his gaze fixed on the bag. "I don't know. I mean, he's always—" He shook his head again, and something almost like pain flashed across his face. "I told him everything. *Everything.* I can't— How could he have?"

I sat down on the edge of my bed with a thump and tossed a sweater over the paper bag. I didn't want to see it anymore. It wasn't just evidence of murder, of violence committed and violence pending, it was a statement of betrayal, executed by one of the few people in this school Logan and I had both trusted implicitly.

"I don't know." I chewed my lower lip as I thought. "I think he's done *something* though. I mean, his scent is on the bag. And when I saw him earlier today with Smith, he was really … odd. And scary. He didn't seem like himself."

"The prospect of gaining power can do that to a person." Logan sat down quietly beside me, close enough that I could feel the warmth of his body, but not close enough to touch. "It can change people in ways you could never imagine."

"I guess you never really know what's going on inside someone else's head." The room in front of me wavered, falling away as I pictured all of my therapy sessions, all of that time spent on Mr. Green's couch. I hadn't always liked talking about what was going on—hell, most of the time I'd despised it—but I'd always liked *him*. He'd been kind. Dependable. Thoughtful. But … "Why would he help me if he wanted to hurt me?"

Logan lay back on the bed and stared up at the ceiling. "I don't know."

I sighed, then lay back too. "I'm sorry."

"For what?"

"For a lot of things." I turned my head to face him. "I'm sorry for dragging you into this mess. I'm sorry for whatever's going on with Mr. Green. I'm sorry for what happened when we kissed in the woods."

Shit.

I hadn't meant to mention that. Ever.

Logan still stared up at the ceiling, his profile carved from marble. "Was it because of what I told you?"

"What you told me?" I blinked, not really understanding what he meant. "Do you mean—"

"The self-harm. The OCD." He looked at me then, his eyes searching mine before turning back to the neutrality of the ceiling. "Because I understand. You wouldn't be the first."

"No," I said vehemently. "It wasn't about that. It would never be about that. I just meant I was sorry I lost control. I didn't mean for my fangs to come out." My face flushed, and I put a hand on his arm. *You wouldn't be the first.* "I don't think we're talking about the same thing."

"My last girlfriend broke up with me when she saw the scars." Logan's voice was flat. "She didn't even know about the OCD. The scars were enough. And the rumors."

"Rumors about you?"

"About me. About both of us. She wanted something fun. And what she got was the opposite of that."

I wasn't sure what to say. In some ways, Logan was an enigma. He seemed to spend his life being whoever other people expected him to be. But I didn't have any expectations.

"Can I ask you a question?" I said.

He turned back to face me, his expression serious. "It depends what it is."

I didn't speak immediately. There was something in his gaze that made me pause, a sense of openness mixed with shame, like a weakness he was trying to both embrace and conceal. I didn't want to say the wrong thing. Because even though I knew I didn't have any expectations, I wasn't sure that *he* knew that. And if I said the wrong thing, he might withdraw from me forever.

I didn't want him to disappear.

"You can ask," he said, already shutting down. "I can guarantee it won't be worse than what I've already heard."

"It's nothing bad. At least, I don't mean it to be."

Heat flared across his skin.

I took a deep breath and hoped he wouldn't hate me. "I just want to understand. Why did you do it?"

Logan frowned. "Why did I do it? No one's asked me that in a really long time." He looked away again, and his next words were muffled. "Everyone has their theories. Some people think I'm crazy. Some think I'm a disappointment. Everyone else just thinks I'm a maladjusted fuck up."

"That's not true," I said softly. "You have friends. Haven. Cayley. *Me.*"

"Fine." His arm was tense under my hand. "But you're in the minority."

I drew circles on his skin with my fingertips. "I don't think it's as bad as you think it is. I mean, I haven't seen anyone shunning you in the halls. Yes, there was the rumor that Courtney and Vanessa and Danielle started, but—"

"Why do you think people were so quick to believe it?" he said, cutting me off. "They could smell the truth on you when you denied it. But that didn't matter. They believed what they wanted. Some of them are nice to my face because I'm the alpha's son, but I know what's said about me behind closed doors. And sometimes that spills over into the light."

"I don't—"

"I had a breakdown," he said abruptly. He sat, and my hand fell away from his arm. "I thought I was going crazy. Or maybe I thought I already *was* crazy. My mind would get stuck on things, like my thoughts were in a loop. They'd just spiral, over and over and over, and I couldn't stop them. I didn't know what was happening. It didn't make sense. I was counting, and changing my clothes five times a day, and I couldn't stop tapping. I wouldn't stand next to anyone on the stairs because I was scared I'd lose control and push them. I was frightened of every single decision I had to make, no matter how small. There was just—it was too much. It was relentless. All day, every day. And I couldn't control it."

"So you—" My breath caught in my throat.

"Yeah. I cut myself. With silver."

Anything else would've healed without leaving a scar.

"I wanted evidence on the outside," he said. "Those marks I made, they made it real. They were something tangible, something I could see and feel and deal with on a physical level. They made it so it wasn't just all in my head."

"So they were like a physical manifestation of your thoughts?" I asked, pushing myself up to sit.

"Yeah, in a way. And it was kind of like a safety valve. A way to relieve the tension." His hands were held tightly together, his fingers twisting. "For a while, it gave me control. Or an illusion of control. But in the end, I couldn't stop it. It controlled me."

A phone rang, loud and intrusive, and Logan fumbled in his pocket, his restless hands missing it on the first try. "Hey, what's up?" he finally said, managing to answer just before the voicemail kicked in.

Whoever was on the other line—Thomas, maybe?— was talking so fast I could barely make out the words.

"I've heard the rumors," Logan said slowly. "And no, I didn't kill anyone."

"I know you didn't kill anyone," the voice exclaimed through the phone. "Has Benedict heard?"

Logan's jaw tightened. "Yeah."

"Shit." It was definitely Thomas. "So is the alpha pissed?"

"What do you think?"

"Okay, yeah. Of course he is." Thomas said something else I didn't catch, then paused. "Are you okay?"

"Of course I am."

Thomas couldn't smell the lie, but I could.

"And Emily? What about—" Thomas paused again. "What about Haven?"

Logan's eyes cut to me. "They're both fine. But if you find out who started that rumor, tell me." He disconnected the call and scrolled through his messages before putting his phone back in his pocket.

I leaned my head against his shoulder. "I didn't mean for you to get mixed up in any of this."

He nudged my leg. "It's better than being bored."

I watched his fingers move against each other, skin against skin, and it struck me how smooth they were, a gentle contrast to the scars he'd shown me the night before. "Do you know why it started?" I said softly.

"Well, first I dropped in on you unannounced. And then we became friends. And then I wouldn't leave you alone until you told me about the prophecy. Simple, really."

It was my turn to nudge him. "You know that wasn't what I meant."

He shifted then, his shoulder moving awkwardly beneath my cheek. He smelled of carnations and mint leaves. Shame and truth. "It started after I changed for the first time. I was scared I wouldn't be able to control it. That I'd lose that connection to my human side and hurt some-one. And then there was the whole alpha thing—the pres-sure that came with knowing it would be my role one day."

He tilted his head to the side, his cheek resting on the top of my head. There was something awkward about it, a tension that meant we didn't fit together quite right, but it was also strangely comforting, that juxtaposition of warm and cold, of his body and mine. I didn't understand his fear of becoming alpha, but I was intimately familiar with the fear of a destiny you didn't want. And I knew what it was like to fear losing control. It was something I'd been scared of since I'd been turned.

Michael Miller had failed the Program.

It could easily have been me.

"I feel like I should've fought harder," Logan said, "but I didn't know what to do." He unclasped his hands, then drew them back together, his knuckles strained and white. "I'd missed six months of school and my parents were ready to send me away for good. But Mr. Green gave me some sessions over the phone, then flew out to Portland to work with me in person. I had to repeat seventh grade, but I wouldn't be here, in school and more-or-less functional, if it wasn't for him."

I lifted my head from his shoulder. "Maybe you're right. Maybe the scent of him on the bag is just a mistake." I didn't believe it, but I wanted it to be true. Mostly because I didn't want to take the value of Logan's experience with Mr. Green away from him. Not when he'd worked so hard and come so far.

"I know you don't believe that."

I just stared at the sweater that was covering the bag.

We sat there for a while longer, our legs touching but each of us lost in our thoughts, until Logan suddenly stood. "What if we're coming at this from the wrong angle?" he said. "What if whoever's behind all of this doesn't want to kill you? Maybe they want to steal the power from you, the way the warlock did from the woman." He looked at me, his brown eyes wide. "Or maybe they just want to destroy the world."

An uncomfortable knot bundled itself in the pit of my stomach. "I'm not sure that helps."

"Oh." Twin lines appeared between his brows. "Sorry."

I got up off the bed and stepped toward him, missing the warmth and the comfort of his touch. "It's okay." I put one hand on his arm, the other on his chest, my gaze settling on his lips. "You're right. It's something we should consider."

What are you doing?

Why are you thinking about kissing him when someone's sending you threats? When someone's killed Dr. Norlgren? When—

"Emily?" Logan's voice was husky. "Should we—"

The door burst open and we sprung apart, Logan stumbling over the sweater-covered bag. Neither of us had heard anyone coming. And we should have.

"Your house master's looking for you, Logan," Haven said as she stepped into the room.

Cayley slammed the door shut quickly behind her. "He wouldn't tell us why, but he's adamant that he needs to see you right now."

The strange moment of longing I'd felt, the desire for something warm and connected and so deeply, deeply *normal*, disappeared as the knot in my stomach tightened.

Was it something to do with the SCC? Did they want Logan to go back for more questioning? Did they think he was guilty? Did they think *we* were guilty?

Logan ran a hand through his hair. "I guess I'd better go."

"No, wait," Haven said. "Cayley and I were talking on our way upstairs and we think—"

"You mean *you* think," Cayley interrupted.

"Okay, whatever." Haven rolled her eyes. "*I* think we need to stick together. No more going anywhere alone until the Sapphire Eclipse is over. For any of us."

Logan sighed and pulled his phone out of his pocket. His pulse still beat a fraction too fast, and his shoulders sat a little too high, but not enough for anyone to notice. Not unless they were looking for it. "Are you sure that's necessary?"

Haven's expression gave no room for argument.

"Fine," Logan said. "I guess I'll get Thomas to meet me downstairs."

Haven lifted her phone and smiled. "It's already sorted. I told him you had a rough night."

"Great." Logan sighed again as he unlocked the window and hoisted himself up onto my desk. "He's going to think I'm losing it again."

"Don't tell him about the prophecy," Haven called as he slipped outside.

"What were you doing before we walked in the room?" Cayley said when Logan was gone. "Were we interrupting something?"

"No!" I pressed the backs of my hands to my suddenly burning cheeks. "We were just talking."

She smirked, then handed Haven the small bag she'd been carrying. It was emblazoned with the red and purple logo of the campus supply shop. "You two would be good together, you know."

"But the timing." I glanced up at the ceiling and tried to will the embarrassment away. "There's too much going on to even be thinking about boyfriends."

Cayley flopped down on my bed and leaned back, her ankles crossed in front of her. "You can't stop living your life just because you're busy. Or scared. It's about time someone gave Logan a chance again."

Haven nodded as she searched through the contents of the bag, then tipped it out onto her desk. "Cayley's right. It would be good for both of you. It's important to have things to look forward to, even when times are bad. *Especially* when times are bad."

Her lips had turned up into a dreamy smile, and the scent of Philip clung to her like cut-price perfume. "Oh, crap," I said, surprised I hadn't realized earlier. "You're in love. Like, *in love* kinda love. Does Philip know?"

"If he's perceptive." She placed an object from the bag —a long, thin stick that tapered down to a point at one end—onto the floor in the middle of the room, sobering quickly. With swift, efficient movements, she set four large candles at equal distances around it, then sprinkled something green and fragrant around each one. Finally, she pulled a thick, leather-bound book from her bookshelf. "I need a map that shows me your old house and your brother's school. And some photos, as well, if you've got them. I want to get your family warded as quickly as possible."

Everything else slipped away, and I sat down on the bed next to Cayley, and we watched Haven work. She studied the maps application I'd brought up on my phone, then moved on to the photos of my family that I'd secretly saved from my brother's socials.

"This shouldn't be too hard," she said, more to herself than to us. She muttered something under her breath as she consulted her book one last time, then smiled. "Another sprinkle of rosemary and we should be good to go."

Like a lot of the magic I'd witnessed at Mistwood, the spell was quiet. Understated. It was based around intention and impact as opposed to spectacle. Haven's voice was low as she chanted softly in Latin, lighting the candles, her words rising and falling with the cadence of the flames. A woody aroma filled the room.

"*Protego*," she said, lifting the thin wooden stick that she'd placed down earlier. "*Contego*." She drew something in the air above the map, and it left a faint trail of golden light. "*Cingo*." The glow intensified, though it was still muted, a delicate version of the lights I'd seen spark across the windows and walls the night Dr. Norlgren had died.

I looked at Cayley, but she just shrugged.

A few more air-drawn symbols and three quiet words

were all the spell needed to be complete. When the trails of light faded away, Haven extinguished the candles.

"One down, one to go," she said. "I'm going to find the Blade."

"Do you need us to do anything?" Cayley asked.

Haven shook her head. "This is an easy one."

She handed my phone back to me before clearing away the rosemary and placing the tapered wooden stick away in her trunk. After retrieving the same pendulum I'd seen her use the other day, she set *Putere: Prophecy and Destiny* down on the floor and positioned her phone next to it, the screen already bright with a zoomed out map of the world.

I'd expected the locator spell to work quickly, like it had the time before, but ten minutes later the pendulum was still hanging limp and motionless in Haven's hand.

"Is everything okay?" I whispered.

Haven kept chanting, the words getting louder and louder.

Then the pendulum sparked, and we were plunged into darkness.

22

"WHAT JUST HAPPENED?" I said, panic constricting my throat. Something was wrong. Seriously wrong. The room was heavy with darkness, the kind of inky blackness that wends its way through you and settles there, until all you are is shadow is fear.

Why can't I see anything?

"Haven?" Cayley's voice was charged, electric and sharp. "Tell me you did that on purpose."

I reached out into the darkness, my heart pounding in my throat. I expected resistance, something solid in the black, but there was nothing there except empty space. "Haven, where are you?" I moved slowly toward the center of the room. "Say something. *Please.*"

She didn't answer. She didn't speak or move or breathe.

I couldn't hear her heartbeat.

"Shit," Cayley muttered. Something clicked mechanically. A light switch, angry and fast. "The power's out."

I breathed in slowly. The scent of magic and fear, of vanilla and smoke and spice, drifted weakly around me, overpowered by something bitter and burned. For once, I didn't wish I was human. Instead, I wished my vampiric abilities were better.

I pulled my phone out of my pocket. "Is your phone working?"

"Nope. Yours?"

I shook my head automatically before realizing she wouldn't be able to see it. "It's completely dead."

There was a gasp. A gulping of air.

A heartbeat.

"Haven?" I crouched down low, my fingers brushing the floor, and moved toward the sound.

Her heartbeat faltered.

Stuttered.

Stopped.

"No," I said, moving faster. "Wake up. You need to wake up."

The doorknob rattled and Cayley swore again, louder this time. "We're locked in."

My fangs descended and I tried to connect with my abilities, to amplify then, to somehow make them better. I didn't know how it would help. All I knew was that I couldn't lose Haven. I wouldn't be responsible for another death.

"Em," Cayley said. "I—"

Haven screamed, high pitched and primal, an explosion of unadulterated power.

The lights came back on.

Haven was standing in the middle of the room, a living, breathing, gasping, beautiful mess. Her limbs were shaking, her cheeks sunken in, and blood trickled from her nose. Her skin was almost translucent.

And for a moment, none of that mattered.

She was alive.

Alive.

I crossed the room, my own body unsteady with fear and relief, and gathered her into my arms. "Are you all right?" I knew she wasn't—I could feel the dread on her skin; it clung to her like smoke clings to hair—but the words still came out, dense and pointless. Because I hoped, despite what I knew, that she'd prove me wrong and tell me everything was fine.

"She knows," she said, her voice raw. "She saw me looking for it."

"Who saw you?" I said, leading her over to her bed.

"I don't know." Haven shook her head like she was trying to clear it. "But she's strong. Stronger than me."

"That wasn't like any location spell I've ever seen," Cayley said, her hands curling into fists at her sides. "What the hell did you do?"

"What I was supposed to! I searched for the Impure Blade." She put a hand over her mouth and coughed thickly. "But—"

"Haven," I said, alarm coursing through me. "You're

bleeding." It was more than just a nosebleed—tiny patches of red dotted the corners of her mouth.

"What happened?" Cayley grabbed Haven's wrist and turned it; Haven's palm was flecked with blood. "Why are you coughing up blood? And what the hell is that on your arm?"

Cayley sounded unquestionably angry—her tone was caustic, almost cruel—but she couldn't hide the scent of her panic. It was brittle yet fierce, a foreign thing that had suddenly become all-encompassing. And that scared me more than anything. Because Cayley was never frightened.

"The Blade is protected." Haven curled her fingers into her palm, then wrenched her arm away from Cayley's grasp. "I tried to get past the spells, but they were strong. Too strong. I made a connection with the Blade, but—" She paused, coughing again. "There was someone with it. A woman. A witch."

I handed her a tissue from the box on top of her dresser and watched as she wiped the blood from her lips. "We need to take you to the infirmary," I said when she was done.

"No! You can't." She tossed the tissue aside and darted back to the center of the room, straightening one of the candles which had been knocked askew. "I have to try again before she makes her protections even stronger."

Cayley glanced at the door. "I'm usually the first to agree to something stupid, but this time I think Emily's right. You need to go to the infirmary."

"I'm fine." Haven picked up the crystal she'd used for the spell, her eyes widening. "Holy crap. She broke my best crystal." She rocked back on her heels and coughed so hard her body bent double. Her breath was a rattle in her chest.

"No more spells." Cayley tried the door handle, the relief evident in her eyes when it opened. "We're taking you to the infirmary. Now."

"But I need to help—"

"You need to help yourself," I said, cutting her protests short.

"But I heard her, Em." Another cough. Another splatter of blood. "She said your name. She knows who you are."

"We don't need the Impure Blade," Cayley said, her voice low. "Isaac's still protecting Emily's family. That'll be enough to disrupt the prophecy."

She sounded so certain.

I wished I felt the same way.

"What if it's not?" Haven said, echoing my thoughts. "I need to do more." She impatiently swiped at a lock of hair that had fallen across her forehead and left a smear of blood, bright red and angry, across her skin.

Then her legs gave way.

"We're going," Cayley said.

We helped Haven stand and maneuvered her toward the door. She was fragile and thin, like she might break beneath the weight of our hands, though she still burned with determination. She moved slowly, one step after another, me propping her up on one side, Cayley on the other.

"She's coming for you, Em," she whispered when we finally made it outside. "And I won't be here to look after you."

The skin on the back of my neck crawled, but I forced my lips into a smile. "I'm a vampire. I'll be fine."

"I'll stay in your room," Cayley added. "Em won't be left alone."

Haven coughed again as we walked down the path, and a few people passing looked at her with concern. We'd been lucky to make it out of Worthington unnoticed—it was lunchtime, so almost everyone was at the dining hall —but we couldn't hide her entirely. And there were already so many rumors.

"What are we gonna tell people?" I whispered as Haven wiped her mouth with the back of her hand. "We need some sort of plausible explanation for this."

Haven shook us both off. "I'll walk on my own. It's not far."

"Don't be an idiot." Cayley slipped a hand under Haven's elbow just as she started to fall. "If anyone asks, we'll tell them you're sick. You're a witch, but you're still technically human. You're not immune to everything like the rest of us."

"And the doctor?" I took Haven's other arm. "What will we tell her?"

We all paused as Mr. Dufort strode into view, carrying his briefcase and an assortment of books.

"Act natural," Cayley hissed, and we both let Haven go, though neither of us moved from beside her.

"Good evening." Mr. Dufort's washed-out eyes were filled with concern. "Is everything all right?"

Cayley's mouth stretched into a smile. "Haven isn't feeling well." Technically, it was the truth. "We're taking her to the infirmary."

The ancient vampire's head tilted slightly to the left as he observed the three of us. He was an otherworldly creature, a being of authority and influence, but his gaze held so much compassion that I almost forgot for a moment he wasn't human.

"Would you like me to accompany you?" he said, tucking the stack of books in closer to his body.

Yes.

"No." Haven shook her head. "We're almost there."

Cayley pointed at the books in his arms. "You look busy. We don't want to take up any of your time."

Mr. Dufort laughed, a rolling chuckle that made his graying cheeks bloom lightly with color. "I'm a vampire. I have nothing but time."

Nothing but time.

It was a light-hearted remark, but it turned the inside of me cold. I didn't know how old Mr. Dufort was—not exactly, anyway—but I figured he was about the same age as Mr. Olaru. They had the same slightly musty odor, like they wore the weight of their years on their skin. But while Mr. Olaru kept his predatory side close to the surface, never hiding the monster that lurked within, Mr.

Dufort was polished and refined, and I wondered what happened that had made them that way.

Will I be one of the ones who loses their humanity? One of the ones who loses it all?

"Thank you," Haven said. "We'll be fine, though."

Mr. Dufort inclined his head. "As you wish. Remember though, when you get to be as old as I am, you find you've already seen everything." His gaze slipped down to the silver marking on Haven's arm. "Nothing surprises me anymore."

Haven moved, just enough to hide the silver swirl. "I'm sure it doesn't."

Mr. Dufort's elegant stride carried him away, and when he was finally out of earshot I turned to Haven. I wasn't sure what I'd missed; I just knew that I'd missed *something*. "What was that about?"

"You mean the way he was staring at my arm?" She shrugged and took a halting step forward. "Some of the older staff have issues with my tattoos, even though they pretend they don't. I try to keep them covered, but …" She trailed off, coughing again.

"Let's go." Cayley took Haven's arm and smiled insincerely at a couple of freshmen who stared openly as they passed. "Didn't your parents teach you not to stare?"

One of them snapped a picture on his phone.

"Great," I muttered. "Now everyone will know."

We hurried to the infirmary as fast as we could. Which was to say, not fast at all. At least four people took pictures, three asked if Haven was on drugs, and two questioned whether we'd killed anyone lately. By the time the medical center came into view, my fangs were tingling and the hunger was pushing to be set free.

"What's our story?" asked Cayley as she reached out to steady Haven at the bottom of the steps.

"The truth." Haven suddenly bent double, her face screwed up in pain. Fresh blood dripped from her nose. "At least some version of it."

"What *is* the truth?" I said. "Besides someone seeing you through the spell."

Haven rose slowly. Everything about her was hollow. "The truth is simple. I wasn't strong enough. I couldn't get past all of the protection spells—there was more than one on the Blade—and when I got close, I was attacked. I couldn't see who did it, but I could hear her. And feel her." She paused to cough, and a chimera, hulking and grim, came over to survey us from the edge of the roof.

"Can they hear us from up there?" I whispered, staring up at the lion-faced guard.

Cayley shrugged. "Probably."

"It doesn't matter." Haven took one step forward. Then another. "I fucked up. I deserve whatever punishment I get."

"That's not true—" I started.

"It *is* true, and you know it. I could feel her pulling at my magic, sucking all the light and energy out of the room. Out of me." She held up her arm, showing us the sinuous marking that snaked its way across her skin. "I fought back with everything I had, but she still left me with this. A permanent reminder that she beat me."

"So she marked you?" I said, still not understanding exactly what the silver swirl was.

"Not exactly. This mark—" Another pause. Another cough. "It's the result of the collision of our magic—mine light, hers dark. It's rare, but when the magic's strong enough …" Haven met my gaze and her expression was bleak, as if all the joy had been leeched from her body. "She's dangerous, Em. You have to promise me you'll be careful."

"I will," I said quietly.

We managed to get her inside the medical center, and the administration assistant at the main desk blanched at the sight of us, then immediately called for the nurse. A few minutes later, Haven was sitting in an examination room, a blood pressure cuff around her arm and a little plastic heart rate monitor on her finger.

"What's this?" Ms. Park lifted Haven's arm—the one without the blood pressure cuff on it—to look at the new silver marking. She leaned forward and inhaled. "It smells like magic. What kind of spell did you say you were doing?"

Haven shrugged, then coughed loudly, avoiding the question.

"Emily? Cayley?" Ms. Park turned to us, her expression firm. "Do you know what she did?"

I glanced at Cayley, who looked as apprehensive as I felt. We hadn't come up with a reasonable explanation, and the thought of lying about what had happened didn't sit well with me. If the medical staff didn't know the truth, Haven might get the wrong treatment. It might even make her worse.

"Well?" Ms. Park checked Haven's temperature, then removed the cuff from her upper arm, before typing up some quick notes on the computer on the nearby desk. When she was done, she turned back to the three of us. "I need to know what's going on."

Cayley opened her mouth, but Haven shook her head. "I was doing a locator spell," she said. "Something went wrong."

Ms. Park nodded. "What were you trying to locate?"

Haven folded her hands in her lap. "I can't tell you."

"And I can't help you if I don't know what's going on." Ms. Park rubbed a hand on the back of her neck and sighed. "Can you tell me anything that might help? Anything at all."

Haven was quiet for a moment, each breath she took rattling as she thought, then she told Ms. Park everything. Well, almost everything. She didn't mention the Impure Blade by name, and she didn't mention the prophecy. When she was done, Ms. Park nodded.

"That gives us something more to go on," she said. "I'm going to get Dr. Patterson now. Stay here, and don't remove the heart monitor."

Even I could tell Haven's pulse was erratic.

"How dangerous is this?" I said quietly when Ms. Park

had closed the door behind her. "The blood, the cough, the mark. What's going to happen to you?"

Haven shrugged and slumped back in her chair. "I don't know. It depends on exactly what the magic did to my body."

"But you're gonna recover, right?" I leaned forward and took her hand. It was cold and clammy, and I squeezed it gently.

She smelled of fear and bitter magic, but she gave me a shaky smile. "Dealing with Mr. Olaru—*and* my parents when they find out what I've done—is gonna make this seem like a walk in the park."

Cayley walked over to Ms. Park's desk and glanced over the pile of papers stacked neatly beside the computer. "He won't do anything to you. Your parents donate more money to this school than everyone else's combined."

Haven screwed up her face, but I held a finger up to my lips. "They're coming," I mouthed silently.

Seconds later, Dr. Patterson swept into the room, her sensible shoes carrying her quickly and quietly across the floor. "I hear there's been a situation," she said to Haven, her tone brusque. "Ms. Park, get me the blood pressure cuff. And you two—" She turned to Cayley and I. "Leave. I need to concentrate."

"No," I blurted out without thinking. "She can't—"

"Now!" Dr. Patterson's eyes flashed.

I flinched, and my fangs slid out, but I let Ms. Park usher me toward the door. Cayley followed close behind.

"Be careful," I said to Haven. "Okay?"

We don't know who we can trust.

"She'll be well looked after," Ms. Park said, putting a hand on my shoulder. "And you can come back tomorrow during visiting hours."

"Em?" Haven said, coughing again. She smeared more blood across her face with the back of her hand. "Tell Philip where I am." Her eyelids fluttered closed, but she forced them back open. "And Logan."

"Ms. Park," Dr. Patterson barked. "I need you over here." She placed a number of implements, some obviously medical, some possibly magical, onto the counter at the far end of the room. "Promptly."

Ms. Park smiled gently, then closed the door in our faces.

"What do we do now?" Cayley said.

I slumped back against the nearest wall, trying to clear my head, trying to focus on what needed to be done—*do I know what needs to be done?*—but I groaned when I realized who was coming around the corner.

"Now we deal with him," I whispered, so low I wasn't sure Cayley even heard.

"You have a gift for finding trouble, Miss Sanderson," Mr. Olaru said when he saw us. "And you, Miss Rodriguez." His voice was as cold and sharp as the bones in his cadaverous face. Long, skeletal fingers folded over each other until his hands were clasped together. "Is there something you'd like to tell me?"

"No, sir," I said quickly.

"We were just leaving," Cayley said. "It's almost fourth period."

She dragged me away, each footfall an echo of danger, and when I glanced back Mr. Olaru bared his teeth, his pale eyes boring into mine. "I will be seeing you again soon," he said. "Very soon."

I didn't blink until the doors were closed firmly behind us. And I didn't breathe again until Worthington Hall came into view.

"So when do you think Mr. Olaru's going to call you in to see him?" Logan said, taking a bite of lasagne, his dark eyes worried as he looked at me across the dining hall table.

"Hopefully never." I shifted in my seat, trying to get comfortable, while my dinner sat untouched in front of me. We were tucked away at the back of the room—Logan, Cayley, Thomas, and me—and all I wanted was to be somewhere else. To be some*one* else. I was scared, sinking under the weight of the prophecy, and terrified that I'd take everyone else down with me.

"What *I* don't understand," Thomas said, spearing a carrot with his fork, "is everything. What happened to Haven? Why is she in the infirmary? And why are you all so secretive all the time?"

Because I'm supposed to destroy the world.

"I—" I started, but I didn't know what to say. I didn't

know Thomas as well as the others. We ate together at almost every meal, we shared three of the same classes, and we'd bonded briefly over our former human lives. He was Logan's brother. But he still didn't know about the prophecy. And I wasn't sure I wanted him to.

Cayley nudged me with her elbow.

Knowing about the prophecy could make him a target.

Thomas frowned and stabbed another carrot with his fork.

But what if not knowing makes him an even easier target?

"There's this thing," I said slowly, hoping I was making the right decision. I didn't want to tell him—too many people knew already. But being friends with me could be enough to put him in danger. Maybe I should've told him weeks ago. "There's a prophecy."

Thomas frowned harder. "A prophecy? About Haven?"

I shook my head and put a finger to my lips and hoped no one had heard him. "About me."

It didn't get any easier, no matter how many times I explained it. But I told him everything, and by the time I was done, Thomas' bright blue eyes were wide with surprise.

"Holy shit," he whispered. "Way to jump in at the deep end."

"Huh?"

"Nine months ago, you were human," he said, his voice still low. "And now you're a vampire. A vampire who's part of an ancient prophecy." He leaned forward, his angular body awkward, his dark hair in disarray. "That's a lot to take in."

"Yeah, I guess." I half-heartedly pushed my food around with my fork, then shoved the plate away. "I'm not going to let it happen, though. *We're* not going to let it happen."

I hope.

Logan tapped lightly on the table with his fingers. Once, twice, three times. "Until the Sapphire Eclipse has passed," he said to Thomas, "none of us should go anywhere alone." He tapped twice more, then clenched his hand into a fist.

"I guess that's why you just happened to be walking past every one of my classes all week," Thomas said, his forehead wrinkling as he glanced at his brother's hand. "I couldn't figure out why you'd been lying to me."

"We need to be careful," I said. "All of us. Being associated with me could make you a target."

Thomas paled. "Do you really think—"

"Nothing's going to happen," Cayley said firmly. "It's just a precaution."

Logan's fist unfurled.

"We just want to make sure everyone's safe," I said.

"What about Haven?" Thomas blinked, his irises flashing yellow. "She's alone in the infirmary. How is that safe?"

"She's fine." Cayley's voice held a thread of uncertainty.

Logan started tapping again, his fingers moving rhythmically against the scarred wooden surface of the table.

"What exactly happened to her?" Thomas' eyes had returned to their regular blue, but his body was tense, his wolf stalking just below the surface. "You said she was sick. Something about a spell that went wrong? She was looking for something?"

I nodded.

Thomas stood. "I have to go."

"You can't." Cayley put a hand on his arm. "They won't let you in to see her."

"They won't let anyone in," I added.

Cayley and I had gone back to the infirmary on the way to the dining hall, hoping to see how Haven was, but Ms. Park wouldn't let us into her room. She wouldn't even tell us if she was awake or not. "I know this is hard," she'd said, "but we can't permit visitors right now. Come back tomorrow. And try not to worry."

Try not to worry.

It was impossible.

The last time I'd seen Haven she'd barely been able to move through her weakness and pain. She'd been coughing up blood. She'd been marked.

And now she wasn't even answering her phone.

My stomach turned.

Thomas shook off Cayley's arm, his eyes blazing with shards of amber. "I'm going," he said. "I don't care if they won't let me in. I'll find a way."

"No." Logan got to his feet, suddenly calm. Warm, fragrant power drifted around him, reaching out to the rest of us. "We need to follow the correct processes. We can't cause a scene."

Thomas glowered. "But she's your best friend. And she's—"

"Being looked after," Logan said, his power still swirling around us. "We'll finish up here, then go back to our rooms."

Thomas looked like he was going to say something, but he slowly sat back down, the amber bleeding from his eyes until they were nothing more than troubled blue.

I dragged my plate back toward me as Logan sat down, the heat of his power still flowing around us. Everything smelled of fur and wolf and forest. There was something inviting about it, something vital and living and *real*, like I was seeing the world through different eyes, but for all its weight, it was also strangely muted. Like he was holding a part of it back.

What would it be like if he let it all free?

I studied him carefully as I took a bite of cold lasagne, and then suddenly, he was just Logan again. The heat, the scent, the power—he'd drawn it all back inside of himself, leaving me cold.

We finished up quickly, none of us talking, then stacked our dirty plates on one of the metal carts at the side of the room.

"Do you need to feed before we go?" Logan asked me as he wiped his hands on a napkin and threw it in the trash. "The feeding room's open for another fifteen minutes."

I shook my head and reached out and took Logan's hand. "I'm fine. Hey, why did your housemaster want to see you earlier?"

Logan's fingers wound around mine. "He just wanted to check that I'm coping with things. He knows about Haven. And he knows my history."

I took a step toward him, closing the gap between us. "And are you?" I said. "Coping with things?"

"It's—"

"Em," Cayley called from where she and Thomas stood waiting by the door. "Are you guys coming?"

Logan squeezed my fingers. "We'd better go."

Nobody paid us any attention as we made our way outside, but my skin felt tight—too hot, too cold, too *much*. I wanted to fix this. *All* of this. Haven, the Sapphire Eclipse, my family, my friends. I wanted it all to be right.

Ten days.

That's all I had to get through. Ten more days.

"Has anyone heard from Haven?" Thomas pulled his phone out of his pocket and stared at the screen. "She hasn't replied to any of my messages."

"Maybe her phone died," Cayley said, her head down as she checked her own phone.

Guilt gnawed at my insides. Haven wouldn't have done the spell in the first place if it wasn't for me. "Maybe she's asleep," I said, scrolling through my messages.

Nothing.

"I hate this," Thomas said, his fingers curling tightly around his phone. "I fucking hate not knowing."

"We all do," Cayley said.

"But I really—" Thomas stopped. Closed his eyes. Dark lashes lay soft above his razor-sharp cheekbones, and his thin chest expanded and contracted with several shallow breaths. "I need to take a walk. Now."

Cayley's expression softened. "I'll come with you." She hooked a hand gently around his upper arm. "We can take a detour through the forest. Head to the dorms the long way."

"Text me when you get to Worthington," Logan said.

"Do you think he'll be okay?" I asked Logan when they were out of sight. "He was really … on edge."

Logan sighed. "I dunno if you've noticed, but he has a thing for Haven. Has done for a really long time."

"Yeah, I know."

"It's not just that, though." Logan swallowed, his fingers tightening around mine. "Do you know about Marcus?"

"Yeah." I'd first heard Cayley mention him the night we'd gone to Adventure Gardens. Later, back in our dorm, I'd asked Haven who he was. She'd seemed almost embarrassed when she'd heard his name, but finally, haltingly, she'd told me what had happened. They'd dated, back when Haven was a freshman and Marcus was a senior. He'd been kind to her at first, a real gentleman. Until the night he'd posted all of her private messages, including photos, online for the entire school to see. All because she'd refused to sleep with him.

"He was such an asshole," Logan said. "Haven was so

humiliated. Thomas found her that night, right after she'd realized what Marcus had done. She wanted to run away and never come back."

I nodded. "She told me Thomas promised her he'd never let her get hurt again."

"They weren't empty words." Logan's hand didn't leave mine as we moved away from the dining hall. "Everyone knows Haven's perfectly capable of looking after herself— once she'd gotten over her initial shock she called out Marcus' behaviour in front of the entire school. But Thomas…" He shrugged, a strangely helpless gesture. "He took that promise seriously."

"No wonder he's so upset." I tilted my head in the direction of a small wooden bench that sat tucked away in an alcove, set back from the path and almost hidden behind a row of leafy bushes. "Shall we sit? It's just … I don't want to go back to my room yet. Haven won't be there."

We walked down the path and sat, Logan's leg pressed against mine, our fingers still tangled together. "We can stay as here as long as you need," Logan said.

I lay my head against his shoulder and breathed in the familiar scent of boy and wolf. The night was still and quiet around us, the alcove bathed in shadow. I wasn't sure how long we sat there, side by side, warm against cold, but it was almost like the world had paused, and for the first time in a long time, I felt like I could finally exhale. Even if it was just for a moment.

"I should've been there," Logan said, finally breaking the silence. "Maybe I could've done something."

I pulled away, turning so I could see his face. "No. This isn't your fault. If it's anyone's fault, it's mine."

Logan's brows drew downward. "You didn't cause this."

The guilt churning in my stomach didn't believe him. "Haven will be okay." I said it to convince myself, because I needed it to be true. "She's strong. And resilient. She's going to be fine."

Logan's expression was calm, but he couldn't hide the sharp intake of breath, or the increase in his pulse. He began to tap gently on the wooden bench, his fingers moving quickly, deliberately. He shifted, trying to conceal it with his body, but it was too late.

He looked away.

"Logan," I said quietly. "Did I say something wrong?"

"I'm fine." The tapping stopped. His fingers clenched.

I bit my lip, but didn't say anything else. I couldn't force him to tell me what was going on.

He sighed, drawn out and tired, a sigh that carried everything he wouldn't—or couldn't—say. And then he whispered, "It's both."

"Both?"

Shame colored his features. "There was something you said … but it's also fine." He thrust a hand awkwardly through his already messy hair. "Honestly, I'm okay. This is just an old habit that comes back when I'm tired or stressed. I've gotten it under control before. I'll do it again."

And he would. I could hear the strength in his voice. But—

"What was it?" I asked. "What did I say that made it worse? I don't want to do it again."

Logan's gaze cut to mine, his eyes darker than usual under lowered lashes. "It's stupid."

I wound my fingers through his and waited. His pulse beat hard against my skin.

"I don't even know how to explain it. I guess, I don't do well with absolutes. You know, things like, *she'll be okay*, or *that won't happen*. Or *I'll do it again*. It makes me nervous." He coughed, clearing the words from his throat. "The tapping helps. For a while, anyway. Until it makes it worse."

I leaned over and kissed him on the cheek. Then he turned his head, and his lips caught mine.

Our phones beeped.

"Shit." Logan pulled away.

We both scrambled around for our phones. "It could be Haven," I said, pressing the home button.

Logan was already reading. "It's Cayley. It says: *meet you outside Worthington in 15 mins. Thomas is okay.*"

I leaned back and lifted my face to the sky. My heart pounded in my ears. "I guess we should go."

Logan tucked a stray piece of hair behind my ear. "We could stay for five more minutes."

When he brought his lips to mine, I wished we could stay forever.

<hr>

Later that night, something woke me, just before dawn. I hadn't been asleep long, maybe half an hour, but I rubbed my eyes and pushed myself up to sit. Cayley was sound asleep in Haven's bed, her chest rising and falling rhythmically, one hand resting under the pillow. Other than that, the room was still.

I checked my phone, then swung my legs over the side of the bed, unable to hold back a small smile. I'd missed a message from Logan. It was just a simple *good night*, but it felt like more. I liked knowing that he was thinking about me, that I was present in his thoughts, even when we were apart. It made me feel less adrift in the world. Less alone. Like I might be able to find a place where I belonged, a *life* where I belonged, even if it didn't look the way I'd always imagined.

Maybe it could look better.

I didn't have my family, not anymore, but I had friends who cared about me, and a boyfriend—the word had come up more than once on our walk back to Worthington—who made my heart happy. Haven was going to be fine—she'd finally been allowed to text us, just before curfew, letting us know she was feeling better and might be allowed out in a day or two. And Thomas had regained his usual control.

As soon as we got through the night of the Sapphire Eclipse, everything would be fine.

I slipped my feet into my sneakers, leaving the laces undone as I stumbled to the door, yawning. Cayley looked so peaceful I decided not to wake her. I was only going to the bathroom. It wouldn't take long.

I didn't realize anything was wrong until I was on my way back to my room. The hallway was quiet. *Too* quiet. It almost crackled with the kind of eerie stillness that falls right before a storm.

I walked faster, my sneakers silent on the wooden floor.

The bulb in the nearest lamp flickered.

I wished I'd brought my phone.

"Emily Sanderson." It was a familiar whisper, one that sent shivers crawling across my skin. "We're ready for you now ... *putere.*"

I opened my mouth to scream.

And nothing came out.

Panic gripped me, seizing my chest and my limbs.

No, it wasn't just panic.

It was the spell.

"You can't get away, *putere*." There was a laugh, quiet and deep and satisfied. "There's nothing you can do. Not this time."

I tried again to scream, frantically drawing breath and forcing it back out, but it was useless. My voice didn't work.

"Hurry up." Another laugh. "We're waiting."

My body turned, my legs no longer under my own control, and I began walking toward the stairs. Each movement I made was a step toward the unknown, a step away from safety. I couldn't smell him or see him, but I knew it was Derek. His voice grated along my skin as he laughed. But … how was he back on school grounds? Who was he working for? Mr. Green? The unknown witch who'd marked Haven?

What were they going to do to me?

I fought against the spell with everything I had, drawing deep on that power that lay hidden inside me, that indefinable spark of magic that made me both predator and human, that gave me speed and strength and fangs. But even though my incisors slid down, I couldn't regain control.

My hand glided along the bannister as I walked down the stairs. I hadn't put it there, and I couldn't move it away. Flames burned in my chest, the anger and terror fighting to find a way out. Because I wasn't just scared of what they—whoever *they* were—might do to me. I was scared of what they might make me do.

I wasn't in control.

And I needed to be in control.

The only thing you can control is yourself and how you respond.

Logan's words came back to me, and I tried to hold onto them as I walked toward the front door of Worthington Hall. I didn't know when I'd be in control of my body again, but at least I could try and manage my emotions. Because even though remaining calm seemed impossible in my current situation, it might be the only thing that could save me. I just needed to wait for Derek to make a mistake.

"You're almost there," he whispered. "Open the door."

No.

"Step outside."

My body betrayed me.

The only thing you can control is yourself and how you respond.

Derek wouldn't win. I wouldn't let him.

"Are you scared, *putere*? You should be."

Terror lodged itself in my throat, but I swallowed it down.

I inhaled. Exhaled.

"You know this is going to hurt," he said.

I wished I could scream.

My legs carried me over the threshold and out into the night, where the stars were almost ready to meet the day. The first strains of light, dusty yellow and pink, bled into the slowly lifting black, and suddenly it all felt too much. It was the first sunrise I'd seen since I'd been turned. It would probably be my last.

"Turn around."

Adrenaline fought through the exhaustion that came with the rising sun, but my body still turned, slow and impatient, until finally I saw him. Derek Watson. He was tall—taller than I remembered—and his broad shoulders stretched his white T-shirt tight. His mouth was curled up in a smirk.

"Asshole," I mouthed, exaggerating the shape of the word to make sure he could read it.

"What's that?" He sauntered toward me, his smirk turning into something more triumphant. He knew he'd already won. "Did you forget? You can't talk, bitch."

"Fuck you," I mouthed.

His hand was fire across my cheek. "Shut up. I only have to deliver you alive. They didn't say you had to be unharmed." He grabbed my arm and pulled me roughly onto the path. "Keep walking."

I didn't have a choice.

The school was deserted as we made our way to the front entrance. We passed quietly beneath the burning lamps that lit the paths. Their yellow glow, soft beneath black decorative casings, had become redundant—the sun slowly crested the horizon. The school's chimera, with their familiar hulking frames, were nowhere to be seen.

"Hurry up," Derek barked.

Tiredness pulled me down, slowing my legs even through the spell.

"I said, *hurry up*."

My feet got tangled up in each other and I fell, landing brutally on my hands and knees. Rough cobblestone bit into my skin, but I dragged myself forward, impelled by a magic that was stronger than I was.

Derek turned and saw me, then cursed loudly, his lips curling into a violent sneer. "It's only a bit of sunlight," he said. "You're so fucking weak." He strode back toward me, and I tried not to cringe at the sight of his boots, black with steel caps, coming closer and closer.

Inch by inch I moved toward him. I was being torn in two, split between the spell that kept moving me forward and the sun that simmered in my blood. The last thing I felt was the heat of Derek's skin as he hauled me up to stand. My feet left the ground and I tried to kick him, my fangs grazing my lower lip with the effort, but neither the spell nor the sun would let me.

I opened my mouth in a silent scream.

And then there was only blackness.

I woke up in a car. It was moving fast, the tires loud against the road beneath us. My wrists and ankles were bound with something rough, probably rope. I kept my eyes closed, but I reached out with my other senses, listening and smelling for something that might tell me exactly what was going on. The heat of the sun itched under my skin.

"—go there. No, dumbass. Not there. *There*. Down that one."

Ugh. Derek.

Everything came back in a flash.

"You drive, then." It was another voice, familiar and threatening.

"Shut up, Smith," Derek said.

"You shut up." The menace in Smith's voice turned dark. "You're so busy worrying about my driving that you haven't even noticed she's awake. Do your job, asshole."

My eyes flew open, and I tried to sit.

I couldn't move my legs, but my arms were finally back under my own control. I desperately strained at the ropes that held them down. "Let me go," I screamed, adrenaline briefly punching through the magic-and-sun-induced grogginess.

"The spell's wearing off," Smith said. He sounded both terrible and matter-of-fact all at once.

"What do you even want from me?" I said hotly, catching the end of a knot between my fingers and thumb. Something burned against my skin, but I didn't let go. It could be my only chance.

"Oh, *putere.*" Derek leaned over into the back seat, one hand cupped in front of him. "Wouldn't you like to know?" He lowered his hand, pursed his lips—

—and I blew, a steady stream of air that pushed the tiny glitter-like pieces of purple dust that had been nestled in Derek's hand back into his face.

He sat back in surprise, eyes wide, while the lilac dust clung to his eyebrows and his skin. It smelled like lavender and something I couldn't identify—something bitter. "What the hell?" he managed to say before he collapsed down onto the gear shift.

Smith looked back at me over his shoulder, then pushed Derek back into his seat. There was a loud smack as Derek's head hit the side window, but Smith didn't seem to care. He just straightened the car and kept driving. "You're nothing but trouble," he said. "You know that?"

I glared at the back of his head and tried to keep my eyes open.

"Oh, so *now* you're not going to speak?" Smith glanced back at me again, snarling violently. "I know you made a complaint about me. My supervisor put me on probation. One more incident and I'm fired."

I smiled and pushed down the fear that had been threatening to overcome me. "Good," I said, putting every ounce of venom I had into that one word. Smith was a werewolf—if he suspected even a hint of weakness, I was screwed.

He laughed softly. "I'm going to enjoy hurting you."

He didn't speak again. He just left the threat hanging there, a sinister promise that I tried to ignore.

Some time later, when Mistwood Academy was a lifetime away and the ropes binding my wrists and ankles were no closer to loosening, Derek woke up and Smith laughed again. "That was such a rookie mistake, man." He clapped Derek on the shoulder, his broad fingers splayed, and shook his head. "Dumbass."

"Shut up, Smith."

I didn't know how long we'd been driving—sleep had overtaken me more than once, despite my best efforts— but the sun was high in the sky when Smith pulled into a gravel driveway. The car shuddered past overgrown hedges and empty fields, the unkempt grass patchy and neglected. We'd left civilization far behind.

No one was going to come and save me here.

Shit.

Smith stopped the car abruptly in front of a dilapidated old house. Gravel and dust kicked up behind us. The house had probably been beautiful once. It had a wrap-around porch downstairs and dormer windows with shutters on the upper levels, but the windows were dark and empty, like so many missing teeth, and the shutters hung loose and crooked. Paint peeled from the sun-scarred weatherboards, though the front door looked solid and new.

"We're going in there?" I said dubiously.

"For a while," Smith replied. "But the fun won't really start until the night of the Sapphire Eclipse."

The ritual.

They were going to do it.

"It won't work," I said, keeping my voice level.

Smith ignored me. "Get her out," he said to Derek. "They're waiting for us."

Seconds later, the door beside me burst open and Derek hauled me out. He deposited me roughly onto the ground, then leaned back into the car. "I'm not your fucking slave, you know," he told Smith. "You carry her this time."

"I can walk." I tried to get up, but the sun and the ropes pushed me back down. Smith and Derek were saying something, but I couldn't understand them. The sun beat down harshly against my skin and my hair, and my eyelids fluttered closed. "Car," I whispered, my tongue like sandpaper. The direct sun was too much, too harsh. I needed shade.

"If I had my way, I'd just leave you here," Derek whispered in my ear.

I tried to move my hand, but nothing worked. Gravel dug into my cheek, and I wondered why I'd ever missed the sun at all. How had I loved it? It was cruel and vindictive, burning me alive from the inside out.

"No point." Smith's voice was far away. "It won't kill her."

"Of course it won't." Something gripped my arm. "It'll hurt like hell, though."

I was still fighting when my eyes opened again. It took my brain a few moments to catch up with what I was seeing, but when it did I realized that, strangely, I was alone. I was lying on top of a crisply-made bed, my wrists and ankles still bound. The room around me was dark and sparsely-furnished, though a velvet-covered wingback chair sat proudly in one corner, the only touch of luxury in an otherwise austere space. There was one window, small and clean, which was closed against the pitch black of the rural night. The single door was shut.

"Where am I?" I whispered.

At least my voice still worked.

I levered myself into a sitting position and snapped my still-bound wrists apart as sharply as I could. Hunger stirred in my belly and in my veins, two very different kinds of need, one very much human and one very much not.

A key crunched and rattled in the lock, then the door opened, squealing loudly on its hinges. "You'll never get those undone," Derek said as he walked into the room. He flipped a switch on the wall, and the single, clear bulb dangling from the ceiling flickered to life. "They're laced with silver thread."

I glared and snapped at the ropes again. Harder. "Why are you enjoying this so much?"

"What's not to enjoy, *putere*?" Derek's strong features were angled into something dark and sinister. "Kidnapping. Assault. Revenge. I couldn't have planned it better myself."

My fangs slid out with a craving for blood and a desire for pain. Derek's pain. I wanted to hurt him. It would be so easy—the predator inside me was so close to the surface. It wouldn't take much for me to let it free.

But I couldn't.

Remember what happened to Michael Miller.

I wouldn't lose control.

"Who did plan it?" I said carefully, breathing in and retracting my fangs. "You know, if you didn't. Was it Mr. Green?"

Derek laughed. "You'll find out soon enough." He crossed the room and looked out into the night. "The moon's not ready yet. But when it is …"

"You'll what? Kill me?"

"*I* won't." Derek's gaze met mine and the unspoken words were clear in his eyes.

Derek wouldn't kill me. But someone else would.

I sat a little straighter and reached up as far as I could with my fingers, scrabbling against the rope at my wrist. It was thick and rough, and the fibres caught under my skin, but I couldn't find the end of it.

I needed to stall.

"So if you didn't plan this," I said slowly, "and you're

not going to kill me, then why are you doing it? Why do you want to hurt me?" There—it was there. The end of the rope. I moved my fingers carefully around its edges and let them drift farther up until I found the bulge of the knot. "What's in it for you?"

"What's in it for me?" Derek sat down in the wingback chair and crossed his legs, his right ankle resting on top of his left knee. He leaned forward, a predatory glint in his eyes. "Power. Revenge. Community."

"Community?" Honestly, I was surprised. Derek didn't seem like he played well with others.

His upper lip curled. "You wouldn't understand. You're a vampire. A parasite. Of course *you* wouldn't care about community."

"I used to be human."

Derek ignored me. "They took it from me, you know. From us."

I kept my face impassive as my fingers fought with the knot, again and again. "Your community?"

"Logan and his family have everything. *Everything*. And then they banished us. They took our entire community away."

I almost felt sorry for him. There was pain, real and tangible, a lightning storm of emotion tucked away behind those words. Derek was hurting. A lot. But it wasn't Logan's fault. And it wasn't mine.

"Maybe your dad shouldn't have challenged Logan's then," I said quietly.

Derek rose, his face contorting cruelly. "Shut up." He

loomed over me, a hulking colossus of menace and pain. "Shut up, shut up, shut up!" He raised his fist.

"Hurting me isn't going to make you feel any better," I said.

His mouth split apart in a smile. "You're wrong." He was showing too many teeth, and his eyes were amber. "Hurting you is going to hurt Logan. And that's the most satisfying thing of all."

We lunged at the same time, him with his entire body and me with little more than fangs and nerve. His fist connected with the side of my head, and the world tilted sideways.

"You're better than this," I said, though it came out strange and slurred, like the words weren't really mine.

"No, I'm not." He hit me again, and I rolled onto the floor. His foot connected with my ribs.

"You don't—" I said. "You don't have to—"

Smith stormed into the room. I couldn't see him—I was facing the other way—but the bitterness in his scent gave him away. "What are you doing?" he snapped, dragging me away from Derek. "They're ready for her."

Derek lunged at me once last time but stopped short, his fist inches from my face. "This isn't over, bitch."

Smith hoisted me over his shoulder and told Derek to stay where he was. "Take a breather. You're gonna kill her before it's time."

I tried to kick at him, but my bound legs wouldn't co-operate. Hunger writhed in my belly. "I won't let—you can't kill me. I'm supposed to—"

Smith growled. "You're supposed to shut up."

I tried again to kick him, but he just held onto me more tightly. My head was swimming, and my ribs burned with every breath, but I couldn't let him—them—whoever—do this. I hoped with every last bit of power I had in me that they didn't know about my family. Because if my family was safe, none of it mattered. Even if they did the ritual, even if they killed me, it wouldn't work. I wouldn't be the last of the warlock's bloodline.

"That's better," Smith muttered.

He walked out of the room and turned right into a narrow hallway. The floor beneath his feet was scuffed and cracked, yet scrupulously clean. I lifted my head and tried to see what was around us, but nausea roiled dangerously in my stomach and I looked back down.

"What is this place?" I asked as the dark wood beneath us shivered and blurred.

"It is what it needs to be," Smith replied. "Nothing more. Nothing less."

He entered another room and the floor grew shinier, richer in color and somehow more luxurious. I wanted to lie on it, lie down and sleep, as it cradled me and whispered lullabies in my ears.

"Put her down over there." I didn't recognize the woman's voice, and I couldn't smell her scent, but there was something about her that frightened me. Something that exuded power and menace and longing. "I'll start the spell."

2 5

<hr>

RED.

That's all there was. Mixing and flowing, spawning copper rivers in my veins and scarlet veils behind my eyelids. It was life. It was death. It was everything.

And it was hungry.

Deliciously, painfully hungry.

I know this.

Need twisted itself like a knife in my gut.

I want this.

I lunged at the nearest figure, but something held me back.

I'll have this.

"Enough."

No.

But something inside of me, something tucked so far down it could hardly breathe, recognized that command. Recognized that voice.

"Bring her out of it."

The red waters rippled and I coughed, disoriented and drowning, the hunger still tearing at my insides. Everything burned. My skin, my throat, my lungs. I couldn't get away from it. I couldn't move.

Why can't I move?

"Faster, gentlemen. I need her more cogent than this."

Rage hovered at the edges of my consciousness, but I pushed it down, blinking rapidly as I was thrust into a world that was too loud, too colorful, too—

"There you are." Mr. Olaru's acidic voice cut through the pain. "I have been waiting for this moment for a very long time ... *putere*."

I swallowed hard, my throat still burning with bloodlust and magic. "Mr. Olaru?"

"I have great plans for you, *putere*." His hollowed out cheeks lifted as he smiled, dark and ruthless and cruel. "And great plans for myself."

I have to get out of here.

Even through the fog and the hunger, I wasn't surprised Mr. Olaru was there. He'd always been so cold, so far removed from anything that might once have made him human. Had he ever been human?

I looked around the room, my gaze still blurred with red, then stilled my head as everything tilted around me. "Are you in charge? I said, tugging carefully at the restraints around my wrists. "Are they all—Mr. Green, Derek, Smith, the witch—are they all working for you?"

"What do you think?"

"I—"

Red.

It hurts.

My fangs sliced through my gums.

I want it.

Red.

I need it.

Someone—a person, a wolf, O positive singing in his veins—lifted his hands. Derek. Was that his name?

I'll take it.

Reality shifted, shimmered, and my stomach pitched.

"Come here, Mister Watson."

My head was spinning, but I watched as Derek made his way toward Mr. Olaru. He walked with bravado, but it was a false confidence. The scent of his fear was strong. *I want it, I want it, I want it.* I lifted my chin and breathed it all in, the dread, the suffering, the trees around us.

The trees around us.

We were in the woods.

I'd been in a house.

And now I was in the woods.

How did I get here?

There was a blank spot in my memories. But the woods looked familiar. Smelled familiar. Was I back at Mistwood?

Mr. Olaru slapped Derek hard across the face, and the sound of it broke the tenuous hold I had on my thoughts. "You were not given permission to put her under again," he snapped.

"Sorry, sir," Derek said. His gaze was fixed on the dirt beneath his feet. "It won't happen again."

"One more error and you will not live to reap your reward. Do you understand?"

Derek nodded, then waited for Mr. Olaru's dismissal, which came in the form of a long-fingered sweep of a hand. Then he walked back toward me.

I didn't speak.

The remnants of bloodlust still coursed through my veins. I could feel it clouding my thoughts and coloring my reactions. *I want to lose control.* Derek was barely human or werewolf anymore. He'd become something edible, a meal I needed and wanted, both tempting and repulsive.

And he wasn't the only one.

I turned my head as something moved in the trees, somewhere on my right.

I need it.

"Not yet, *putere*." Mr. Olaru's pale gray eyes glittered in the leaf-shadowed moonlight. "Mister Watson is not the sacrifice."

The sacrifice?

The sacrifice?

Was I missing something? I closed my eyes, trying to clear the cobwebs from my mind, but all I knew was that something was missing. Something important. Something big.

The wind blew, shifting the branches, the leaves, the dirt, and I smelled them—*him*—again.

I had to get away.

I had to save him.

But I still couldn't move. For the most part, anyway. I could control my head and my eyes, my mouth and my lungs. I could feel everything—the cool breeze that bit through my tank top, the itch behind my left knee, the ropes that bound my wrists and my ankles. But I couldn't walk. Couldn't even move an arm.

"What are you talking about?" I said, trying to stay calm. "What sacrifice?"

"The one you must make in order for the transformation to occur," Mr. Olaru said.

"That's not how it works." I shook my head. "That's not how the *putere* is made." I tried to believe it with everything I had, though I knew he'd be able to smell the lie. But I couldn't sacrifice someone. I wouldn't. Anyway, this couldn't be the night of the Sapphire Eclipse. It was still … I shook my head again, trying to clear it. "What day is it?"

"Enough." Mr. Olaru turned. "The sacrifice is ready."

As if in response, the trees to my right parted slowly. Then they faded. Disappeared. There was an odd after-image of shifting leaves and branches, and for a moment I wished it made sense, but then—

It doesn't matter.

None of it does.

Because tied to a solid oak set just past the now smooth soil that had recently held trees was …

"Logan," I whispered, my heart in my throat.

I'd known he was there; I'd smelled his scent. But

seeing him made everything worse. He was rumpled and bruised, his skin scratched and his clothes dirty. A dark purple mark smudged its way up his jaw, ending just below his cheekbone, and the hollows around his eyes told me he hadn't slept in days. He struggled against the ropes when he saw me, but Smith, standing next to him, stopped him with nothing more than a look.

"I'm sorry," Logan whispered. "We tried to stop this. All of us did. We tried to find you, but ..." He trailed off, the pain behind the unspoken words etched plainly on his face.

I wanted to reach out and touch him. "Why haven't you turned? You could go. Get help. Save yourself."

"They did a spell. I can't change."

"But they're not witches! They can't do magic! Not properly, anyway." I closed my eyes for a moment and tried to remember how to exhale. When I looked back up, Logan was staring at me, his muscles straining against the ropes.

"It's not their spell," he said. "I heard them talking. They got it from someone else. They got all their spells from someone else. I think it was the witch who hurt Haven."

"Quiet." Mr. Olaru's voice crackled with danger. "The sacrifice may not speak again."

I wanted to scream. "He's not—"

The headmaster snapped his fingers. "Derek. You may put her under."

I knew what to expect this time, but it hit me just the

same. By the time Derek pulled me out, I was shaking with rage. "Stop doing that!" I screamed. "I won't sacrifice Logan."

Mr. Olaru laughed. It was thin and rusted, like he was using a part of his voice that had lain dormant for centuries. "*Putere,*" he said coldly, "you do not have a choice. You are under my control. And in nine minutes, the Sapphire Eclipse will begin." He glanced down at his watch. "We must make haste."

The Sapphire Eclipse? In nine minutes?

How had I lost so many days?

My gaze caught Logan's, and he nodded. "It's tonight," he whispered.

Smith backhanded him across the face, and I screamed, fear and fury making me bolder. "Leave him alone! You don't need a sacrifice! Don't you realize that none of this—whatever *this* is—is going to work? I'm not who you think I am. I can't be the *putere*. I'm not the last living relative of the warlock who started it all. I have a family." Unless … unless Cayley's cousin had failed. "Logan?" I whispered. "Are they still alive?"

"They're alive," he said, earning himself another slap across the face. This one was followed by a punch to the gut, and he grunted, but didn't let it stop him. "Cayley talked to Isaac an hour ago."

Mr. Olaru laughed again, and it grated inside my skin. "Have you ever wondered why you look nothing like your father, *putere?*"

"What? No. Why? I have his …" *No.* Whatever I'd been

going to say was a lie. My dad was six foot three, with bright blue eyes and curly blond hair. I looked nothing like him. But it had never mattered before. I'd always assumed I'd taken after my mom's side of the family.

But that means ...

Mr. Olaru smiled, an odd twitch of the lips that managed to be both gruesome and self-satisfied.

"Why, then?" I refused to consider the implications of his question. "Why are you doing this?"

"Why does anyone do anything, *putere?*" He pulled something sharp and dangerous out of the brown leather bag that sat at his feet. "For power, of course. I do not have enough, so I am going to steal yours. I will need to kill you, of course, so I do hope you have said your goodbyes."

I swallowed hard as the Impure Blade glinted in the moonlight. *He has the Impure Blade. Derek's in control of my bloodlust. And I don't have a plan.*

We were so fucking screwed.

"You recognize this, don't you?" Mr. Olaru's lips flickered briefly in another grotesque smile. "It would seem your *adjutor* did manage to teach you a few things before Derek and Smith killed him. What a pity he did not choose to join our side. He could have been useful."

"Yeah," Derek said. "He could've handled all this magic shit for us."

"You killed him?" I asked.

Derek narrowed his eyes. "Of course we did."

"Be quiet, Mr. Watson." Mr. Olaru pointed the sharp

end of the blade at Derek, his nostrils flaring. "Unless you would like to be the sacrifice instead?"

"No, sir."

"I thought as much." Mr. Olaru strode toward me, his black suit swallowing up the darkness. "Let us proceed."

Derek and Smith joined the headmaster in front of me. Together they were a multi-headed monster, all of them vicious and wrong, and all of them more powerful than me.

What the hell am I supposed to do now?

My gaze cut to Logan as Derek and Smith lifted me, their hands rough beneath my armpits and legs. "You don't need a sacrifice!" I screamed, unable to struggle no matter how much I tried. "You just need me. Me, the Blade, my blood, and the Sapphire Eclipse. That's enough to take the power from me."

Mr. Olaru scowled. "We will proceed as planned."

"I'm sorry," I whispered to Logan. My feet hung lifeless above the dirt.

"Don't be sorry." His gaze never left mine. "This isn't your fault."

I blinked back tears as Derek and Smith set me down directly in front of him.

"Say goodbye to lover boy, bitch," Derek said, his lips close to my ear. "Enjoy sucking the life out of him. It'll be the last thing he'll ever know."

They're going to make me do it. They're going to make me do it. They're going to make me do it.

"Look at me," Logan whispered. "Look at my eyes. You're—"

Smith raised his fist, but the blow never came. His fingers loosened, slack like his mouth as he stared at someone behind me. "What's she doing here? We did all the spells. No one should be able to come in or go out."

I turned my head, and though I couldn't twist far enough to see who it was, the familiar floral perfume sat heavy in my lungs, a toxic mix of synthetic fragrance and alcohol. "Vanessa?" I said, frowning as I tried to decipher the scent that accompanied her. "And … Philip? Is that you?"

"The one and only." His voice was clipped and cold.

But … he was Haven's boyfriend. He couldn't be involved in something like this. Could he?

"Shit," Logan said, his face turning pale. "Your eyes, Philip. You're a tiger. How did you … ? Why are you here?"

"There's only one reason why we could be here," Vanessa said silkily, her voice close to my ear.

"What have you done to Haven?" Logan yelled, the muscles in his neck cording as he strained against his bonds. "Where is she?"

Mr. Olaru was suddenly beside me. "The werewolf girl must be removed. Philip, take her away." Everyone fell silent. "It is time."

"A kiss before I go, then." Vanessa had sidled up to Derek, who was standing just behind Smith. "For luck."

Inexplicably, I almost laughed. Something pale and

metallic bubbled up within me, a kind of tinny hysteria that grated my teeth and sent acid burning through my chest. This is what my life had become. *This*. An absurd sort of pageant where nothing made sense, where the players were deceitful and everything I'd ever known had been lost or abandoned.

I would be lost or abandoned.

For a moment, I wanted to give into it. I could relinquish control and at least it would be my choice.

But Logan stretched forward and his forehead touched mine—we were standing so, so close—and he burned all of my weakness away.

"Fight it," he said. "When they bring on the bloodlust, fight it with everything you have."

"Silence!" Mr. Olaru roared. He was beginning to unravel, his coldness giving way to a fervent hunger he'd given up trying to moderate. His fingers pulsed with it as he grabbed my shoulders and forced me away from Logan.

"Let me go," I said, my voice shaking with effort.

"It is almost here." Mr. Olaru looked to the sky. "Can you feel it?"

He didn't seem to notice when Derek fell to the ground, his skin deathly white and his pulse shallow, or when Vanessa punched Smith in the face. He just pushed the smooth, dark wooden hilt of the Impure Blade into my hand and curled my fingers around it.

"Two minutes," he whispered, his gaze still on the heavens. "Put her under."

Nothing happened.

There was no red. No searing hunger.

Derek was unconscious. He couldn't do the spell.

"Get off me," Smith yelled, his voice echoing through the night. He struggled against Vanessa, who'd managed to pin him down.

"It's me, Smith," she whispered, her blonde hair turning dark. "I came to help."

"But, you—and Derek—" His forehead wrinkled with confusion as Vanessa's features changed. "Shelley? Baby, what are you doing here? What did you do to Derek?"

"It was a spell, honey." Her nose lengthened and gained a small bump on the bridge; her jaw grew wider, her shoulders broader. "He didn't deserve this. You do." She lowered her mouth to his.

I locked eyes with Logan. What the hell was going on? Who was this woman? And why was she kissing Smith?

"For Christ's sake," Philip said. "I'll put her under. I know the spell. Everyone stay back—the hunger will focus on whoever is closest. We need that to be Logan."

"Yes," hissed Mr. Olaru. "Do it. Now."

Logan's eyes burned with something I didn't understand. "You're stronger than their spell," he whispered. "I believe in you."

The air around us turned blue as the Eclipse began. And then Philip whispered the words that turned the whole world red.

I want it.

"You can stop this, Emily. Find your way back."

I could hear him through the crimson, a faraway sound both familiar and comforting. *Home.* But the hunger was stronger.

I need it.

I wished I could've kissed him one last time.

"Do it," Mr. Olaru hissed in my ear. "Stab him in the heart. Then you may drink."

The Impure Blade was heavy in my hand, humming with a magic I didn't recognize.

Philip's voice sounded again, farther away this time, almost like it was underwater. Then the ropes suddenly fell to the ground and I could move.

"Go." Mr. Olaru hit me on the back with a cold, hard hand. A strange purple glow stuttered to life around his fingers. "Do it. Do it now."

Hunger roared in my veins, dark and wild and enchanting. I was terror. I was longing. The Impure Blade coursed with power, imploring me to use it.

"You can fight this." Logan's voice was firm, infused with heat and power, and the scent of it cut through the spell.

"I can't." I tried to focus on his face as I gulped down air. I was carved in two, split between girl and monster. And the monster—the part that scared me, the part that I tried to control, the part that still filled me with shame— was winning.

Philip's voice grew louder.

So did the hunger.

The Blade was warm in my hand.

"Do it now," Mr. Olaru hissed, spreading his fingers wide, the purple glow stretching from his hands to his wrists. He lifted his arms, and I raised the Blade. I was his puppet. A plaything. A means to an end.

I could almost taste Logan's blood.

"Emily," Logan whispered. "You're Emily Sanderson. Hold onto that."

His face wavered in front of me.

He was food; he was something *more*; he was food; he was something more …

"Philip," Mr. Olaru barked, his voice inhuman and sharp. "What did you do wrong? Why isn't she fully under?"

My predator rose up at the sound. It didn't like the competition.

"It's working," Philip replied tersely. "Give it time."

Mr. Olaru looked up at the sky, where the moon, the clouds, the air shone blue. "There is no time. She must drink now. I will not wait seven hundred years for a second chance at this." His lashed out with a bony hand, pushing me forward even after his touch had left my back.

Logan grunted. The sharp smell of copper filled my senses. It was wolf and oak and pain.

"No," Mr. Olaru hissed, lifting his hands. "Higher. Go for the heart."

I drew back the weapon. Its shining silver blade was marred with blood.

I looked at the werewolf in front of me.

His blood is mine.

"Don't do this," he said.

I bared my fangs. My arm moved forward in unison with Mr. Olaru's glowing direction. *Is it another spell?*

"Emily Sanderson." The werewolf's power flowed around me, strong and warm and commanding. Familiar. "You will not give into this."

I shook my head. Everything was wrong. The world was blue. Purple. Red. And I was so, so hungry.

"Emily."

The werewolf put his forehead against mine. His blood—blood that I had spilled when Mr. Olaru had driven me forward—spoke of comfort and home. It wasn't a place I could remember, but a feeling, a sense of belonging, of everything being *right*.

"Emily Sanderson."

He was more than blood.

He was more than food.

"I believe in you," Logan said.

I leaned forward and pressed my lips to his. For three long seconds, I breathed him in. I was human, I was vampire, I was whole again.

"I'm sorry I stabbed you," I whispered, my mouth still against his.

He kissed me again, then quickly pulled away. "I'll be fine. But we have to go. Now. Can you—"

An eerie screech shattered the moment. "It's almost over! Drink! Drink, damn you." Mr. Olaru seized my arm, twisting it higher. The Impure Blade pointed tip-first at Logan's chest. "Philip! The spell. Do it again."

No.

With a scream that tore blood from my vocal chords, I wrenched myself away from the headmaster's grip.

"Emily!" Logan said. "Watch out—"

Philip crashed into me, a full-body blow, and I fell forward, my body slamming into Mr. Olaru's with bone-shattering force. My fangs embedded themselves in his shoulder as we tumbled to the ground. Philip put his hand around mine. The Impure Blade thrust into Mr. Olaru's chest.

Red.

Philip's voice in the background.

Blood on my tongue.

I love it.

I hate it.

I drew it all in. The blood and the darkness and the last splintered remnants of a long violent life.

And then the pain began.

I WAS BEING DESTROYED from the inside out. Lightning filled the spaces behind my eyes and I doubled over, barely breathing. My muscles contracted, closing in on themselves, and I pressed myself into the ground, wondering in a far-off way if the pain would ever end. And if there'd be anything left of me when it did.

"Emily!" Logan yelled.

I didn't answer. I just rested my cheek on the dirt and wished it was colder.

"Emily!" he yelled again.

Another voice joined him. "Hold on," it called, high and feminine and out of breath. "I'll be there in a minute."

Cayley?

Someone grunted and I opened my eyes, but the world was too blue. It was worse than the flashes inside my head. My teeth chattered loudly, and I squeezed my eyelids shut. Sweat dripped down my back.

I could hear the unmistakable sounds of fighting—skin meeting skin, hearts beating louder, bones cracking on impact—but I couldn't turn my head. "Logan," I rasped. "What's going on?"

I already knew.

I'd lost control. I'd killed Mr. Olaru. And I'd set the prophecy in motion.

The putere *will come to power on the night of the Sapphire Eclipse. As the power ascends, a darkness will rise, and with it will come the destruction of our world.*

Someone laughed; I think it was Philip.

"Cayley!" Logan yelled. "Shit. Philip, what the fuck are you doing?"

"Removing obstacles." Philip's voice was cold. "Your turn will come. First, I have to deal with *her.* Then the damn succubus. She sucked half the life force from Derek and Smith. And she fooled me. *Nobody* fools me."

Logan's rage was audible. It flowed through his veins and quickened his heart. "Em," he said urgently. "He's got the Impure Blade. You have to get out of here."

"I can't. I can't move." The pain gripped me tighter, and I dry retched in the dirt. "Cayley—is she—?"

"She's alive," Logan said. "She tricked Philip into letting her in. He thought she was Vanessa, coming to help Derek. She's unconscious, but she's breathing."

"She won't be for long," Philip snapped. "But first, the *putere.*"

A hand—Philip's hand—slid into my hair. It was gentle

at first, but then he pulled, twisting my head until I gasped in pain. I opened my eyes, and he smiled.

"Why are you doing this?" I said, glaring up at him.

"Money, mostly." His eyes flashed yellow, though not in the way the wolves' eyes did. These eyes were different. A tiger's eyes. And I'd seen them before.

"That was you," I said slowly. "In the mirror maze at Adventure Gardens. I saw your eyes in the mirror. You brushed up against my leg."

Philip's expression turned sour. "I was supposed to kidnap you that night. But I couldn't get you on your own. She docked my pay because of that."

"Who did?" Logan said. "One of those strange girls that was there? Or … the witch who hurt Haven? Why isn't she here?"

"Shut up, Logan." Philip set Mr. Olaru's brown leather bag down next to me and pulled a dark green ceramic vessel from it. The vessel was small, maybe eight inches high, with a wide mouth that tapered down to a thin, uneven base. It was beautiful, imperfect, and very, very old. It carried the weight of its years in the clusters of cracks that spread web-like across its glaze.

"What's that for?" I asked, though the look of satisfaction on Philip's face told me I didn't want to know.

"It's for you," he said.

"Em." Logan's voice was tight with too many things I couldn't even begin to describe. "Move. Please. Try. You have to get away."

Philip smiled and produced the Impure Blade, still shining and slick with Mr. Olaru's blood. "It's too late for that. But don't worry, your power will live on." He leaned over me and grabbed my left wrist with his free hand. "This won't hurt a bit."

It was a total lie.

The Impure Blade bit into my wrist, slicing my skin with swift efficiency. It burned, though not as much as I'd expected. The clean line of the cut welled up quickly with blood, and Philip held it over the ceramic jar. Apparently it wasn't enough—he frowned up at the sky with fierce dissatisfaction.

"Come on, dammit," he muttered. "It's almost over."

I tried to pull my arm away. "I never liked you."

Philip held on tighter and slashed at my wrist again, faster and deeper. Once. Twice. Three times.

"Let her go!" Logan yelled.

Ignoring the pain that clung to me with beast-like claws, I sat. Then I punched Philip in the jaw. He reared back, but didn't let go of my left arm. "Smith said you were trouble," he growled.

I punched him again. "What are you going to do with my blood?" Every word was a battle. "Why do you need it?"

"It's not for me, if that's what you're worried about."

The sky around us was slowly darkening—the blue that had spun its way through the air was beginning to fade.

"What happens if you don't collect enough in time?" I said, still trying to pull out of Philip's grip.

He looked down at the ceramic vessel, his blue eyes assessing. "That won't happen. I'm almost done. Anyway, she's strong—she doesn't need all of it."

I wanted to ask who he was talking about. But while the pain was finally beginning to subside, my limbs were heavy and weak. Black spots danced in front of my eyes.

"Hold on," Logan called. "Em, just … hold on."

I can't.

There was hardly anything left of me. I reached for the ceramic vessel; at least I could ruin Philip's plans before I—

"No!" Philip pushed me back. His knee smacked into the brown leather bag and it toppled over, spilling a variety of papers, gems, and little fabric pouches onto the ground. "She'll kill me if you ruin this."

I grabbed the first pouch I could reach and nudged the top of it open with shaking fingers. It was half-filled with a fine lilac powder that smelled familiar—like lavender and bitterness. I didn't even think. I just tipped some into my hand and blew it toward Philip.

His mouth opened in surprise. And then he crumpled to the ground.

"What did you do?" Logan said.

"I don't—" I couldn't finish what I'd wanted to say. The black spots grew larger, merging until there was nothing but darkness. My ears roared.

And then I keeled over, too.

I was barely breathing when someone pressed a warm hand against my forehead. "Mom?" I said. "What are you doing? Where's Dad? And Sam?"

"She's freezing, James. Here—hold this for me."

The warm hand lifted and a shiver worked its way across my skin. It wasn't Mom. It would never be Mom. "Miss Lassila?" I managed to open my eyes. "Is that you? Is this … am I at Mistwood?"

"You are." She brushed my hair back from my face, then looked up at someone behind me. "Put the vessel over there by the candles. We have to do it now, James."

"It won't work," I mumbled. "The Eclipse is over. It's finished."

Miss Lassila shook her head. "The spell's still in you. It's in your blood. It's strong. *You're* strong."

Another voice spoke. One that made me flinch, even though I was barely a trace of a person. "The vessel's protecting that which was taken," it said.

No, not it.

Him.

Mr. Green.

Does that mean …

The world started closing in again, and I struggled to think. My heart was barely beating.

"Stay with me," Miss Lassila said, patting my cheek.

My eyelids fluttered, but I couldn't keep them open. "I trusted you," I said, the words thick in my throat. "How could you do this?"

Has anyone at Mistwood ever been what they seemed? Or did they all just want my blood? My life? My power?

I rubbed my fingers against my palm and forced my eyes open. "I won't let you take it. The prophecy—it ends with me." I raised my hand and—

"What are you doing?" Mr. Green grabbed my wrist. "We're trying to help you."

I blew helplessly at the remnants of the lilac powder in my hand. "I won't let you do it."

"Wait." Logan's hand was on my shoulder. "They explained everything while you were unconscious. They're telling the truth."

My eyes burned with tears. I hadn't noticed he was there. I couldn't see him or smell him or hear the blood rushing through his veins. "Are *you* telling the truth?" I whispered.

I don't know anything anymore.

Haven's hand covered Logan's.

"When did you get here?" I asked, my voice a faraway echo.

And then there was nothing. No sound, no movement, no light.

The world had ceased to exist.

As the power ascends, a darkness will rise, and with it will come the destruction of our world.

Was this—this silence, this darkness, this *nothingness*—what the prophecy had meant?

Had everything been destroyed?

I didn't know how long I floated there, bodiless and

senseless, alive and not, but eventually the world came back in snatches. There were fragments of conversations, of familiar voices; flashes of light, of faces that felt like home; of magic and fire and blood; the scent of the woods, of witch, of wolf, of succubus, of haltija; and underneath it all was the feeling of love, of a warmth that wouldn't let me go.

"She's coming around," said Haven, her voice high with relief.

I blinked slowly, and her face came into focus. "Hey," I mumbled. "Did I destroy the world?"

She smiled briefly, light and shadow flickering over her face. "Not yet."

It was only a joke, but a shiver ran down the back of my neck, crawling over my skin and burrowing down, deep into my heart. I'd killed someone. I'd lost control. We hadn't been able to stop the ritual—maybe it had never been in the cards.

"I'm sorry," I whispered.

Logan came into view, stepping up behind Haven. "This isn't your fault."

I wanted to say that it was, that I'd failed us all, but nothing came out. The world felt so uncertain. I felt so uncertain. Like I was balanced on a knife-edge, where one wrong move would destroy everything.

I don't know who to trust.

"We love you, Em," Haven said. She looked down at me, bathed in heat and light, and I couldn't figure out why.

My eyes were already closing.

When the world came back again, sometime later, it was sharper than before. Each leaf above me was bright, clear. The dirt beneath me was loud with the movement of insects. Every heartbeat around me was deafening. I could see everything, hear everything, feel everything.

I lay there, my senses firing, and remembered other nights that had felt just like this. The nights just after I'd been turned. It had been so overwhelming. So unstoppable. It had made me lose control. Again and again and again.

I wish I had my cello.

I imagined the bite of the strings beneath my fingers, the smoothness of my bow, and tried to make the world smaller. I had to turn it back into something manageable.

"It's okay," Mr. Green said softly. He stood a few feet off to the side, with Cayley fidgeting next him. "This is all part of the process. Just breathe slowly—in and out, in and out."

I didn't believe him. But somehow, everything began to settle. Enough for me to be able to sit, at least.

"Wait," Miss Lassila said. "We're not quite done."

She stood next Haven. The ceramic vessel was wedged in the dirt between them. Haven's fingers were held out in front of her, her fingers spread; fire crackled its way from her skin to the earth, surrounding the vessel in a vivid embrace. She wasn't commanding the blood, though— that was Miss Lassila's domain. It looked almost easy, the way the haltija drew the red liquid from the vessel with nothing more than murmured words and a few flicks of her fingers, though the faint and irregular twitching of the pulse point in her temple suggested otherwise.

I looked down and saw the blood—*my* blood—flowing into the still-open cuts on my wrist. It was strange, uncanny, like a film reel in reverse. "What are you doing?" I asked, unexpectedly relieved to hear the words come out the right way around.

"They're saving you," said Mr. Green.

This time, I knew it was the truth.

I glanced around the woods. Mr. Olaru's empty body lay a few feet to my left. He was still where I'd left him, all bone-white skin and staring eyes like an unspeakable nightmare. Derek, Smith, and Philip's bodies lay nearby, alive but unconscious. Their wrists and ankles were tightly bound.

I swallowed down bile. "Why would you save me after all of this?"

"Why wouldn't we?" Haven said. She looked down the neck of the vessel, then smiled. "It's done."

The blood had stopped flowing, but the wounds on my wrists still lay open. They'd been made with a silver blade—they wouldn't heal quickly.

"Come on," Miss Lassila said, taking my hand—the one belonging to my non-injured arm—and helping me to my feet. "Let's get you out of here." She pointed to the four bodies lying in the dirt and nodded at Mr. Green.

"Already on it." He held up his phone. "The SCC are

sending a couple of agents in to do clean up, no questions asked. Derek, Philip, and Smith will be behind bars within the hour."

Miss Lassila nodded firmly. "Good."

Two weeks later, I was standing backstage in the school theatre, sorting through my sheet music one last time, when Vanessa tapped me on the shoulder. I didn't flinch; I'd already known she was there. "What do you want?" I said, sounding as bored as I possibly could.

"To apologize," she said softly. "I haven't seen you since …"

"You were suspended?" I finished, still not turning around. "I know you came back to school yesterday. You can't really blame me for not seeking you out. You know what you did." She was the one who'd broken into my room—using a spell Derek had given her—and left the lock of Dr. Norlgren's hair in an envelope under my pillow. She was also the one who'd conveniently delivered that lock of hair back to me in a bag that smelled like Mr. Green, trying to confuse us. She'd brought it to my door that time, because Derek's spell hadn't worked against Haven's strengthened wards.

"I didn't know he wanted to hurt you," she continued, a whine creeping into her voice. "I thought it was a prank. He told me you lied about him and got him expelled."

I finally spun around to face her. "You're a werewolf. You should've known he wasn't telling the truth."

"He told me on the phone!" Her hands turned to fists at her sides. "You can't smell lies over the phone!"

She still didn't know what had really happened. She didn't know that her boyfriend had been working for a homicidal, power-hungry vampire—aka Mr. Olaru—who'd promised him little more than a glorified servant's job and a place for his ostracized family to live. And she didn't know that he—and Philip and Smith—had double crossed that homicidal, power-hungry vampire for what had apparently been a better offer.

No one on my side knew what that offer had been.

Or who had made it.

Not even Miss Lassila or Mr. Green, both of whom worked for the SCC—doing what exactly, I didn't quite know. From what I could gather, they'd been keeping tabs on Smith for a long time. And on Mr. Olaru for even longer. Both of them had apologized to me for not being able to find me when I'd been abducted. They still couldn't figure out whose house I'd been in. And both of them had apologised for not getting to me faster during the Sapphire Eclipse when they'd finally figured out I'd been brought back to Mistwood—apparently the spells around the woods had been more complex to get past than they'd anticipated.

"Whatever," Vanessa said hotly, breaking into my scattered thoughts. "Be like that, then."

She stormed away, pushing angrily past a group of

violinists who'd just come in from outside. *Should I have accepted her apology?* I didn't like her, but I guess it took guts to turn up and face me after what she'd done.

I almost went after her. But in the end I couldn't. I wasn't ready to forgive anyone for their role in what had happened.

Including myself.

"Is she giving you a hard time?" asked Mia, who was standing at the edge of the room, her violin case in her hand.

I shook my head. "She's just being Vanessa."

"If it was about Derek … or Mr. Olaru …"

She left the words unsaid, an unspoken offer, but I didn't know what to do with it, so I just shook my head again. The official story was that Derek had killed Mr. Olaru and had almost killed me. That his use of black magic had led to extreme issues with anger and aggression, leading him to sneak back into the school to attack those of us who'd been involved in his expulsion.

No one knew that Philip had been involved, so nobody thought it was strange that he'd suddenly transferred schools the day after it had happened. He wasn't the only one. A couple of juniors and one of the seniors had been pulled out by their parents, who apparently no longer trusted the staff at Mistwood Academy to look after their children. The only difference was, Philip hadn't really transferred. He was now locked up in an SCC-owned penitentiary, awaiting trial.

We hadn't had to come up with a story about Smith—no one at Mistwood knew who he was.

"Ten minutes, people," Mr. Longley said as he swept past, his long legs carrying him to the small corridor at the back of the building. "If you're not on stage by one o'clock, we'll be starting without you."

Mia faded away into the bustle of musicians who were suddenly milling around, all nerves and energy and excitement, while I just sort of … watched. I'd been an outsider at Mistwood when I'd started, a human turned into something other, and I was even more of an outsider now.

I was the *putere*.

I was a secret.

I was a murderer.

"Hey," Logan said, coming up behind me and sliding his arms around my waist. "You've done nothing but practice for the last two weeks. You're gonna be great."

I rested my head back against his chest and sighed. "That's not what I'm worried about."

"I know," he said softly. "But you're still gonna be great."

"Totally." Haven popped up beside us, straightening the frilly collar on her black performance shirt. "The prophecy's over. The darkness didn't rise. You didn't destroy the world." She smiled brightly. "Everything's fine."

"But—"

"Prophecies aren't always accurate," she said. "They're an art, not a science."

Mr. Longley rushed past again, harried strands of hair falling down over his eyes. "On stage now, everyone. This is it. Have fun."

"Let's go," Haven said, squeezing my hand. "You'll be fine. I promise."

And I was. At least while I was playing. Thomas and Cayley watched from the front row, side by side, their fingers entwined. Something about what had happened on the night of the Sapphire Eclipse had changed their relationship, and they'd been together ever since.

I smiled at them as they applauded, and flipped over to the next piece of music in my folder, ignoring the pain in my still-healing wrist. Everything *was* fine. Haven was right. It would all work out okay.

I almost believed it.

And then I moved to the front of the stage to do my solo and nearly tripped, my feet catching on nothing. *They can't be here. They can't.* Not at my school, in my auditorium, watching me play. It wasn't possible.

Mr. Longley smiled at me. "You ready?" he whispered.

I nodded, but my heart was frozen in my chest. I wasn't wrong. They were definitely there, sitting two-thirds of the way back—my mom, my dad, and Sam.

I'd missed them, I'd loved them, I'd grieved for them. Seeing them here was everything I'd wanted. But … they'd lied to me. Mr. Olaru couldn't have turned me into the *putere* if I hadn't been the last of the warlock's line.

I had questions. So many questions I couldn't ask.

Not here.

Not now.

Mr. Longley lifted his baton, and the audience stilled. The music started. I took a deep breath and began to play.

Thank you for reading *The Sapphire Eclipse*! If you have a few moments, I'd love it if you could leave a review on Amazon or Goodreads.

To be the first to know about new releases and updates—and receive a free copy of a prequel novella—sign up to my mailing list via my website!

www.amyhartbooks.com

ACKNOWLEDGMENTS

A huge thank you to Clare, for reading every single version of this book. Your enthusiasm for these characters and your unwavering belief in my writing means everything to me.

Many thanks also to Amanda Ashby. Without your support and advice this book would probably still be a draft!

A big thank you to my parents for always being so supportive, for helping with the kids, and for always believing in me.

Thank you to Hamish, Zoe, and Alex for always being awesome, always being supportive, and for being some of the funniest (and most fun!) people I know.

Thanks to Rianna for being my very first pre-order!!

An enormous thank you to Ian, for everything. For always making me laugh. For patiently putting up with the late nights, the worries, and the endless loads of dishes. I couldn't have done this without you.

And lastly, thank you to Connor and Ava for always cheering me on, and for being the best kids a mum could ever ask for.

ABOUT THE AUTHOR

Amy Hart is the author of young adult paranormal novels about vampires, witches, and other magical beings. Her love of paranormal fiction began at an early age when she would routinely check out the maximum number of books allowed on her library card. After growing up and completing a Bachelor of Arts, a Bachelor of Music, and a Master of Arts (Hons) in Art History, she found her way back to fiction. Born and raised in Auckland, New Zealand, she adores cookies, singing, and collecting too many journals.

For more books and updates:
www.amyhartbooks.com

facebook.com/amyhartbooks
instagram.com/amyhartbooks
goodreads.com/amyhartbooks

* 9 7 8 0 4 7 3 5 6 5 5 3 4 *